FIRST DEGREE MUDDER

I laughed out loud when I looked at my arms and legs. Thin, runny mud melted from the steam ran down my arms. Mother would pay big money for this kind of experience at a spa. Mud baths and masks were all the rage at her club. What a mess.

My laughter quickly faded away as the steam continued to dissipate, and I realized I wasn't alone. Billy lay on his back on the far bench. Why hadn't he said anything when I came in?

"Listen, Billy," I said. "I'm so sorry that I cut out early. My feet are killing me."

Billy didn't move.

"I know what you're going to say," I continued. "I'm only cheating myself. I know that. Really, I do, but that was too much this morning—the mud, Tim, everything."

Billy didn't say a word.

That wasn't like him.

Something was wrong.

I stood and walked over to him. His eyes were staring straight at the ceiling and he looked as stiff as the cedar bench beneath him.

"Billy, are you okay?" I shook him. He didn't move and I threw my hand over my mouth.

Billy wasn't yelling at me because he was dead . . .

Books by Kate Dyer-Seeley

SCENE OF THE CLIMB

SLAYED ON THE SLOPES

SILENCED IN THE SURF

FIRST DEGREE MUDDER

Published by Kensington Publishing Corporation

First Degree Mudder

Kate Dyer-Seeley

KENSINGTON PUBLISHING CORP.
http://www.kensingtonbooks.com

KENSINGTON BOOKS are published by

Kensington Publishing Corp.
119 West 40th Street
New York, NY 10018

Copyright © 2016 by Kate Dyer-Seeley

All Kensington titles, imprints, and distributed lines are available at special quantity discounts for bulk purchases for sales promotions, premiums, fund-raising, and educational or institutional use. Special book excerpts or customized printings can also be created to fit specific needs. For details, write or phone the office of the Kensington Special Sales Manager. Kensington Publishing Corp., 119 West 40th Street, New York, NY 10018. Attn: Special Sales Department. Phone: 1-800-221-2647.

Kensington and the K logo Reg. U.S. Pat & TM Off.

ISBN-13: 978-1-4967-0509-9
ISBN-10: 1-4967-0509-2
First Kensington Mass Market Edition: December 2016

eISBN-13: 978-1-4967-0510-5
eISBN-10: 1-4967-0510-6
First Kensington Electronic Edition: December 2016

10 9 8 7 6 5 4 3 2 1

Printed in the United States of America

Chapter 1

Fort Vancouver National Historic Site
Old army barracks

My feet squished inside my drenched kicks as I limped through the damp grass. *I'd like to give Billy a swift kick in the shins,* I thought, cranking the volume on my phone to high. Maybe Dean Martin's "King of the Road" would give me a final boost. Doubtful. I didn't feel like the king or queen of the road. Quite the opposite.

The rest of my Mind Over Mudder teammates were nowhere in sight. Thank God. I checked behind me twice, just to make sure. I probably could have taken the shortcut straight to the barracks, but I didn't want to risk being seen. That might have been a mistake. The historic grounds gave off an eerie aura, especially the dilapidated army hospital Building 614, to my left. It was rumored to be haunted. I understood why. Built in 1904 during an influenza outbreak, the three-story brick building had served hundreds of infantry men over the decades.

I shuddered to imagine the torture some of them must have endured. Was that a moan? A prickly feeling ran down my spine.

"I think that's a moan," I said aloud as I glanced up at the broken top-story windows. Something ghoulish floated past.

Run, Meg!

I willed myself forward, ignoring the blisters on my heels or the chafing under my sports bra. It felt like I was breathing underwater. I didn't care. I crested the hill and turned onto Evergreen Boulevard.

Relax, Meg. It's just your mind playing tricks on you. I had read one too many ghost stories when researching the history of Fort Vancouver and its surrounding grounds. The hospital had been abandoned for years, but people swore that things were amiss. Faucets were said to turn on in the middle of the night, bathroom doors banged shut for no reason, faces, like the one I'd just seen, appeared out of nowhere in the windows. The place was haunted. Definitely haunted.

You're fine now, I told myself, slowing my pace.

I followed the flour on the sidewalk that marked the route of our predawn run. It took us past the fort's parade grounds complete with an old-fashioned bandstand and Officer's Row—a row of stately Victorian officers' houses. That's when I saw the creepy old lady again. I'd seen her watching us from her ground-floor apartment before. The twenty-two stately mansions that make up Officer's Row were now used for a variety of purposes. The Grant House had become one of Vancouver's premier restaurants and the Marshall House a favorite spot for weddings. The remaining properties had been converted into commercial and residential space.

Yesterday when I jogged past the creepy old lady's apartment she peeled back one lace curtain and watched me and my teammates. It was unsettling to say the very least.

I stopped to tie my shoe under an ancient oak. Its leaves looked parched from summer's endless sun. My throat commiserated with the tree. I could use an ice-cold glass of water right about now. Pushing myself to standing, all the hairs on my arms stood at attention as a creaking sound came from the creepy old lady's front door. She appeared out of nowhere on the wraparound porch.

Were my eyes playing tricks on me? Where had she come from? I jumped back in surprise. Her glassy eyes bore into me. She wore a faded pink bathrobe and appeared to have been old enough to be one of the original members of the Hudson's Bay Company.

"Hi." I offered a tentative wave.

She didn't move.

I tried again. "Good morning."

Her eyes remained locked on me, but she gave no indication that she'd heard my greeting.

Was she a ghost?

I had no intention of waiting around to find out. I plowed ahead, crossing Evergreen Boulevard and practically hurdling the waist-high wooden fence that ran the length of the grassy parade grounds.

My feet revolted as I stumbled down the hill. It felt like someone was sanding my heels with sandpaper.

Pick up the pace, Meg.

The only thing that kept me upright was the promise of a hot shower and the fact that a ghost might be in hot pursuit. I needed to get to the barracks and get out of these shoes. Mud and sweat oozed from every pore. Thankfully, I'd learned my lesson after the first day on the training course and ditched my cute pink tank top and capris for old raggedy sweats and a T-shirt. Everything ended up discolored from the mud. There was no point in trying to look cute while under Billy the Tank's watchful eye and blaring bullhorn.

I cut through the grass, something Billy definitely frowned on. "Reed!" he bellowed in his bullhorn when he caught me sneaking around the back of the barracks last week. "When you take a shortcut you're only cheating yourself."

That was fine by me. I happily owned cheating on myself.

There was a single light on in the otherwise deserted collection of buildings down the hill. The reserve encompassed 366 acres of land. It included Fort Vancouver, Pearson Field, Pearson Air Museum, the barracks, army hospital, Red Cross building, Officer's Row, an old chapel, stables, and non-commissioned officers' houses. The grounds are considered the Pacific Northwest's most important historical site. And this morning I couldn't shake the feeling that there were whispers from the past surrounding me.

My target was the barracks building where the

single light glowing golden yellow looked like a welcoming beacon. Billy and his business partner, Dylan, had leased the barracks to use as base camp for their three-week intensive training class Mind Over Mudder. They promised that by the end of the session (*If* you survived, which at the moment looked doubtful for me.), not only would you be in "fighting shape" to finish a mud run, but you'd also drop pounds and pant sizes. So far the scale hadn't budged when I stepped on it, and I was so exhausted at the end of the day that I felt like dropping dead.

Using the wooden railing, I placed one hand over the other and slowly hauled my body up the ramp. The rotting wooden slats buckled. Please hold, I said a silent prayer to the Universe. The last thing I needed was to crash through the ramp.

Compared with the other buildings, the barracks were in great shape. Everything had sat empty since the army abandoned its post in Vancouver decades earlier. The National Park, along with a trust, had begun renovations on the massive site. The barracks were first on the list, and Mind Over Mudder the first and only tenant at the moment. A sharp splinter lodged itself in my palm. It protruded from my mud-chapped skin. I stopped and yanked it free. Ouch!

Yet another reason to love this training program, I sighed as I opened the front door and stumbled inside. Every muscle in my body quaked. Billy had promised us that muscle pain was a sign that our metabolism was revving up and we were replacing fat with muscles. "Embrace the quakes" was his motto. Easy for him to say. Billy, aka "the Tank," was the fittest person I'd ever met. That was saying a lot given that I write for *Northwest Extreme* magazine and am constantly surrounded by hard-bodied adventure junkies.

Billy instructed us to call him Tank on the first day of training. He looked like a tank. His stout body bulged with muscle mass. There wasn't an ounce of fat on his body. Let's just say that he was a bit intimidating when he sounded the whistle around his neck, wearing skintight army shorts and a sleeveless shirt specifically designed to show off his enormous muscles.

I scanned the dimly lit hallway to make sure Tank wasn't there. By my estimate, the rest of my teammates should be on the course for another thirty minutes. That should give me ample time to shower, soak my aching soles, and hightail it out of here before anyone was the wiser. I clicked off my music, tugged my earbuds out, and clutched my phone in the hand without the splinter.

The barracks have an ominous vibe even when they're packed with my teammates and coaches. Shuffling down the long, empty hallway made it feel even creepier. Like the army hospital, the barracks are said to be haunted. The top floor was used for gun testing. There are still bullet holes in the walls upstairs, and it was said that you could hear phantom gun shots.

A loud thud sounded below.

I jumped and let out a scream.

My heart pounded in my chest. *Relax, Meg.* Maybe one of my teammates had the same idea.

I continued on, checking over my shoulder to make sure no one was behind me. The locker rooms were located in the basement. Not exactly where I wanted to be at the moment, but I hobbled down the hardwood stairs anyway.

When I was a few feet away from the locker room doors, they swung open, nearly smacking me in the face.

I jumped again.

Was it the ghost? How were the doors opening? One of the rumors that I'd heard about the haunted buildings was that doors were known to open and close at will.

I backed up.

At that moment someone barreled through the doors and knocked me off my feet.

"Hey!" I caught myself on the wall.

The guy leaped over me and raced down the hallway before I could get a look at his face. I had a pretty good guess who it was—Tim Baxter, one of my fellow teammates. I recognized his bulk and black hooded sweatshirt. What was he doing in the locker room, and why was he in such a hurry?

I pushed to standing. "Tim, where are you going?"

He paused at the front doors.

I noticed a package under his right arm. "Tim!" I called again. "What's going on?"

He froze. I thought maybe I'd made a mistake. My contacts were thick with sludge. I don't see distances very well even when my contacts are perfectly clear. Dirt had formed a thick filmy layer, making my vision blurry. I blinked twice.

The door slammed shut. Tim, or whoever had run into me, was gone.

Weird.

I brushed myself off and continued into the locker room. Steam enveloped the front area where three massage tables sat empty. Long mirrors stretching the length of the room were completely fogged over. It smelled like stale sweat, moldy wood, and eucalyptus. Someone, probably Tim, must have left the steam room doors open.

Using my hands as a shield to avoid tripping over a bench, I made my way past the massage tables and into the shared steam, sauna, and whirlpool room. Doors on either side of the room led to the men's and women's changing rooms and showers. Originally the barracks housed only men, so when Mind Over Mudder renovated the basement locker room they'd had to get creative with the design. The actual changing areas and showers were private and on opposite sides of each other, but the steam room and hot tub were coed, which meant that bathing suits were always required.

My cheeks burned with heat. Muddy sweat dripped onto the floor. The wet air filled my lungs, making me cough.

I fumbled through the dense layer of steam. My hands landed on the cedar steam room door, which was indeed wide open. Someone had propped it open with one of the locker room benches. Really weird. I pushed the bench away. It made a sound like nails on a chalkboard on the tile floor.

My feet slid across the wet floor. I landed on my tailbone as the steam room door swung shut. Awesome. Two falls in a matter of a few minutes.

That had to be a new record for me. At least my phone was safely secured to my arm. I just got a new phone after a little accident with my old phone. Smartphones aren't cheap, especially for a girl on a tight budget. I couldn't risk damaging this one, so I undid the Velcro strap around my arm and placed my phone and earbuds on a bench nearby.

Steam billowed from underneath the door. It reminded me of dry ice on Halloween. Whoever turned it on must have cranked the heat to full blast. I braced myself as I opened the door to shut it off.

I couldn't see my hand in front of my face, but I knew where the dials controlling the heat and steam were. The steam room and I had become besties over the past few days. Nothing soothed my training aches and pains like the moist, warm air.

I found the thermostat and switched it off. I know I shouldn't have, but I climbed onto the cedar slatted bottom bench and drank in the steam. Billy would be furious if he caught me wearing my muddy clothes in the hot, humid room, but I couldn't help it. I was freezing. *Just five minutes, Meg,* I told myself as my breathing steadied and I sank onto the warm bench. This is exactly what I needed, I could almost feel my muscles begin to relax.

Within minutes the steam began to evaporate and the air began to thin. I opened my eyes. My contacts were like glue. Blinking as hard as I could, I tried to loosen their grip. It didn't work. They felt like sand. I might have to ditch them, I thought as I stood up.

The small cedar room came into soft focus.

Someone else was in here with me. I blinked again. "Billy?"

Billy was lying on his back on the top bench with his eyes closed. Why hadn't he said anything? He must be pissed that I snuck out early.

"Listen, Tank, I'm really sorry I took the short-cut. My feet are killing me this morning. I have, like, a thousand blisters."

Billy didn't respond.

"Tank, I'm a reporter, remember. I'm here for a story. It's not like the rest of my teammates." I stood. Spots danced in my vision.

Again Billy didn't respond. I moved closer. Suddenly, I knew why he wasn't responding. Billy wasn't resting.

As I came closer, a horrific sense of dread came over my entire body. Billy was dead.

You would think that I would have learned my lesson by now. But no. Signing up for Mud, Sweat, and Beers was entirely my idea. I wanted to prove myself as a serious member of the *Northwest Extreme* team after returning to Portland from a whirlwind week in New York.

It might be hard to believe (it still was for me) that I turned down a job offer at ESPN. ESPN! What was I thinking? Did turning down their generous offer make me wise beyond my years or a total idiot? I wasn't sure, but I was sure that I belonged in Portland.

New York had been exactly as I imagined it— busy and crowded with a constant pulse of people and energy. I loved it. I loved watching throngs of businessmen and women in sharp, smart suits and fancy shoes navigate sidewalks and honking taxis. No one honks in Portland. Cars *always* yield to pedestrians. Merging into the flow of foot traffic in the Big Apple was as challenging as trudging up deserted wooded backcountry trails in the Pacific Northwest. I almost got run over twice. Thanks to a bystander with quick reflexes I was spared being mowed down by a speeding Uber driver.

Fortunately, I'm a quick study and the social media team at ESPN gave me a quick course in how to blend in like a New Yorker. My first rule was to *never* look up. Apparently, no one in New York stares at the massive skyscrapers that tower over the city. I couldn't help myself. Some of them seemed as high—if not higher—than Oregon's majestic peaks. I found myself bumping into strangers as I walked with my head tilted up trying to catch a glimpse of the sky through the giant columns of steel and concrete. They were as impressive as the Cascade Mountains and equally intimidating.

My new friends also advised caution at crosswalks. I wasn't in Portland any longer. That was for sure. After two near misses, I learned to stop and wait for the light to change before crossing intersections that hardly ever clear. In no time, I began to feel like a bona-fide New Yorker. And the fashion. Swoon. I could definitely get used to the big-city wardrobe.

Very few Portlanders wear suits. Not true in New York. I appreciated the city's sophisticated style. I usually feel overdressed in my vintage A-line dresses at *Northwest Extreme* where most of my coworkers arrive in shorts and hiking gear. Many of them don't even bother to shower. Fashion in Portland had been defined by an influx of hipsters who sported shaggy beards, knit caps, flannel shirts, and skinny jeans.

New York brought out the girl in me. I have a serious addiction to pink. I've tried to temper it with my outdoor apparel, but in New York I embraced my love of all things pink, wearing my favorite cashmere cardigan and flared skirt with strappy pink sandals to happy hour and sporting a pink polka dot 1950s number to lunch. I even chopped off my hair on a whim. One afternoon I passed by an upscale hair salon. Without a moment of pause, I walked in the doors and asked the stylist for a modern pixie cut.

The social team at ESPN was a blast. Unlike at *Northwest Extreme* where most of my colleagues were older than me by a decade or two, everyone at ESPN's new satellite office was my age. Hanging with my fellow millennials made for an eventful week and required copious amounts of coffee in the morning to deal with the hangover from hitting the club scene every night. New York was alive no matter the hour. No wonder they call it "the city that never sleeps." I didn't sleep at all during my stay.

I'm pretty sure that was due in part to trying to make a major life decision. As flattered as I was by ESPN's offer, and as enamored as I was with the city, I just couldn't quite picture myself living in New York. Maybe I wasn't as athletically inclined as the other writers at *Northwest Extreme,* but I'd come to really enjoy my job and the outdoors. There was something about the wide-open space on the West

Coast that I couldn't bear to leave. Portland was home, and everyone I loved was in Portland.

At the end of the week, I packed my suitcase and turned down ESPN's offer. The entire cab ride and flight home I debated with myself. Had I made the wrong choice? What if I never got another opportunity like this?

But when the pilot announced we were starting our descent into Portland, I pulled up the shade and looked out the tiny window. We circled over evergreen trees as far as my eye could see. Mt. Hood stood like a mighty snow-capped pillar at the base of the deep blue waters of the Columbia River. The vast clean sky seemed to stretch to the ocean. I had what Gam calls a "knowing." I had made the right decision. I was home.

Chapter 2

I didn't have much time to reflect on my decision. I was due at *Northwest Extreme* bright and early Monday morning for our monthly all-staff meeting. Greg, my editor and boss, hears our story pitches at the all-staff meeting. I'd been so consumed with my interview in New York that I hadn't exactly done a ton of research into what I wanted to pitch.

My flight got in at seven on Sunday night. I had less than twelve hours to come up with a story idea. Having recently wrapped a feature on windsurfing in the Columbia River Gorge, I knew I wanted to write about something closer to home. Most of my assignments had been based outside of Portland. My time in New York had given me renewed appreciation for my funky city. I wanted to explore that. The question was how.

Portland boasts a variety of outdoor events throughout the year. Rain or shine Portlanders are usually game for any adventure. After unpacking and a quick glance at the junk mail that had piled up while I was gone, I got to work. I needed something unique to pitch to Greg. I leafed through the newspaper. Call me crazy, but I still get the paper delivered to my front door. There's nothing like flipping through its thin pages or the feel of residual newsprint on your fingers.

Plus, reading the paper always made me feel closer to Pops. He'd been the lead investigative reporter for *The O,* Oregon's oldest newspaper, until his untimely death right before I graduated from college. My fondest memories of him are him sitting at his desk at *The O.* His desk was always a mess. It used to drive Mother crazy. "Charlie," she'd gripe. "You need to set a better example for your daughter." Then she'd try to tidy up his piles of handwritten notes and clippings.

He would wave her off. "Darling, stop. There's a method to my madness. Our little Maggie knows this, don't you?" He would wink at me and suggest that we all walk for an ice cream. He was brilliant at distracting Mother. I wished I had his same talent.

The paper was much thinner these days. Pops would have been disappointed to see dwindling subscription numbers and the fact that the entertainment pages took up more space than serious investigative pieces. The landscape of the media had changed drastically in the past few years. Maybe in some ways it was better that he wasn't around to see his beloved profession transformed into a battle between "citizen journalists" to break news first on Twitter and experienced, well-qualified reporters who logged long hours researching and doing due diligence for each story that made it to print.

An even scarier fact that I'd recently read was that computer-generated stories were becoming commonplace in well-respected media outlets. Computers were spitting out stories that were being published in Pulitzer Prize–winning publications. Most of the stories were statistics-based, centering around sports or finance, but as computers become more sophisticated and able to exhibit creativity, more and more creative jobs were at stake. Pops used to say that computers were taking over the world. He was right. It was becoming impossible to find a field where machines weren't taking over.

With that comforting thought in mind I turned to the week's event guide. There were a number of bike rides and runs listed. All standard fare for late August in Portland, but nothing worthy of a *Northwest Extreme* feature. I found a brief write-up about a midnight brews cruise where people paddled across the Willamette River under the moonlight and stopped at three different pubs for late-night pints. It sounded intriguing but not extreme enough for Greg.

My eyes felt heavy, despite the coffee. I was about to call it a night. Just as I folded the paper and placed it on my desk I noticed a small ad on the back page that read: *Mud, Sweat, and Beers. Are you ready to get sweaty? Announcing Portland's inaugural mud run!*

Reading the fine print, I discovered that Mud, Sweat, and Beers was the ultimate endurance event. The course would take participants through miles of obstacles like scaling ten-foot walls and army-crawling through thick, muddy ravines. Jackpot! I'd found my story. I cut out the ad and crashed for the night.

The next morning I formulated my pitch on the

drive to *Northwest Extreme*'s headquarters on the Willamette River. It's a good thing that one of my best skills is quick thinking. I had a feeling that Greg would bite on the story, but I knew that I needed a unique angle.

What if you do it, Meg? I asked myself as I waited for an iced mocha with extra whipped cream at my favorite drive-through coffee cart. The race was in three weeks. That would give me plenty of time to prepare and train. Maybe that could be my story. I could document my training experience, give our readers a first-hand look at the process. That should also make for great social content. I could post daily updates and pictures of my training routine. There was only one small problem. I had no idea how to train for a mud marathon.

Armed with an iced coffee, I hurried into the office, waving greetings to my coworkers.

"How was the trip, Meg?" one of them asked as I sprinted past.

"Great!"

"We missed you. It was quiet and—uh—not pink, while you were gone." He nodded at my pale pink sundress and sparkly flip-flops. "New haircut, huh? It looks good."

"Aw, thanks. I'm happy to be back and happy to have Portland coffee again." I held up my coffee in a toast.

"Greg's got some big announcement this morning. The entire office is talking about it."

"What about?"

"No one knows. He's been pretty buttoned up about it." He glanced at his watch. "I guess we'll find out soon. Meeting starts in fifteen."

"Shoot. I've gotta run. I have something I need to look up before my pitch. See you in there."

"Good to have you back, Meg."

I grinned and continued to my desk. My laptop slowly chugged to life. We needed new machines. Compared to ESPN, *Northwest Extreme*'s computers were dinosaurs.

Sucking down the sweet dark chocolate mocha, I did a search for mud marathon training courses. To my surprise the first thing that popped up was Mind Over Mudder located right across the river in Vancouver, Washington. Vancouver was only about a ten-minute drive north, and happened to be where my grandmother lives. Gam is an energy healer. She owns a new age bookshop, Love and Light, on the Vancouver waterfront where she hosts Reiki workshops and meditation classes; sells crystals, gems, and spiritual books; and always lends a listening ear to anyone who comes into her shop.

She would say that I was in alignment with my story idea. It all came together so easily. It must be the story for me. I finished my coffee, then printed out info sheets on Mind Over Mudder's training schedule and pricing, and the entry form for Mud, Sweat, and Beers. "Thank you, Universe," I sang as I practically skipped to the conference room.

Northwest Extreme's computer equipment might be outdated, but our office space wasn't. When Greg took over as editor in chief he purchased an abandoned warehouse and converted it into the magazine's headquarters. The space is the perfect balance of new meeting old. Greg kept the historic exposed brick walls, but outfitted the east side of the building with giant windows that look out onto the river. He chose the building for its charm and location. One of the benefits of working for the magazine is that Greg encourages his staff to head outside for a lunchtime run on the waterfront path or to take off early to mountain bike in Forest Park. I hadn't exactly taken advantage of that benefit. That was going to change as of today. I was resolved to continue my quest to become more athletic. I had turned down a major promotion in New York after all. And if I was going to compete in Mud, Sweat, and Beers, I didn't want to look like a fool.

"Meg, welcome back." Greg stood near the windows of the conference room. "You cut your hair."

My heart skipped. Greg is unsettlingly gorgeous. I mean as in ridiculously gorgeous. No one should be as beautiful as he was. His rugged looks should be passed around and evened out a bit. When I first started working for him I had a serious crush. I'm over it now, thanks in part to the fact that my friend Matt doesn't trust him, and because he's too old for me. Oh, and he's my boss. Still, it was impossible not to react to his evenly bronzed skin, chiseled jawline, and casually confident personality.

"Yep, totally. I'm super happy to be back. You know New York was great, but it kind of smells." I should mention that I have a tendency to babble and say stupid things whenever I'm around Greg. Another habit I needed to break.

"Smells, hmm. That's not usually the first description of New York I hear." Greg smiled.

"Well, you know what I mean. It was August and hot, so the garbage . . ." *Stop while you're ahead, Meg.*

Greg raised his brow, but before he could respond a group of my coworkers entered the conference room. We all gathered around the long table in the center of the room. Greg stood at the head of the table. He shifted his weight from side to side. Normally, Greg is very centered, as Gam would say. He seemed nervous.

Chris, an ad sales guy, sat next to me. He leaned in and whispered, "Get ready."

"Get ready for what?"

"The ax." He made a chopping motion with his forearm.

What did he mean by that? Cuts? That would be just my luck. Had I turned down a once-in-a-lifetime opportunity with ESPN only to get cut at *Northwest Extreme*? So much for my brilliant plan. I took a deep breath and awaited my fate.

Chapter 3

Greg cleared his throat and waited for everyone to stop chattering. I studied his face. The sun had left its indelible mark on his cheekbones and forehead. Greg spent as much time outside as possible. His skin was usually bronzed and chapped from weather. It suited him. So did his casual attire. Like most of my colleagues at *Northwest Extreme,* Greg's wardrobe consisted of relaxed khakis and dress shirts with the sleeves rolled up.

"Morning, everyone," he said, pushing up his sleeves. "I know there have been a lot of rumors swirling around the office for the past week or so."

I caught Chris's eye. He nodded as if to say I told you so.

"Changes are coming, but I want to talk through them with you." Greg picked up a file folder resting in front of him.

"Are we all getting laid off?" someone asked.

Greg sighed. "No, at least not right away."

My stomach dropped. This was bad.

"Listen, let me explain what's going on and then

I'll take questions," Greg said. He opened the file folder and passed each of us a piece of paper.

"What you have in front of you is a copy of the offer I've been given by a Japanese company interested in buying out the magazine."

"A buyout?" Chris blurted out.

"That's right." Greg nodded at the paper. "Everything is spelled out in the offer. I haven't accepted yet. I wanted to tell you all first. Some of you have been with me since the beginning, and as much as I love running *Northwest Extreme,* I have to seriously consider the magazine's future. The industry is changing faster than I ever expected, and quite honestly, I'm having a hard time keeping up." He paused and caught my eye.

"Thanks to our young one, Meg here, at least we've been able to get with the times and have seen some nice traction online."

I could feel my cheeks burn with heat. I kept my eyes focused on the paper in front of me.

"I've been thinking long and hard on this. The last thing I want to do is sell the magazine, but I have to be realistic. Print ad sales are still down. Way down. Even as the economy has improved ad sales have continued to slump. I have to be realistic. Print just isn't what it used to be. *Northwest Extreme*'s future is online." He paused and sighed. "I don't think I'm the guy to lead that charge."

Silence filled the room.

Greg continued. "I know there have been some crazy rumors floating around. One of my personal favorites is that I'm actually working for the Secret Service. I assure you, I'm not. The reason that I've been traveling so much is that I've been having meetings with interested buyers all over the globe. If I do sell, I want to make sure I sell to someone who has the vision and talent to take *Northwest Extreme* into the future."

I had wondered for months why Greg was always taking off on unexplained trips and sneaking away to have secret phone conversations. I wanted to text Matt right away. Matt, my good friend and current crush, had been convinced that Greg had a secret identity. He'd been worried that Greg was connected to Pops' death, and for good reason. Matt found a photo of Greg with the editor of *The O* and Pops in the newspaper's archives that proved that Greg and Pops not only knew each other, but had worked together a decade ago.

Matt made me promise not to confront Greg about the photo. So far I had kept that promise, in part because Greg had confessed that he had been asked by someone unknown at *The O* to watch over me. He swore that his only goal was to look out for me, and that whatever he wasn't telling me about his involvement with the Meth Madness investigation, or his relationship with Pops, was for my protection. I wanted to believe him, and for the most part I did, but Matt's doubt and the fact that Greg was so tight-lipped about what he was doing and where he was going made me wonder if my instincts were wrong.

Meth Madness had been Pops' last story and in all likelihood had gotten him killed. What started as an exposé about the rise of methamphetamine addiction in Oregon led to *The O* devoting a huge chunk of its reporting staff and hundreds of features to its coverage on the powerful stimulant.

Initially Pops and the paper were recognized for shedding light on the growing epidemic. The state passed legislation that banned over-the-counter sales of pseudoephedrine, one of the key ingredients in cold medication used to manufacture meth. Congress followed suit, allocating over one hundred million dollars to the fight against the drug and extra law enforcement.

Pops went underground, tracking mega-labs in Mexico and California and revealing deep ties with overseas pharmaceutical factories. He was committed to the story and the families whose lives had been ripped apart by the illicit drug. Then things took an unexpected turn. Local media watchers claimed that *The O* (and namely Pops) had inflated and even falsified statistics and misled readers. Pops was placed on temporary leave as *The O* fought allegations of skewing the truth from the *New York Times* and *Wall Street Journal*. His work was discredited and his reputation destroyed. In a strange way meth had had a devastating effect on him just like it had on its users' bodies.

Part of me wished that Pops had never started on his quest to sound the alarm on meth usage in Oregon. He could have left it to another reporter, and maybe he'd still be here today.

Hearing that Greg had been trying to save *Northwest Extreme* made me pause. That could explain his covert behavior—at least some of it.

Chris raised his hand. "Who is the buyer?"

"Good question," Greg replied. "If I sell—and it's still if—I feel confident about Hoshino, the company interested in acquiring *Northwest Extreme*. Check out their stuff. They have an excellent portfolio. They've transitioned quite a few print publications online seamlessly."

"Why can't we do that ourselves?" I cried out. This couldn't be happening. Why would Greg sell the magazine? Our social media numbers were exploding. I'd been working on posting multiple times a day, asking interesting questions, sharing fun links, and offering our followers exclusive give-aways. It was working. In the last quarter alone we tripled our numbers, and more importantly we started tracking their engagement. I explained to Greg that getting people to actively engage is the key to any successful social media campaign. If we had one hundred thousand followers but only a handful of them interacted with us, it was pointless. On the other hand, if we had thirty-five thousand followers (the number we just hit) who shared links, commented, and liked what we were posting, that was a major success and would be appealing to advertisers.

Greg smiled. "I appreciate your enthusiasm, Meg. I've considered that option, and like I said, you've done an incredible job. In fact, the Japanese investors were very impressed with how quickly our social media numbers have grown. But to be honest, I'm not sure that my heart is into making the magazine digital. I don't think it's much of a secret that I have some serious concerns about what's happening in the digital trend. We're destroying the environment and natural habitats in our quest to get the perfect selfie. I'm sure I've had a conversation with everyone in this room about it. I don't know if

I can be part of this cultural push to go digital, and I don't know if the magazine can survive if I don't." He looked at his feet.

"What does this mean for our jobs if you sell?" Chris asked.

"Yeah, that's another good question and one of the things I've been trying to work out. This company has a history of magazine buyouts and they have a good track record. They've assured me that they would keep the core team in place. Full disclosure— nothing's written in the contract about keeping staff. I've been negotiating on that point and they haven't budged."

Chris rolled up his piece of paper like a telescope. "So we're all going to get laid off?"

"No." Greg shook his head. "I'm going to do everything I can to ensure that doesn't happen. I trust these guys. I don't think that's their intention. I just think that, contractually, they want to reserve the right to let staff go if it's not a match."

"Would we have to move to Japan?" I asked. If I couldn't handle city life in New York, I was fairly confident Japan wasn't for me either.

Greg shook his head. "No, that I know for sure. They want to keep the operation here. Now, I'm not sure if they'll keep this building or if they'll have everyone work from home. There will be some redundancies in staffing. They already have accounting and ad departments in Tokyo."

Another member of the ad team who was sitting on the other side of me muttered something under his breath. "So there *are* going to be cuts," he said to Greg.

"Not necessarily. The only person who will be cut for sure is Angie in accounting. She and I have already had a discussion about this. She knows and she's fine with it since she only works part-time. Listen, ultimately this is a small operation. You're likely to get better benefits working for a bigger company, and as far as ad sales go, the investors in Japan are interested in having a team on the street here in Portland to build relationships with some of the huge outdoor companies based here."

"A likely story," Chris whispered to me. "I don't trust a word he's saying. Listen to how much it's changed in a few minutes. It started with no cuts. Now Angie's out and I guarantee we are too."

I wasn't sure what to think. Greg asked if there were more questions and was greeted with a palpable silence. Gam would be able to sense the negative energy humming in the room in about a second. After an awkward pause, Greg shifted gears. "I'm in my office all day today, so feel free to stop by if you want to chat individually. I'm going to sit on this decision for a week or two, so no one needs to panic. There's plenty of time to figure out what's next for the magazine. Let's move on to your ideas for the November issue. Anyone want to go first?"

There was more silence as Greg scanned the room. Usually on pitch day we're all clambering over each other to go first. Greg's news had squashed the healthy competition between us.

"Anyone?" Greg asked. "No one has a story idea?"

I felt bad for him, so I raised my hand.

"Meg! Thank you. Go for it. What's your idea?"

I explained how I wanted to sign up for training classes with Mind Over Mudder, my plans for documenting the experience online, and then competing in Mud, Sweat, and Beers.

Greg practically did a dance when I finished. "Love it. Love everything about it. These kinds of races have been popping up all around. It's about time Portland finally got in the game. It's yours. Send Angie your expenses and I'll get them approved right away."

I wasn't sure if Greg was really that excited about my idea or if it was more that he was happy that I was willing to break the silence in the room with my pitch. The rest of the team reluctantly offered up their story ideas. Greg said yes to every pitch. He'd never done that before.

As I walked back to my desk after the meeting, Chris caught my arm. "Don't listen to his corporate sales pitch. He's selling. There's no reason he would have told us if he wasn't. Trust me. And take my advice, start looking for a new job now. We're all going to be on the street in a couple weeks."

I started to protest, but he walked off toward the kitchen before I could respond. I wasn't sure what to believe. I had trusted Greg and felt validated that my intuition was right. Greg wasn't a bad guy. He didn't have a secret agenda. He wasn't involved in a cover-up about Pops' death. He was a struggling business owner trying to do the right thing for his employees and the magazine's future.

What I wasn't sure of is whether or not he was

being truthful about the future of *Northwest Extreme*. I had to agree with the ad team. It sounded like Greg was planning to sell. That meant it might just be back to couch surfing and meager meals of soup and grilled cheese for me.

Chapter 4

I tried to put the meeting out of my mind and focus on organizing my story outline. There wasn't much I could do in the short term other than panic about being jobless again. That wasn't going to do me any good, so I decided my best bet was to rock this story and impress the Japanese investors. Greg said they liked what I had done with our social media. Maybe I'd be lucky and get to keep my job after all.

You're not going to have any job if you don't get to work, Meg, I scolded myself, and opened my top desk drawer where I keep a collection of Sharpie pens. Then I collected a stack of crisp file folders and labeled each one with a different-colored Sharpie with *Research, Notes, Photos, Social,* and so on. Everyone teases me about my old-school organization, but the system works for me.

My next task was to register for Mind Over Mudder. The next group training session started tomorrow morning. Talk about good luck. Training sessions were every morning for the first two weeks and then twice daily, aka "daily doubles," for the last week. That meant I would be training for two hours in the morning and two hours in the evening. Fortunately, my schedule was extremely flexible. I updated my online calendar, marking myself out until ten every morning and leaving at three every afternoon.

I called the number listed on Mind Over Mudder's Web site to register for the course. No one answered, so I left a message explaining that I was a journalist and would be writing a feature story on my experience. If I didn't hear back today, I would just show up early for tomorrow's training session.

With the menial work complete, I got started on my favorite thing—research. I'm a research junkie. I can spend hours, days, or even weeks researching a story. I had also learned over the course of working for *Northwest Extreme* that I did much better if I created a rough outline of my story before diving into the process of actually writing it. That's not to say that I didn't allow myself leeway, but it made a big difference to know where I was headed with a story. For Mud, Sweat, and Beers I wanted to give readers an insider's look at training for such an extreme event from a novice's perspective. And I definitely qualified as a novice.

For the rest of the day I scoured the Web, made preliminary phone calls to the race organizers and other mud marathon racers throughout the country, and sketched out the questions I wanted to ask the staff at Mind Over Mudder tomorrow.

Before I knew it, the clock read 5:30. Time to call it a day. Jill, my bestie, was meeting me for pints at our

new favorite Eastside pub. She texted at lunchtime:
Big news. Pints? Migration. 6!

I shut down my laptop, filed my research notes,
and grabbed my supplies (aka my notebook and
pencil) for tomorrow. The late-summer sun hung
high in the sky. Soon it would start to slip on the
horizon as we inched closer to fall, but for the time
being Portlanders were taking advantage of the
extra hours of sunlight. The waterfront path was a
sea of color. Bikers, moms pushing baby joggers,
and runners navigated past one another as the sunlight sparkled off the Willamette River.

Migration, the pub where Jill and I were meeting, was located on the opposite side of the river. I
considered walking. It was a gorgeous evening and
I knew that all too soon the rain would return.
But I stayed longer at work than I had intended. If
I didn't get moving I'd be late. I hurried to my car,
rolled down all the windows, and blasted Taylor
Swift as I drove across the Hawthorne Bridge. Usually, I'm more of a big band fan, but I have to keep
up with my peeps, and all my friends were jamming
to Taylor's latest hit.

Warm air breezed through the sunroof. My hair
barely moved. After attempting to grow it out, I had
had enough. The pixie style framed my face and
made getting ready in the morning a total breeze.
Jill hadn't seen it yet, so I couldn't wait to surprise
her. Speaking of surprises, what could her surprise
be? Jill and I have been besties forever. They say
that opposites attract. That's Jill and me. I'm short,
accident prone, and always seem to be getting
myself into trouble. Jill is tall, graceful, and much
more serious. Gam says we balance each other—I

know how to bring out Jill's goofy side, and she usually talks me out of doing ridiculously stupid things. Or at least she tries to.

I made it to Migration with three minutes to spare. Finding street parking in any of Portland's popular neighborhoods is a nightmare. My timing was impeccable, just as I was driving in front of the busy pub, someone pulled out of a parking space. I didn't even have to parallel park. Thank God.

Southeast Portland, where Migration was located, had become a hub for hipsters with pubs on every other corner, funky shops, and food carts selling everything from home-style fried chicken to bacon milkshakes. Long picnic benches in front of the pub were packed with the after-work crowd kicking off the night with a fresh pint.

I spotted an empty space at one of the far tables and went straight for it. Beer could wait. An outdoor spot was highly coveted. I knew that Jill would want to soak up as much of the lingering summer sun as possible.

"You want us to move?" the guy sitting on the bench asked as I squeezed onto the end.

"No, I'm good. As long as I'm not crowding you."

He shoved his buddies down a couple inches. "I'll be crowded by a cute girl like you any day."

I'm sure I blushed.

At that moment the energy outside shifted. I knew immediately that Jill had arrived. The guy flirting with me and all of his friends sat up a little straighter as she approached the table. I shook my head and laughed. Jill has no idea what her effect is on men. The guy sitting across from me slid so far next to his friend to make room for Jill that their shoulders were touching. She was completely oblivious that all of them were drooling over her when she greeted me with a kiss and giant hug. "Meg! I feel like we haven't seen each other for ages."

"We haven't." I squeezed her back and winked at the guy next to me as I sat down. "It's been like two weeks. That's like an eternity. What have I done to deserve this?"

Jill laughed. She'd obviously come straight from work. Her tailored black skirt, periwinkle silk blouse, and the single string of pearls around her neck were a dead giveaway. She shook her long expertly highlighted hair free from a ponytail. I swear all the guys around us let out audible sighs.

"I love your hair. It's absolutely adorable." She reached across the table and ran her fingers over my new cut. "Adorbs! When did you chop it, and why didn't you consult me first?"

"Do you like it?" I wrinkled my nose. "I mean, really? Is it too short?"

"Meg, it's perfect. Seriously. It's so you! I just can't believe you didn't text me. I would have come to the salon with you."

I knew she wouldn't lie. Jill is the textbook definition of honest, at least when it comes to her friends. When we were in high school I thought it would be fun to experiment with hair color and decided to try going a few shades darker than my naturally blond hair. My first mistake was attempting low lights from a box at home. My second mistake was not consulting Jill. When she saw the blotchy dark streaks in my hair she made me promise that I would never attempt to color my own hair again and that I would never go lighter than a shade of ash blond. I'd followed her advice.

If only she could follow her own advice when it came to doing what she loved. She has always been my biggest cheerleader, encouraging me to follow my dreams, but she hasn't allowed herself the same freedom. Jill has been struggling with her career path since we graduated from college. She has a great job at one of Portland's best law firms thanks to her parents' connections. They are quite pleased that Jill is following their expectations and studying around the clock for the bar exam. The only problem is that Jill doesn't want to be a lawyer. She wants to create art, and she's one of the most talented artists I know. However, she hasn't worked up the courage to break the news to her parents, who have been priming her since we were kids to pursue a "respectable" career like becoming a lawyer or doctor.

The guy sitting next to me interpreted my thoughts. "I think your hair is great. You look like that actress. What's her name? You know, she and Heath Ledger were a thing," he asked his friend.

His friend pushed nerdy black glasses onto the tip of his nose and studied me. After a minute he said, "Michelle Williams."

"Yeah, that's the one." The guy next to me raised his pint glass. "You look like her."

My cheeks radiated with heat. "Thanks."

Jill gave me an "I told you so" look.

"Can we buy you two lovely ladies a pint?" the guy asked. "We were about to head out to a new pub, but we'll stick around if you want."

I waved him off. "No, thanks. We're good. Girls' pint night, you know?"

Jill nodded in agreement. We had some serious catching up to do and didn't need the distraction of hipsters trying to hit on us. Or, more like—her.

The guys took off. I went inside to order our pints. It was my turn to treat, and it felt good to be in a position to buy a round of pints myself. For the first year after we graduated Jill let me live on her couch rent-free and always found subtle ways to pay for me when we went out. She was a good friend. The best.

I decided on Blood, Sweat and Red. The menu board described it as a rose-colored red ale with a light citrus aroma. That sounded ideal for alfresco pints in the evening August sun. Not to mention that it sounded like a classic beer to pair with my feature. In fact, if I liked Blood, Sweat and Red maybe I could work it into my Mud, Sweat, and Beers story. I could see the caption now: *Power through with a perfect pint!*

With two frothy beers in hand, I circled back to the table. Jill had her head down staring at the glowing screen on her phone. I knew this was a tactic she used to appear unavailable.

"Oooh, what a gorgeous color," she said, looking up from her phone as I placed the pints on the table. She tucked her phone into her purse and hid it under the bench.

"If you like the color, you're going to love what they named it."

"Rose City?" Jill asked.

"Nope, even better. More like a title from one of your British mysteries. Blood, Sweat and Red."

"Love it!" Jill raised her glass and clinked it to mine. "I'll drink to that."

"Me too." I took a long sip of the cold beer. It lived up to its name. I could smell a hint of orange, followed by a nice hoppy finish. "It's delish. You'll love this even more. Guess what my next assignment is?"

Jill looked at her beer. "A pub crawl?"

"Almost. Good guess, but no."

She frowned. "Wait a sec, am I going to approve of this assignment, or is this another one where you're going to be in way over your head."

"I think you're going to approve, actually." A brew cycle pedaled into the pub. Beer bike tours were all the rage in Portland. Beer lovers hop aboard a twelve-person bike and pedal from pub to pub. The rowdy group must have already made a few stops. They stumbled off the bike wearing half-eaten pretzel necklaces and singing at the top of their lungs.

"You're not doing one of those, are you?" Jill asked, pointing to the drunk crew. "Those are for tourists."

"Nope."

"Really?" She narrowed her eyes and waited for me to say more.

"Mud, Sweat, and Beers."

"Huh?"

I could barely hear her over the off-key chorus of brew cyclers making their way inside. "That's my next assignment. Mud, Sweat, and Beers. Isn't this beer the perfect accompaniment to the story?"

"What is Mud, Sweat, and Beers?" Jill asked, taking another drink and frowning.

"A mud marathon race."

"Meg!" Jill almost spewed her beer all over me. "What? A mud marathon. You don't even run."

"I know, but wait. It's not really a marathon. I'm just calling it that for the sake of the story. It's only a 5K."

Jill rolled her eyes. "Only a 5K? Again, can I please state the obvious? You don't run. A 5K is over three miles. Aren't these races like army boot camp? Don't you have to scale buildings and stuff?"

I grinned. "Yep! And crawl through muddy pits, slides, you name it. It's going to be a muddy mess. Don't you think I can handle a three-mile run? That's doable. I'm going to train for it too. My training class starts tomorrow."

Jill didn't look convinced. She picked up her beer and slowly drank it. I wondered if she was trying to buy time to come up with the right response. "Actually, you know what, I think you're right. I think you can manage a 5K. This might be really good for you. When I think of what you've done so far with *Northwest Extreme,* maybe this will give you a nice confidence boost, especially if you train. You're really going to train, right?"

I crossed my fingers over my chest. "Promise. It's a three-week training course—Mind Over Mudder—isn't that hilarious? They claim that everyone who completes the course will be ready and in fighting shape to participate in the race."

"Hmm." Jill held her pint glass. "Okay. I'm in support of this idea. In fact, if you want, I'll even do the race with you."

"You will?" I grabbed her forearm. Beer sloshed from the side of her glass. "Sorry."

She smiled and wiped the glass with a napkin. "Sure. It'll be fun. A bunch of people from work did one together last year in Seattle and they said it was a blast. And muddy."

"Muddy! Let's do it." I toasted her again.

"I'm in! But, Meg, you have to promise that you'll follow through with the training."

"Pinky swear." I held out my pinky. We linked our fingers together. I understood why Jill was hesitant. In the past I'd had a tendency to embellish my outdoor ability and borrow some of Jill's expertise when it came to athletic adventures. No more. I was a changed woman after my time in New York. I would keep my promise to Jill and myself and do this right.

We ordered appetizers and another round of pints. Happy chatter and the aromatic scent of hops surrounded us. Inside, the brew cycle tourists had managed to corral a group of locals into singing spontaneous karaoke with them. The garage-style doors on the front of the building were open, allowing pubgoers inside to drink semi-alfresco and giving all of us a front row seat to the impromptu performance. The steel corrugated siding on Migration's natural wood walls glinted in the sun. A dog lapped water at a table nearby. No wonder I turned down the job in New York. Portland at this time of year was as close to perfection as it gets.

I took a sip of beer. "So, dish, what's the deal with your surfer? Are you eloping to a tropical island anytime soon?" After breaking up with her pretentious boyfriend last summer, Jill had been casually dating a windsurfer whom she met in Hood River.

Jill laughed and shook her head. "No. He's cute, but you know you can only hear about the gnarly winds so many times before it becomes a snooze fest." She paused. "I do have some other news, though."

"What's your news?" I asked, biting into a pulled pork nacho and clapping my hands together. "I love news!"

Jill picked off a jalapeño. "I'm not sure you're going to like it."

"What, the nachos? They're awesome." I made a goofy face in my attempt to tease her.

"My news." She sounded serious.

Uh-oh. Please don't let it be that she's back together with Will Barrington, I prayed internally. Will and Jill (their names match—gag) had been on a long break ever since I caught him having intimate drinks with a sexy lawyer from his firm. I'd never been a fan of Will, but seeing him hurt Jill made me want to punch him in the face. It seemed like she was over him, but she hadn't been very forthcoming about their status. They weren't "Facebook official" (meaning Jill's Facebook page listed her as single) anymore, which I took as a good sign.

"I'm seriously thinking about dropping out of law school."

"Really?" That wasn't huge news. Jill had been talking about following her passion all summer. "Did you finally talk to your parents?"

"Not about this."

I chomped another deliciously fatty nacho piled

with cheese, pork, and cilantro sour cream. "About what? Are you thinking of doing art school instead?"

"It's more than that." Jill stared at the plate of nachos.

"And . . . ?"

She leaned in. "Meg, you're not going to believe this."

"Try me. You're killing me. You're never like this. Put me out of my misery. What is your big news?"

"I've been offered a one-year study abroad scholarship at the art institute in Italy."

"Italy!" I shouted.

She gave the group sitting next to us an apologetic look. "Shhh! I haven't told anyone yet."

"Italy? You haven't told anyone that you're going to Italy? Are you crazy?"

"I'm not even sure I'm going."

"Jill, Italy! Come on, *Italy*. You're going. You're totally going. It's not up for debate."

"You haven't given me a chance to tell you the details."

Tapping my hands on the table, I gave her what Mother calls the stink eye. "Start talking."

"Remember how I sold that painting a couple weeks ago? It turns out that the person who purchased it is a curator at a museum in Rome. He showed the piece to his friend who happens to be a professor at the art institute, and it spiraled from there. I got an e-mail asking if I was free for a Skype call. I didn't even know what we were going to talk about. I kind of hoped that maybe they wanted to display the painting in the museum, but it was even better. They offered me a full scholarship with room and board for the entire year."

"Jill, that is amazing. I'm so happy for you! I told you that your work is incredible. Now do you believe me?"

She smiled, but there was a sadness behind her eyes.

"What is it?" I asked.

"It's a huge decision, Meg. This impacts my entire future."

"In the best way possible," I interrupted.

"What if it's a huge mistake? Maybe I should just follow what my parents want me to do and finish law school."

"But they can't say no to this, Jill. A full ride? Art school in Rome? That's major! We're not talking about you dabbling with watercolors in my basement or something. This is an opportunity you can't pass up. Imagine the connections you'll make in the art world."

Jill pushed around her nachos. My side of the plate had a giant hole in it. Jill's was untouched. "Look, I understand that this is a life-changing decision, but it's the best kind of life-changing decision."

"Easy for you to say. You just turned down a job in New York."

"I know, but that's different. ESPN isn't my dream job. If the *NYT* came calling, you know that I'd jump all over that—or *The O,* but it's not like I've always imagined being a sportswriter. You've wanted to be an artist since you wore your hair in braids and played with American Girl dolls."

"I know." Jill rubbed her temples. "I don't have

much time to decide. School starts at the end of September."

"That's in a month!"

"Right."

I ran my finger along the rim of my pint glass. Jill and I had been inseparable for as long as I could remember. September was a month away and Italy was an ocean away. Suddenly, I realized why Jill was torn. I was thrilled for my best friend, but I didn't know if I could handle being on different continents for a year.

Chapter 5

After happy hour with Jill, I drove home in a daze. What was happening? My entire world was shifting. Was this just the normal evolution of our twenties? I knew I had to encourage Jill to take the scholarship, but it wasn't going to be easy. I was going to have to bottle my own feelings and focus on what was best for her.

I didn't sleep much. I spent most of the night scouring the Web for information about Italy. Flights weren't cheap, as in over a thousand dollars apiece. I did some quick math and calculated that I could probably swing two visits if I saved every penny—every single cent—I earned at *Northwest Extreme* and cut out happy hour. That would be a small price to pay to see my bestie, and to visit Italy. Aside from the cost of the flight, I could stay with Jill, which would drastically cut costs. By morning I had it all mapped out. I would visit her at winter break and again in the spring. Two Roman holidays in one year. It sounded very Audrey Hepburn. In fact, I sent Jill a text: **Movie night my place tomorrow. Cary Grant and Italian wine.**

By the time my alarm buzzed at 5:15 the next morning, I was already up and dressed. It felt like the first day of school. What do you wear to a mud race training class? I opted for black yoga pants and a hot pink T-shirt that read: REAL WOMEN DRINK CRAFT BEER. That should set the right tone for my first workout session.

Moonlight bathed the street as I tossed my gym bag with a change of clothes in the back of the car and made my way north to Vancouver. I knew the route well. Gam lives on the Vancouver waterfront in a funky condo on the banks of the Columbia River. Mind Over Mudder's headquarters were housed in old army barracks at Fort Vancouver National Park.

When working on my research yesterday I learned that the Vancouver Barracks were the first U.S. Army post in the Pacific Northwest. The post was established in 1849 to help aid American settlers as they made their way into the Oregon territory. Over the next hundred years it was used for supplies and headquarters during the Civil War and the Indian wars. Later it became a lumber mill and training facility in World Wars I and II. Today, it's a national landmark and the barracks are managed by the National Park Service, which has a long-term plan to rehabilitate the buildings for preservation and potentially to house future retail shops and restaurants.

Mind Over Mudder opened its doors six months ago as part of a pilot program with the National Park Service. It had a temporary one-year lease in the south barracks. I was interested to see how the training company had updated the barracks. According to my preliminary research the guidelines for renovating the historic buildings were very stringent.

My memories of Fort Vancouver were from childhood when we'd visit Gam for Sunday brunch. Pops loved history. He would always take me on a living history tour of Fort Vancouver. I felt like I was stepping back into the pages of my favorite childhood book, *Little House on the Prairie.* A few times a year the fort would actually come to life with volunteers who reenacted the time by dressing in period costumes for candlelight tours. I remember the scent of the candles in the lanterns and bread baking in wood-fired ovens, the clanking sound of iron and flaming sparks that danced across the dark room in the blacksmith's shop, and the musty smell of fur in the trading post.

Pops' fascination with life in the mid-1800s under British rule was infectious. "Imagine, Maggie," he would whisper as he guided me up the wooden ramp to the McLoughlin House. "Imagine how different life was not that long ago. Writing with a quill pen using only the flame of a dripping candle to guide you. It's a far cry from our modern e-mail, isn't it?"

I would nod and follow after him stopping to admire a porcelain doll and miniature doll house in the bedroom of the Chief Factor's daughter.

It had been at least a decade since I'd visited the fort. There wasn't any traffic on the freeway at the early hour. Not to mention that I was driving against the flow. Most commuters traveled from Vancouver into Portland on the morning commute, not the other way around.

I took the first exit off the freeway and looped past Officer's Row to the park's entrance. Officer's Row is exactly as it sounds: a row of stately white restored nineteenth-century homes that sit adjacent to the park grounds. Trees lined both sides of the street, making it look like a parade scene from an American movie set. I could picture flags flying from each wraparound white porch and a general in full uniform marching his troops down the idyllic street.

At the north end of the park a circular bandstand sat in a grassy field, offering visitors a covered spot for a picnic or a picturesque place to pose with Mt. Hood looming in the background. A single-lane road cut through the park down to the barracks. The gate was locked.

I followed the main road around the picnic grounds and found street parking at the base of the hill across from Fort Vancouver. I glanced at the historic gardens in front of the fort's massive wooden stakes. A canopy of hops created a romantic archway. There were rows of corn stalks, pumpkin vines, and planter boxes of herbs. Back in the days of the Hudson's Bay Company the gardens would have stretched from the Columbia River for a mile up to what was now the busy intersection of Mill Plain Boulevard. Today, the gardens are tended by volunteers, and each harvest the bounty is used to recreate authentic 1800s fare. I'd been reading up on the fort's history and had learned that the intimidating twenty-foot wooden spears guarding its perimeter weren't actually historically accurate.

Since it wasn't a military fort the formidable fence wouldn't have been there. I was excited to pepper details like that into my feature.

Before grabbing my gym bag from the back seat, I snapped a couple of pictures of the fort, the park, and the barracks on my cell phone. Then I posed for a selfie, making sure the text on my T-shirt was visible. Clenching my jaw and grimacing, I took a selfie with my best "I'm about to freak out" face. I posted the selfie on *Northwest Extreme*'s Instagram with the caption: *IT'S ABOUT TO GET MUDDY! WISH ME LUCK AND BEERS.*

Showtime, Meg, I said to myself as I looped my gym bag over my shoulder and walked up the hill toward the barracks.

The grassy hillside to my right looked ravaged from the summer's intense sun. The Pacific Northwest had experienced one of the driest and hottest summers on record. Forest fires had raged throughout Oregon and Washington, rivers and lakes ran low, and everyone complained about the heat. Fortunately, the weather had shifted in the last few weeks as we inched closer to fall, with cool morning breezes blowing in from the coast.

Dew coated the brown grass. In another month or so the field would be brilliantly green again. That's the beauty of the Pacific Northwest; every season brings its own display of colors. Summer's dull, chapped browns would soon give way to fall's symphony of green, yellow, orange, red, and brown. I could almost smell the shift in the air. Fall is my favorite season. I love the cool mornings, pumpkin lattes, Oktoberfests, apple picking, and so much more.

Fall, glorious fall, was right around the corner. I couldn't wait.

You're going to have to wait, Meg, I told myself. *You have some serious training ahead.* I inhaled through my nose and proceeded toward the barracks. The barracks used to house 240 soldiers. A group of four buildings had been constructed in the early 1900s. Most of the buildings were in desperate need of repair. Plywood had been boarded over the windows of three of the buildings. The exterior paint was chipped. Large sections of wood-planked siding were missing and rotted. *This could be a great setting for Halloween,* I thought.

Only one of the buildings had lights on inside and actual panes of glass in the windows. That must be where Mind Over Mudder was located. I made my way up a wooden ramp and onto the wrap-around porch. White beams divided the porch into six-foot sections. I paused for a moment and took in the view of the grounds. A century ago the empty field would have been alive with soldiers out for their morning calisthenics routine. I clicked a couple of photos. I wasn't sure if they would turn out in the dusky light, but if they did, I could search the library's archives and see if I could find a picture of an active army regiment to run side by side. That would be a nice touch.

I opened the front door and stepped inside. I couldn't believe my eyes. Obviously, renovations had been done to the building. The restored tin ceiling above sparkled against the glowing yellow lantern light fixtures, and the white-oak original hardwood floors gleamed like new. Shiny, wall-mounted radiators ran along one side of the hallway.

A handwritten sign with an arrow pointed to the stairway: MIND OVER MUDDER DOWNSTAIRS TO THE RIGHT.

Running my hand along the creamy chair rail, I followed the sign toward the staircase. I appreciated the fact that the barracks had been restored to their original glory. There's such a push these days to knock old buildings down and throw up something new in its place. But in my opinion, nothing compares to the history of a building. Men walked these halls for decades. I was following in their footsteps.

At the base of the stairs another sign pointed to the locker room, gym, and office. I headed for the office. The sound of angry voices startled me. I paused in front of the door and peered inside the half window. Two men stood inside arguing.

"Dylan, I know what you're doing. It's not right. I'm not going to be part of it." One of the men stood in front of a wall filled with rows and rows of vitamins and supplements.

The other man, I guessed Dylan, sat at a circular table in the center of the room. He opened a large bottle of vitamins and shook a couple into his hand. "I don't know what you're talking about, Billy." He popped the vitamins into his mouth and swallowed.

Had I walked in on some kind of personal dispute? I started to back away from the door, but my cell phone slipped out of my pocket and landed on the floor. Both men stopped talking and looked expectantly at me.

I reached down to pick it up just as the office door swung open. "Hi," I said, holding up my phone and trying to play it cool. "Meg Reed." I extended my other hand. "Journalist with *Northwest Extreme.* Did you get my message yesterday?"

The guy who had been standing on the far wall gave me a once-over, ignoring my extended hand. He stepped to the side to let me in. "Billy the Tank," he said with a two-fingered salute. "We don't shake around here. We salute. That's your first lesson."

"Got it." I returned his salute.

"Second lesson. Lose that shirt."

"My beer shirt? But we're training for Mud, Sweat, and Beers. Isn't that the whole point?"

"Not around here. I don't let any of my clients put that kind of crap into their bodies." He looked at the guy sitting at the table and gave him a look I couldn't decipher. "Isn't that right, Dylan?"

"Right." Dylan twisted the cap on the vitamin bottle and pushed his chair back. "You're a journalist? Which one?"

"Which one?"

"Yeah, are you with KPDX or that outdoor magazine?"

"*Northwest Extreme.* KPDX is doing a story too?"

Dylan folded his hands into a prayer pose. "It's our lucky week." He looked to be in his mid to late forties, but I'm a terrible judge when it comes to guessing someone's age. Dylan wore a loose-fitting hemp shirt and sandals. His long, wavy hair fell to his shoulders. *Total hippie*, I thought. And what was a hippie doing with Billy the Tank? Billy was the opposite. He was short, squat, and all muscle. Bulges stretched from his T-shirt and army shorts. His hair was shaved in a tight crew cut.

Billy scoffed. "I'll tell you this right now and I'll tell whoever shows up for KPDX the same thing. If you get in the way of my training, you're out. One strike and you're out. Got it?"

"I guess." I shrugged. "I'm not sure what you mean by getting in the way of your training?"

"I had a journalist hang around a while back," Billy replied. I didn't like the way he said "journalist" like it was a bad word. "She kept getting in my way. Trying to stop me and my clients in mid-run for interviews. That's not going to happen. I run a tight ship around here."

"Okay. No mid-run interview. Got it. Anything else I should know?"

Billy frowned. He studied me for a moment. "You should prepare for the worst days of your life."

"Right." I laughed.

"No joke. You will hurt. I'm gonna put the hurt on all of you. You'll learn how to work through the pain. Think of this as boot camp, only ten times harder." Billy folded his arms across his chest and walked out of the room.

I chuckled and looked at Dylan.

Dylan shook his head. "He's not kidding. Billy is the best there is, but our clients tend to hate him." He held up a bottle of vitamins. "That's what I'm here for. My natural herbs and supplements will help ease the pain."

"Maybe clients don't respond well to his kind and gentle personality."

He laughed. "That is Billy's kind and gentle personality. Wait until you get out on the course this morning. You haven't seen anything yet."

"Great. Sounds like I'm about to have some serious fun."

Chapter 6

"I think you mentioned wanting to do an interview on the phone," Dylan said, taking a seat. He motioned to the empty chair across from him. "You've got about thirty minutes. You want to do it now?"

"Sure." I pulled out my notebook and flipped it to the page of questions I'd worked on yesterday. "You and Billy are business partners, is that right?"

Dylan laughed. "Our clients call us the odd couple, but it works."

"How so?"

"Like I said, Billy is a world-class athlete and trainer. He served in two Gulf wars. Came home and started competing in triathlons, Iron Mans, and mud races. He decided to start training novices a few years ago. He's been at it ever since. You're definitely going to hurt after today, but it'll be worth it. Every single one of our clients has finished the race after working out with Billy. That's a huge accomplishment."

I took notes as he talked. "What's your role?"

"I'm a naturopath. Billy and I met at an Iron Man a few years ago. I had a booth and was selling my personal line of supplements. Billy was looking for someone with my kind of knowledge to help his clients with eating plans, vitamin regimens, that kind of thing."

"So these are all your personal line?" I pointed to the shelves of vitamins behind me.

"No, not all of them." Dylan pushed the bottle of vitamins across the table. It was a black bottle with the Mind Over Mudder label on the front. "This is our exclusive line."

I examined the bottle.

"It's a special mix designed to help build muscle, burn fat, and speed up weight loss. We've had great success with it. You'll get a sample in your welcome packet. Give it a try. I think you'll be really pleased with the results."

I handed him back the bottle and jotted down a few notes. What I didn't tell him is that I probably wouldn't take the supplement. Growing up with Gam had left me leery of traditional medicine. She believes in a holistic approach to healing. When I would complain of a sore throat she would wrap her warm, gentle hands around my neck to give me a "zap" of Reiki; then she would prescribe herbed tea with lots of lemon and honey, and remind me to call on my body's innate ability to heal itself. Gam is convinced that through the practice of meditation and visualization, our bodies can do amazing things. I'd witnessed her ability to heal enough to be a believer. Maybe that's why I don't like taking medicine or even vitamins. Of course I'm not sure that Gam's whole-body healing approach includes things like drinking beer or rich, dark coffee. She tends to opt for green smoothies and white jasmine tea. Whether my aversion to traditional medicine came from Gam or just my own neurosis, there was something that freaked me out about taking anything in the shape of a pill.

Dylan spent the next fifteen minutes giving me an overview of Mind Over Mudder's history and training regimen. My hand flew over the page as he rattled off stats about how many finishers they had not only compete, but win mud races. Two of their past clients had even gone on to win national titles. I made a note about following up with them. That could make an interesting sidebar to accompany my story.

"You should probably get down to the locker room," Dylan said when I finished questioning him. "Billy doesn't tolerate any late comers."

"Just like being in the army," I joked.

Dylan narrowed his green eyes at me. "One morning with Billy and you'll be wishing you were in the army." He handed me a receipt. "For your records."

"Thanks." I folded the receipt and placed it in my notebook. There was no way I wanted to forget to turn it in to *Northwest Extreme*. If Italy was in my future, I definitely needed a reimbursement for the training course.

"Good luck," Dylan said as I left. "I'm sure I'll be seeing you back here for my special pain relief multipack. Don't forget to take the sample that will be in your welcome bag. We'll see how you do on those and then we can create an individualized supplement plan for you."

"Right." I walked out the door. Was Dylan being dramatic? I hoped so. Otherwise, what had I gotten myself into?

The locker rooms were at the opposite end of the hallway. I could hear Billy shouting out orders. It was a few minutes before six. I hurried down the corridor heeding Dylan's advice not to be late. I ducked inside. Billy snapped his fingers at me. "You're late! One minute. Drop and give me ten."

"What?" I caught the eye of a woman sitting on one of the wooden benches. She gave me a sympathetic look and then pointed to the floor.

"Ten! Go. Do you want to make it twenty?" Billy barked.

"Uh . . . I," I stuttered.

"All right. Twenty, then. Drop and give me twenty right now."

I placed my notebook on the bench and knelt onto the cold tile floor. I assumed that Billy meant push-ups. Push-ups aren't exactly my thing. I spaced my hands wide on the floor and lowered my body toward the ground.

"Stop!" Billy shouted. He walked over to me. My arms quaked. Billy positioned his foot on the small of my back. "I want your back as flat as a table. There's no slumping. Got it?"

I nodded.

Billy counted off my push-ups. I struggled to keep my back in contact with the sole of his shoe and to stop my arms from shaking. Muscles that hadn't been used in years revolted as I lowered myself down again and again.

"You have signed on to train with me," Billy addressed the room. In addition to the woman sitting on the bench there was an overweight middle-aged man, two young guys who looked like runners, and three moms wearing matching T-shirts. This was my training group for the next three weeks, and I wasn't exactly making the best first impression. Billy paused and looked down at me. "Keep your back straight. You've got eight more."

My heart rate climbed with each badly formed push-up. Blood rushed to my head. Sweat dripped from my brow onto the tile floor.

"As I was saying," Billy continued. "You are mine for the next three weeks, and you are going to hate every single sweaty minute you spend with me. This is going to be the toughest time of your life. Some of you will drop out. Only the toughest of you are going to survive. You're going to be bruised and bloodied. You'll have battle wounds and scars that will stay with you for a lifetime. You are going to hurt. But those of you who last *will* finish Mud, Sweat, and Beers, that is a promise."

I was glad I couldn't see his face. I could imagine him staring down each of my fellow teammates as he spoke.

"That's twenty!" He tapped my back with his shoe. "On your feet."

On your feet, yeah right. Easy for Billy to say. My arms felt like noodles. I crawled on my knees and somehow found my way to standing.

Billy yanked at the whistle around his neck.

"When we're out on the course and you hear me blow this, it means drop and give me ten wherever you are. If you don't, you go back to the start." He made the rounds, giving each of us black Mind Over Mudder T-shirts and bandanas. "This is your uniform. You'll wear it every day."

I squeezed next to the woman on the bench. She looked as white as the tile floor.

"I heard he was a drill sergeant, but I didn't think he was going to be this intense," she whispered.

"I know. It sounds like we're going to have so much fun." I couldn't keep the sarcasm from my voice. "It's like being in the army, right?"

"Right." She held out her left hand. An enormous diamond sparkled on her ring finger. "I'm Jenny."

"Meg Reed," I replied. "Journalist with *Northwest Extreme*."

"You're being paid to be tortured for the next three weeks. I signed up for this. I'm *paying* to do this. What is wrong with me?"

"You're a glutton for punishment?"

She sighed. "More like a glutton. I can't seem to lose this baby fat." She jiggled her thigh.

"How old is your baby?"

"Ten."

"Ten months? That's nothing," I assured her. "Doesn't it take at least a year to lose the weight you gain when you're pregnant?"

Jenny pinched her stomach. "That's what everyone told me, but let me clarify, my 'baby' is ten *years* old and I'm still working this off."

"Gotcha." I smiled.

I had a good feeling about Jenny. She and I could team up and stick to the back of the pack. Before we could chat more, a woman wearing a navy blue tracksuit and more makeup than a beauty pageant contestant pranced into the room.

"Sorry I'm late, everyone." She waved and pointed to a man with a professional video camera with the KPTV logo behind her. "We had some technical difficulties with our live shot this morning."

Billy glared at her.

She didn't notice. She thrust papers into all of our hands. "Your eyes aren't deceiving you, I am indeed Kelsey Kain from KPDX." Giving us a cheesy grin, she continued. "It's your lucky day. You all are going to be on morning TV for the next few weeks. If you'll just sign these release forms, we'll be all set for you to make your debut."

Was it just me or was there an actual glare coming from her brilliantly white teeth.

Billy snatched a release form from her hand. Kelsey startled.

"Listen, lady, I run the show around here. I told Dylan I'd give you one shot just like our other reporter here." He pointed at me. "No one gets in the way of my training, understood? You keep up. You stay out of my way, or you're out. Got it?"

Kelsey smiled sweetly at Billy. "Of course. You won't even know I'm here." She turned to me. Her makeup cracked as she gave me a forced smile. "I didn't realize I had competition. I was under the impression that KPDX had an exclusive. This story is mine."

"Don't worry," I said. "I write for *Northwest Extreme*. I'm pretty sure we have very different audiences."

"*Northwest Extreme*, the outdoor magazine?" Kelsey asked.

"Yep, that's the one."

"Ah, I see." She gave me a half smile and turned back to Billy. "I'm glad to hear that KPDX is the only serious news outlet with an exclusive."

"What's her problem?" Jenny asked.

"Welcome to the world of media. Everyone wants an exclusive story."

"Isn't she on that goofy morning show where they play pranks on each other and eat doughnuts on the air?" Jenny tugged at her T-shirt, pulling it away from her waist.

"Yeah." I grinned. I was liking Jenny more and more by the minute. "Trust me, everyone in the world of media thinks they are a serious journalist."

"But I watch her show while I'm making breakfast for my son in the mornings. Last week she was getting makeup and fashion advice from drag queens."

"Well see, that's serious journalism." I winked.

Billy blew his whistle. We all jumped. "On the floor! Drop and give me ten."

Everyone looked at each other. After an awkward pause, Billy let out a long, shrill whistle. "I said drop and give me ten. On the floor—now! Drop, or it'll be twenty."

This time everyone followed his order. I had no idea how I was going to force my aching muscles to do another ten push-ups, but I at least made it to the floor. Fortunately, Kelsey Kain saved me. I faked my push-ups as Billy yelled in her face. "On the floor, newsgirl! Everyone on my team participates."

She batted her false lashes. "Oh, sorry, I didn't realize you meant me."

Billy folded his arms over his chest and waited.

"Okay then." She dropped to the floor and executed ten perfect push-ups.

Of course. She was perky, pretty, and athletic. Just my luck to get stuck on assignment with someone like Kelsey Kain.

"On your feet!" Billy ordered when our push-ups were complete. He held up his black bandana and demonstrated how he wanted them tied on our heads. "If I catch you on the course without your bandana, you'll drop and give me twenty and go back to the start. Understood?"

We all nodded in terrified silence.

"Tie 'em," Billy commanded.

Jenny unfolded her bandana on her lap. "I don't think I can do this."

"I'll tie it for you." I grabbed the bandana from her lap.

"No, I mean this training. This is crazy. I thought it would be kind of a laugh. You know, modeled after a military boot camp. I didn't think we were actually going to be in boot camp."

"You can't quit now. We haven't even started," I said. I agreed with her, but there was no turning back for me. I needed someone like Jenny to survive Billy's constant barrage.

She leaned forward so that I could reach behind her and fasten her bandana. "Okay, I'll give it a couple days, but I'm not making any promises."

I squeezed her hand. "Deal. We'll do this together. It won't be so bad. And if Billy's right, you'll have a svelte pre-baby body by the time we're done. That's motivation, right?"

Jenny helped tie my bandana. "I guess, but I don't have a good feeling about this."

Chapter 7

I should have listened to Jenny. She was right. We spent the next week running mile after mile—uphill, downhill, on flat ground, up stairs, and down stairs. Billy had us lifting weights, doing squats, arm hangs, pull-ups, push-ups, and a variety of other tortures that I was sure would invade my nightmares for years to come. Every cell in my body ached.

Billy was right. By the end of the week I was bloodied, bruised, and blistered. My skin was chapped from chafing against my Mind Over Mudder shirt. My feet had taken a beating. It was all I could do to limp from the locker room to my car every morning. Once I made it to the office, I planted myself at my desk and didn't move until it was time to go home. At home I would soak my feet and crash on the couch before the sun set.

The week may have been the most excruciating of my life, but honestly I was too tired to remember most of it. My days consisted of icing body parts, trying Gam's healing techniques on my raw muscles, and downing Advil. So much for not wanting to take medication. I even considered trying Dylan's "cocktail" for pain relief. The only reason I didn't was because I would have had to walk an extra twenty feet to his office to get it.

At least the week went by fast, and my story came together quickly. It helped that I couldn't move from my desk. I didn't have any option other than busting out my word count. Greg was in Japan negotiating with the buyers. Most of my colleagues were out on assignment, which meant the office was relatively quiet—something that helped me focus. And at least I wasn't embarrassing myself in front of the entire staff.

There was no faking how much pain I was in. I moved like a robot, trying to bend as little as possible. When the following Friday rolled around, the few people left in the office discussed their weekend plans. Not me. I'd never dreaded a weekend before. Billy had informed us that our daily doubles were due to start on Saturday.

I wasn't sure how my body was going to hold up. If it weren't for social media I would have quit. I had enough material to finish my story. It would have been easy to simply opt out for the last week of training. But that wasn't going to happen. I'd been posting daily updates to our social pages, and they were attracting a crazy amount of traction. One photo, a selfie of me at the end of a run drenched in sweat with a bruise the size of a small apple on my left arm, had been shared almost a thousand times. The comments kept popping up in my e-mail. My favorite one was from a guy in Germany who said, "Someone buy that girl a good beer."

Jenny, to my surprise, had stuck with it, and was already looking much thinner. I couldn't believe how quickly the weight was dropping off her. She wasn't enjoying Billy's insane workout sessions either, but the fact that she could slide into her jeans was very motivating.

"Meg, can you believe it? I never thought I would fit in these jeans and it's only been two weeks," she said as we laced up our tennis shoes in the locker room on Saturday morning.

"You look great," I replied. "I mean, honestly, I can't believe it's only been two weeks. I hear Billy's damn whistle in my sleep. I'm surprised any of us are upright and that we have any fat left on our bodies. I'm pretty sure I sweated all my fat off on this morning's run alone. Maybe it's all an illusion that we're losing weight. It's because we're all so tight and stiff we have to walk like statues."

"Have you tried Dylan's vitamin regimen? It does help. I've been taking it twice a day and I'm not hurting at all." She stuck her fingers into her belt loops to show how loose her jeans were.

"What? You're not the least bit sore?" My back throbbed as I tightened the knot in my shoelace.

Jenny shook her head. "Nope. I was at the beginning, but as soon as I started taking the vitamins, I've felt great. In fact, I have more energy now than I have in years. You've got to try them. I can't believe you're not using them. That's an important part of the Mind Over Mudder training protocol."

"Wow. That's amazing. I feel like I'm about ninety. No amount of ice or Advil seems to be working, but I'm not really a supplement kind of girl."

"I'm telling you, I think it's the vitamins. They're

magic." She reached her leg out onto the wooden bench and touched her toes in one smooth fluid motion.

I pushed myself up with wobbly arms.

"Do you want to run together?" Jenny asked. She finished stretching and pranced from side to side on the tips of her feet. "I can't wait to get out there. Did you hear we're doing the mudflats this morning?"

I shook my head.

"Yeah, it's supposed to be a giant mud pit." Jenny nodded enthusiastically. "I guess they hosed down that field over by the airfield. I can't wait to finally get dirty. All we've been doing is running and lifting weights. Now we're getting to the good stuff. So you want to hit it?"

"You go ahead." I waved her on. "I have a couple of questions to ask Dylan for my story. He's been so busy this week that I haven't had a chance to talk to him. I saw him in the office this morning." That wasn't exactly a lie. I did have a few questions for Dylan. Nothing that couldn't wait, but I had a plan for getting out of daily doubles. I figured if I could hide out in the barracks until everyone left, I could kill time by interviewing Dylan and then hook up with them at the end of the course. No one would need to know that I hadn't been along for the entire five-mile morning run. It was a brilliant plan if I did say so myself.

"Have him give you a sample while you're there." Jenny pinched her waist. "Trust me. It's magic!"

She jogged out of the locker room. I watched her go. She had definitely made the biggest transformation out of any of us in two weeks, but I had a feeling the "magic" had more to do with revving up her metabolism with endless runs and workouts. If there really was a vitamin supplement that worked weight-loss miracles like Jenny's, it would be selling out in every market in the country and making head-line news.

You're just jealous, Meg. I tied my other shoe and headed down the hall to Dylan's office. I probably was jealous. There was no debating that Jenny had had incredible results. Granted, it wasn't as if I had a lot of extra baby weight around my middle like Jenny, but I wouldn't have complained about losing a couple pounds. If anything, I think I had gained since starting training. Jill had promised me that was because I was building more muscle. I hoped she was right.

More like building blisters.

I hobbled toward the office but stopped in mid-stride at the sound of Billy's whistle behind me.

"Where do you think you're going?"

Uh-oh.

I turned to see Billy standing in the door frame of the locker room. His hands were placed firmly on his hips and his face fumed with anger.

"I was just going to see if I could grab Dylan for a quick interview. I have a couple of follow-up questions that I need him to answer for my feature."

"You know the rule, Reed. You get outside and get on the course—now!"

"I know, but—"

Billy cut me off. "The only butt I want to see is yours heading out that door."

My shoulders slumped. So much for my brilliant plan.

"Move it!" Billy let out another shrill whistle.

I lurched forward in response.

Billy stomped after me.

Outside the rest of the group was waiting for us. Jenny jogged over to me. "I thought you were interviewing Dylan."

"I was," I whispered. "Until I got caught."

Billy glared at us. "Listen up! This morning your real training starts. You're about to get muddy. I don't want to hear any complaining. Not a single word. Understood?"

No one spoke. Everyone looked at the grass as Billy continued to shout out orders. "We're warming up with our five-mile run. We'll stop halfway for burpees, then hit the mudflats."

Burpees were my worst nightmare. I was convinced that they were an ancient form of medieval torture that Billy had resurrected. The four-count exercise involved a squat followed by a thrust where you were supposed to kick your legs back into a push-up and then frog jump into another squat. For someone with arms as short as mine I felt like a T. rex when I tried to do them. Billy always found fault with my technique. I'd become familiar with the sound of him yelling, "Kick it out, Reed! Lock down those abs!"

He continued his speech to us, while I tried to think of any excuse to get out of doing burpees. "You are going to need every ounce of strength to get through this mud. It's thick—I mean thick." Billy paused and coughed. At first I thought he was being dramatic. Then he clutched his chest.

Tim Baxter, the overweight businessman, ran up to him. He reminded me of something out of one of Matt's sci-fi movies with the hulking gray wireless headphones covering his ears. He looked like an alien. "Are you okay?"

Billy rolled back on his heels. He looked like he was about to pass out.

Jenny stifled a scream. Tim caught Billy as he fell backward.

Was he having a heart attack? Probably from all the stress and yelling. And the whistling—the constant blare of his whistle would give me a heart attack.

Billy cleared his throat and stood. He elbowed Tim. "Back off, tubs. I'm fine. I'm fine."

Tim looked unsure, but he repositioned his headphones and backed away.

Billy tapped Tim's chest. "I'm fine. Get out there. You and beer gut need to move it—now!" He blew his whistle three times and yelled at the group. "Get moving. Let's go!"

Jenny and I started jogging up the hill. "You think he's okay?" I asked.

"I don't know," Jenny replied. Her stride was much longer than mine. Being short sucks sometimes, especially when it comes to running. I took two steps for every one of hers. "Even if he isn't, he's not going to let anyone know it."

"Do you think he should be running? It looked like he was having a heart attack or something."

"That's what I thought too." She glanced up ahead. Billy was jogging backward leading the pack up the hill. "He looks okay now."

"Yeah, I guess," I replied. Pain spread up my legs each time my feet hit the pavement. We followed the flour marking the route up the hill. The first portion of our morning run looped on the road through the park, then up through Officer's Row, past the college, and back to Fort Vancouver. We'd stop at an abandoned field, aka the mudflats, near historic Pearson Field airport to cap off the morning's fun.

Mother likes to remind me that sarcasm isn't one of my most flattering attributes, but really, who coined the phrase "fun run"? I'd like to suggest alternative forms of morning fun, like a cup of French press coffee and the newspaper for starters.

My breath became shallow as I lagged behind the pack. Jenny had caught up with Billy and was chatting with him as they crested the hill. Talking and running at the same time is not an option for me. I wondered if she was checking on him. Kelsey Kain, the KPDX reporter, ran next to Tim. She had to slow her pace and held her phone with one hand to get video of him. Tim, believe it or not, was even slower than me. She thrust her phone in his face. Why was she interviewing him as we were running? She was playing with fire. Billy wasn't going to like that.

I focused on my breathing, trying to fill my lungs with as much oxygen as possible. At the top of the hill Billy sounded his whistle again, pointing us to the left. There was no need. We all knew the route by now. Billy paused and leaned against an oak tree. This wasn't exactly abnormal behavior. He often stopped on runs and waited for those of us in the back of the pack to catch up. I noticed Kelsey run over to him. Their expressions were serious as I passed them and crossed the street. Was Kelsey concerned about him too?

I jogged on the sidewalk in front of an old colonial-style officer's mansion that had been converted into apartments. Lace curtains on the front window swayed open. I squinted to see inside. At that moment, an elderly woman locked her eyes on mine.

I almost tripped over a crack in the sidewalk. I stopped and caught myself. When I looked back at the window the curtains were closed and the woman was gone. When I was a kid one of my classmates told me that all of the houses on Officer's Row were haunted. I shuddered. Had I just seen a ghost?

Meg, stop stalling and run, I told myself. There's no such thing as ghosts.

The old lady had spooked me. I picked up my pace and sprinted to catch up with everyone. We ran past the high school and community college as the sun appeared in the sky. Birds called out to us. Tiny droplets of dew danced on the dry grass fields. Soon students would return to the buildings with heavy backpacks and the promise of a fresh start for the new school year.

I cranked up the tunes on my phone so that I didn't have to talk to anyone. It's not that I didn't want to be social, but I honestly couldn't catch my breath. Sweat pooled on my back and dripped from my forehead. My shoes dug into my heels through my paper-thin cotton socks. I tried to ignore the pain and run on. Once we made it past the community college, it was downhill to the mud field. Thank goodness!

I blasted some Frank Sinatra. My body went into

autopilot. I breezed down the hill. We were almost to the halfway point. After we navigated the mud-flats, our run would lead us toward Fort Vancouver, through apple orchards, over the land bridge, and to the waterfront trail.

If it weren't for the fact that I hated running and was terrible at it, I would have enjoyed the gorgeous loop. Growing up in the Pacific Northwest made me conditioned to the stunning natural beauty around me. Sometimes I had to remind myself to stop and drink it in. The landscape on our short five-mile run changed from charming historic mansions and old-growth trees to the swelling waters of the Columbia River, and then finally looped us through downtown Vancouver's welcoming shops where abundant hanging flower baskets lined Main Street.

You really are lucky, Meg.

That thought stayed with me until I reached the brown dirty field of the mudflats.

Chapter 8

Things were about to get worse. Much worse. I drew in a breath as I slowed my pace. Billy hadn't been exaggerating about the mudflats. Thick, gooey mud in the size and shape of an Olympic swimming pool had been carved into the field.

Jenny was the first in. She did a full body leap, more like a belly flop, landing face-first in the mud. She came up grinning and looking like a swamp monster. I watched as she sunk up to her chin in the mud. She crawled forward on her elbows. "Come on in, guys! It's awesome."

I considered taking off my shoes and socks but knew that Billy would yell at me if I did. My phone was another story. I found a dry stretch of grass on the far side of the field and set it there. My last phone hadn't survived sweat. Let's just say that I didn't pick a perfect spot to stash it when I was covering King of the Hook in Hood River. I thought it would be safe tucked into my sports bra, but I was wrong, and there was no way I was chancing my new phone with mud.

I waited for everyone to go before me. I definitely wanted to be last on this one. Tim Baxter ditched his headphones and dove in in front of me. His belly became lodged in the thick mud. "Help!" he shouted.

Billy, who was watching the madness from the far side of the mud pool, yelled at him to rock on his hands and knees. "Don't fight it, tubs. You're making it worse."

Tim tried to follow Billy's instructions, but he sank deeper. Billy grabbed a long stick, ran over, and pushed me out of the way. I thought he was going to pull Tim up with the stick, but instead he prodded him like cattle. "Use your arms, tubs!" Billy poked Tim's butt with the stick. "It's only a foot deep. You're not going down."

Tim flailed his arms.

Billy poked him again. "Move, tubs! On your elbows—now!" He blew his whistle.

I flinched at the sound. Billy was taking it too far. Tim was obviously anxious.

"I can't. I'm stuck!" Tim's face was bright red and splotched with mud. He was starting to panic. I couldn't believe that Billy wasn't helping him. He began to wheeze. His eyes had a wild look.

Without even thinking I jumped into the mud. It was probably due to my training as a lifeguard. I'd spent every summer in high school and college guarding at the community pool. Mud and water were similar, right?

Wrong.

My body hit the mud—hard.

Shock waves rippled on the surface and up my spine. The mud was much less forgiving than water.

It felt like hitting a brick wall. Mud clogged my nose and coated my eyelids. I coughed trying to clear it from my airway. What had I done?

Everything happened in a flash. I heard the muffled sound of Billy's voice and felt a hand grab the small of my back. The next thing I knew I was thrown onto the grass.

Coughing and sputtering for air, I wiped the thick, oozing mud from my eyes and tried to blow it free from my nose.

Gross.

I blinked. Mud seeped behind my contact lenses. Everything looked blurry and hazy. Billy dragged Tim from the mud and onto the grass next to me. Tim was in bad shape. He wheezed. It sounded like he was struggling to breathe.

"Keep going!" Billy yelled to everyone still in the mud pit. "Don't stop!" He crouched down and slapped Tim on the back. Tim choked and coughed violently. Mud spewed from his mouth. It must have been lodged in his throat.

"On your feet!" Billy didn't give Tim a chance to catch his breath. He pulled him to standing and prodded him toward the mud. "Get in there, tubs. Crawl. Crawl like a real man!"

Tim stumbled forward. His coughing slowed, but he sounded raspy. What was Billy doing? Tim needed to stop and catch his breath.

Mud dripped from my forehead. I wiped my hands and forearms on the grass. It didn't really help. I felt like I'd been dipped in a vat of chocolate. I wished it was chocolate. The mud had a distinct odor like dirt and feces.

Speaking of taste, my palate was coated with a

gritty layer of earthy dirt. I swished saliva in my mouth and spit on the ground.

"What do you think you're doing?" Billy yelled at me.

"Trying to get the mud out of my mouth." I stuck out my tongue.

"Get back in there, Reed!" Billy pointed at the mud pool.

"Do you think it's a good idea to push Tim? He doesn't look so great."

Billy blared his whistle in my face. "Get moving! Now."

People actually pay for this? I thought. This was getting out of hand. I had a sinking feeling that someone was going to end up seriously injured or worse. Billy's drill sergeant act had gone too far this time.

I followed after Tim. He crawled on his hands and knees. His bandana fell off halfway through. He didn't bother to stop and pick it up. It was tough going. My body sank in the thick mud. It took all my strength to free my hands from the mud.

Billy watched from the side, constantly screaming at us to go faster. The rest of the team had made it through the mud pit and started on the second half of the run.

I caught up with Tim. "How you doing?" I asked as mud ran down my arm like a waterfall.

"This is insane," Tim said, glancing at Billy. "He's literally insane."

"Yeah, I know."

"I'm going to kill him. I can't believe I'm paying for this." Tim reminded me of a dinosaur as he trudged through the mud. Each thud sent shock waves rippling through the mud. His heavy body lunged ahead one step at a time. He hadn't experienced the same results as Jenny. His bulky stomach jiggled with each slow movement.

"I was thinking that exact thing. I mean, not about killing him, but about volunteering to do this."

Tim panted. His shirt was plastered to his toneless body. He was a big guy. At least six feet and probably pushing three hundred pounds. "I'm serious. I'm going to kill him. Or sue."

"Sue? Billy? For what?" I tried to wipe mud from my eye. It just made my vision worse.

"Torture."

I laughed.

Tim gave me a hard look. "I'm serious. This can't be legal."

"Why don't you just quit? Like you said, you're paying for this. Billy can't make you do something you don't want to."

"I can't."

"Why not?" Mud had seeped into every inch of my T-shirt, capris, socks, and tennis shoes. I could feel it squishing in my bra. Gross.

"Because if Billy doesn't kill me, my wife will."

"I don't understand."

He heaved forward on his elbows. Mud splattered everywhere like a science experiment gone wrong. "My wife signed me up for this insanity. She's on a mission with my doctor to make sure I don't drop dead from a heart attack, but if we keep going like this I probably will."

"We're almost done." I pointed ahead. The mud

was thinning as we inched closer to the shore. In the distance I could make out Pearson Field airport. A small plane was taxiing down the runway.

"For now, but we're going to come back and do this again tonight. I can't handle another round of this, can you?"

I sighed. He had a point. One mud session was plenty for me. My mind worked overtime trying to craft an excuse why I couldn't participate in the later training session. Nothing came to mind. That was probably due to the fact that my mind was muddy. No wonder Billy and Dylan called their business Mind Over Mudder.

Tim and I made it to the end of the mud pit. Thank goodness.

I shook myself like a dog. Mud flew off me in every direction. How were we supposed to run with our bodies layered in mud? It squished between my toes and ran down my back and arms. I had mud in places that I cared not to discuss.

Billy's unrelenting whistle didn't give me time to think. I plodded on, slipping on the grass.

We ran for another half mile past Fort Vancouver. Once we made it to the orchards surrounding the fort, I came up with a plan. The path looped over the freeway and down to the waterfront. From there everyone would run parallel with the river and then back through downtown to the barracks.

I knew a way out. I would hide in the orchard until everyone had cleared the footbridge. Then I could take my own sweet time walking back to the barracks the way we came. I estimated that it would take everyone about thirty minutes to finish the run. That would give me plenty of time to shower, soak my feet, and head out before anyone returned. If Billy asked, I would tell him I had a deadline at work. Sure it was Saturday, but journalists work around the clock. He would never know. And quite frankly, I was in so much pain that I didn't care if he did find out. He could yell at me as much as he wanted. He wasn't my boss. I only had to answer to Greg, and Greg would never put me through this much pain. At least I didn't think he would.

Chapter 9

I waited until everyone was out of sight and took cover behind an apple tree. Fleshy apples decorated the tree. I breathed in the scent. I could go for an apple right now. The plane that I'd seen taxiing on the runway sputtered above me. Its wings tilted at a steep angle as it banked toward the river. I heard Billy's whistle in the distance. They had to be on the footbridge by now.

After I was sure that everyone was gone, I started to limp back. It wasn't my proudest moment. My feet revolted with each step. The blisters that had developed on my heels rubbed against my muddy, wet shoes. I stuck my earbuds in, hoping that music would help distract me from the pain.

I took the long route, not wanting to risk being seen on the hill leading back to the barracks. My contacts felt like lava stones. No amount of blinking helped clear the mud caked in the corners of my eyes.

It's probably a good thing you can't see, I thought as I

hobbled past Building 614, the old military hospital. The place was beyond creepy. I wished I hadn't researched its history. The first two floors of the decrepit brick building had been used as wards and operating rooms. Mental patients were kept on the third floor, supposedly in cages. Among the many reports I had scoured about the hospital, the most disturbing one that I'd read involved the basement where apparently early twentieth-century physicians collected blood from the operating theaters. There were reportedly pipes in the theaters that allowed blood to flow into the basement chambers. My body convulsed at the thought.

Today, security guards who patrolled the building claimed that doors would unlock on their own and that they would hear doors bang and creak, the sound of men coughing, and footsteps. I wanted to get out of here—fast!

At that moment something drifted past a broken third-floor window. *It's your imagination running wild, Meg,* I told myself. Then I heard a moan. Forgetting the fact that my feet were wrecked and that my skin was being sloughed off by the coarse mud coating my body, I kicked it in high gear and ran up the hill.

By the time I rounded the corner on Evergreen Boulevard I was out of breath and practically vibrating with adrenaline. Pops used to say that the gift of creativity was also a curse. "Maggie, you are a visionary. This cleverness, your sharp mind, it will open many doors, but you have to learn when to close some too. Be tender with yourself and your gift."

It had only been recently that I really understood

what he meant. I was still learning how to be tender to myself and which doors needed to be closed. Maybe familiarizing myself with the fort's gruesome and haunted history wasn't my wisest move.

I stopped to tie my shoe. Just as I was about to continue on, a creaking sound sent a shiver down my spine. I looked up to see the creepy old lady staring at me in her bathrobe from her front porch. At least I thought it was the creepy old lady. She didn't respond when I waved and called hello. Granted I was a bit spooked, but I'd had enough ghosts for one morning, so I leaped over the wooden fence and flung myself through the grass.

When I finally made it up the rickety ramp to the barracks, I checked the hallway before stepping inside. On the off chance that I hadn't timed my escape well, I didn't want to run into Billy. The dimly lit hall was empty.

Thank goodness.

I shuffled downstairs, leaving a trail of muddy footprints behind me. I wondered if Dylan and Billy had accounted for the fact that everyone would be covered in mud when we returned to the locker room. Oh well. *Nothing you can do about it now, Meg,* I told myself as I turned off my phone and supported my weight on the handrail.

Then I looked more closely. There were two sets of footprints. Someone else was here. A chill ran through my body. Time to hit the shower. I must already be cooling down. That, or there really was something to the ghost stories. I wasn't alone. At that moment a loud thud sounded in the locker room.

I jumped and let out a scream. Who was here? Or was that a ghost?

Chill, Meg. I waited and listened for a minute. There was no other movement. It was probably Dylan.

"Hello!" I called out. "Dylan, is that you?"

The sound of a locker door being slammed shut reverberated down the hall.

What was going on?

My heartbeat picked up. It felt like I was back out on the course. I inched closer to the locker room doors. "Dylan!" I called again. "It's Meg! Is that you?"

The locker room doors burst open and someone with a sweatshirt covering his head ran out. He headed straight at me, knocking me off my feet. Before I could stand up he was up the stairs and out of sight.

I think it was a "he" anyway. It looked like Tim, but Tim had been with the group. I saw him jogging toward the sky bridge when I was hiding behind the tree. How did he beat me back here, and why was he in such a rush?

I continued on. A trail of large, muddy footprints led in and out of the locker room. It had to be Tim. No one else had feet his size.

Whatever. I couldn't blame him for sneaking out either. Maybe that's why he ran away so fast. He probably didn't want to get caught.

As I stepped into the locker room a cloud of steam assaulted me. It caught in my lungs. I waved my hands in front of my face in an attempt to clear it. No luck. Steam poured from the ceiling and rose from the floor. It was like being on the set of a slasher movie. For the record, I'm not a fan of scary movies. Shocker, I know.

Just breathe, I told myself. Tim probably left the steam door room open when he heard me. I'm sure it's nothing.

Yeah right, my brain bantered back. A lot of steam had built up. That couldn't have happened in a few minutes.

I kept my hands in front of me in order to keep from slamming into the lockers, or crashing into the massage table. Maybe I should have paid better attention to my footing. I slipped on the tile floor and landed with a thud.

Can this morning get any worse?

I picked myself up and stepped cautiously toward the steam room. Sure enough, the doors were propped wide open. Steam funneled out of the small cedar room. The wet heat hit my face causing more mud to drip onto the floor.

I found the dial inside and turned it off. Then I decided I might as well take advantage of the warm steam. I climbed onto the cedar bench and let my head fall back onto the cedar wall.

Mud pooled at my feet. Okay, so it probably wasn't cool that I was wearing my clothes in the steam room, but at the moment I didn't care, I just wanted to be warm. I closed my eyes and tried to focus on my breathing—a centering technique I learned from Gam.

The steam began to evaporate.

I laughed out loud when I looked at my arms and legs. Thin, runny mud melted from the steam ran down my arms. Mother would pay big money for this kind of experience at a spa. Mud baths and masks were all the rage at her club. What a mess.

My laughter quickly faded away as the steam continued to dissipate, and I realized I wasn't alone. Billy lay on his back on the far bench.

Oh no!

Why hadn't he said anything when I came in? I must be so busted.

"Listen, Billy," I said. "I'm so sorry that I cut out early. My feet are killing me." I lifted my foot from the floor to show him.

Billy didn't move.

"I know what you're going to say," I continued. "I'm only cheating myself. I know that. Really, I do, but that was too much this morning—the mud, Tim, everything."

Billy didn't say a word.

That wasn't like him. I was surprised he wasn't whistling for me to drop and give him twenty right here in the steam room.

Something was wrong.

I stood and walked over to him. His eyes were staring straight at the ceiling. He looked as stiff as the cedar bench beneath him.

"Billy, are you okay?" I shook him.

He didn't move.

I threw my hand over my mouth. Billy wasn't yelling at me because he was dead. His Mind Over Mudder bandana was knotted around his neck. Someone had strangled him.

Chapter 10

I scrambled out of the steam room. "Help! Someone help!" I screamed, but my voice sounded muffled as if it were coming from somewhere far away.

I slid across the wet tile floor and out the locker room doors.

"Hello! Is anyone here? Dylan!" I screamed again.

My voice echoed in the empty hallway.

Think, Meg.

Duh. Call 911.

I ran back to the locker room and grabbed my phone. It was damp with moisture. I wiped it on a towel and punched in the emergency code.

An operator answered on the first ring. "Nine-one-one, what's your emergency?"

"There's a dead body here."

"Slow down, miss. Where are you?"

"I'm at Mind Over Mudder."

"Can you repeat that?"

"The barracks. I'm at the Vancouver Barracks."

"Okay, and you need assistance?"

"Yes! Billy the Tank is dead."

"Billy the Tank?"

"I'm blanking on his real name. That's what he goes by. He's in the steam room. Someone strangled him." I could hear the panic in my voice.

"Calm down. I'm going to need you to stay calm in order to get help to you, okay?"

"Okay," I sighed.

The operator made me repeat my location, twice. Then she asked me to check for a pulse. Why hadn't I thought of that? My hands shook violently as I went back into the steam room and felt for a pulse in Billy's wrist and then neck. Nothing. My intuition was right. Billy was dead. After the operator walked me through her checklist, she told me I was free to wait outside until the authorities arrived.

Gladly. There was no part of me that wanted to wait in the basement of a haunted building with Billy's dead body.

I tried unsuccessfully to dry my muddy clothes with a towel and then walked upstairs. Where was everyone? I'd lost all track of time. Had five minutes passed, or an hour? The sun had risen, but rain clouds loomed on the horizon. Mt. Hood was veiled by dark gray clouds. I shivered as I scanned the park grounds, wrapping the wet towel around my shoulders.

Off in the distance, I noticed someone leaning against an oak tree. I squinted to get a better look. It was Tim. His wireless headphones made him look like an alien.

"Tim!" I called out.

He flinched.

"Tim!" I shouted again.

He pretended to notice me for the first time and headed toward me. He stuffed the headphones into his gym bag.

"What are you doing?" I asked as he came closer.

"I could ask you the same thing. You're a mess."

Tim hadn't showered either. Dried mud coated his face like a mud mask at a spa. His workout gear was filthy, and there was a sweatshirt that looked very similar to the one whoever ran me over was wearing, tied around his waist. A black gym bag hung over his shoulder.

"I know. I'm a total mess. Did you see Billy?"

"What do you mean?" Tim clutched his gym bag.

"Billy. Did you see him in the locker room this morning?"

"I wasn't in the locker room this morning."

"You had to be."

"Nope." He shook his head. "I finished my run and was stretching over by the tree before I headed in to shower."

"So you just got back?"

"That's what I said."

The sound of sirens wailed in the distance. I tried to process what Tim was saying. He had to be lying.

"Where's everyone else?"

He shrugged. "I guess I beat them back."

"You went from last to first." My body began to tremble with cold. I wrapped the towel tighter, but it was futile—everything was soaked with water and mud.

"The mud motivated me." He hugged his gym bag closer to his body. If he wasn't in the locker room this morning, how did he get his gym bag? I was about to ask him when an ambulance, fire truck, and two police cars zoomed down the hill.

"What's going on?" Tim asked.

"Billy's dead."

"What?"

"Billy. He's dead," I repeated.

"How?"

Before I had a chance to answer, a team of EMS workers ran toward the barracks with a stretcher and defibrillator. I knew that neither would be helpful.

"Which way?" one of them yelled at me.

I pointed to the building behind us and ran with them.

They took the stairs three at a time. "Which way?"

"In the steam room," I called, pointing straight ahead. I let them continue on, and waited by the locker room doors.

A minute or two later a man in a dark blue suit and a police officer came down the stairs. I guessed the man to be in his early forties. He was handsome in a hard way. The police officer looked much younger. Probably closer to my age, with a crew cut and thick framed glasses. He looked like a comic book character.

"Are you my witness?" the man in the blue suit asked.

"I guess so," I replied. The towel was soaked and seemed to be making me colder. I dropped it on the floor and massaged my arms to keep warm. Had it been this cold in here earlier?

"Name?" He motioned to the young police officer to take notes. The officer jumped into action, pulling a pad of paper from his back pocket.

"Meg Reed."

"Is that your full name?"

I shook my head and tried to control the waves of cold assaulting my body. "Mary Margaret Reed," I replied through chattering teeth.

One of the paramedics returned from the locker room and waved in the detective and officer.

"Wait here, Ms. Reed."

"You bet."

He scowled.

"I just meant I don't want to go back in there with, well, you know, with Billy."

"Wait here. We'll be back in a moment."

I complied.

There was a commotion upstairs. I could hear the sound of voices and footsteps. The rest of the Mind Over Mudder team must have returned. It sounded like the police were holding them back.

"I'm with the media." I heard Kelsey's high-pitched voice above the crowd. "I need to get down there, immediately."

I couldn't hear the police response, but Kelsey's plea must have been declined. Heavy stomps thudded toward the outside doors.

Could this really be happening? Billy was dead, and I was in the middle of a murder again. *Terrible luck, Meg. Terrible luck.*

Chapter 11

It seemed like it took the detective hours to come back. I shivered on the wall. My body had cooled down completely. Mud congealed to my skin. I needed a hot shower and a coffee—stat. How long did it take to confirm that Billy was dead?

As if reading my mind, the detective stepped from the locker room and cleared his throat. "Okay, Ms. Reed, let's get down to business."

"Business?"

He snapped at the police officer. "Kenny, take notes." Then he appraised me with trained eyes. "Hold on, go grab her a dry towel or something. She looks like a Popsicle."

I gave him an appreciative nod. Kenny sprinted off and returned with two dry towels. My hands were wrinkled like prunes and turning a grayish color. I gladly took the towels from Kenny and wrapped them as tight as I could around my shoulders.

"Ms. Reed, are you with me?" He unbuttoned the

top button of his crisp white shirt and loosened his tie.

"Huh?"

"Are you ready to give us your statement?"

"Sure. Yeah. No problem." I shivered again.

"Do you need a coffee or something? We have a thermos in the squad car, don't we, Kenny?" I appreciated the detective's offer and was seriously tempted by the thought of a warm cup of coffee, but I could tell from his tone that he wanted to get this over with. It made me appreciate Sheriff Daniels, Gam's boyfriend who had been the lead detective on the last few murders I'd been involved in. That sounded bad. It's not as if I went around seeking murders. For some reason they seemed to find me. I blamed it on *Northwest Extreme*. Writing for the adventure publication had put me in the path of adrenaline junkies prone to doing things like launching themselves off the side of cliffs and scaling mountains. Accidents were bound to happen, and lately they had been happening around me.

Billy's murder was no accident, though. A wave of nostalgia washed over me. Billy was dead. He wasn't my favorite person on the planet, but he certainly didn't deserve to die.

"Ms. Reed, are you with me?"

"Yeah, sorry. I guess I'm a little shaken up, that's all."

The detective frowned. "Are you able to answer my questions or do I need to take you to the station?"

Take me to the station? Was I in trouble?

"I don't understand. Why would you take me to the station? I didn't do anything. I found Billy."

"Right now all I have to back that up is your word, Ms. Reed."

"Well, it's true!"

"Calm down." He held up one arm and caught Kenny's eye.

Did they think I was a killer?

"Look," I said, standing a little taller. "I'm not a suspect. I've done this before. I know the drill."

"Done this before?" The detective raised his brow. "Care to elaborate on that?"

"No, not like that. It's just that I've been a witness in a murder investigation before. I know that you need to ask me a bunch of questions. I get it, but I'm not a murderer. How could I have even strangled Billy? He's three times my size and about a hundred times stronger than me."

The detective pursed his lips and studied me. "I don't recall saying anything about a strangling. Kenny, do you?"

Kenny shook his head.

"The bandana, around his neck. Wasn't he strangled?" The caked mud on my exposed skin had started to crack. I had to resist the urge to pick it.

"I don't recall seeing a bandana around the victim's neck. Kenny, do you?"

"No, sir." Kenny shook his head again.

"Wait. There wasn't a bandana around Billy's neck? It was there when I found him, I swear."

"There's no need to swear, but I assure you there

was no bandana around the deceased's neck or
anywhere nearby."

"That can't be right," I protested.

"Would you like to come take a look at the
scene?" The detective motioned to the locker room
doors.

My stomach churned at the memory of Billy's
lifeless body. "No, that's okay. But this might be an
important clue in your investigation. When I found
Billy there was a black Mind Over Mudder bandana
tied around his neck. I just assumed that someone
killed him with it."

Kenny took notes while I spoke. The detective
sighed and rolled his head from side to side. "Why
do I always end up with these cases?" he asked
rhetorically. "Ms. Reed, there are no 'clues' in a
professional police investigation. There's hard evidence. Things like DNA, fingerprints, and blood
splatter."

I swallowed.

"And when it comes to a suspicious death, let's
keep the word 'assume' out of conversation, understood?"

"Yep." I wanted to tell him that I knew Sheriff
Daniels. Maybe he could call the sheriff and have
him verify that I wasn't a killer. But there was something about his hard dark eyes that gave me pause.
I had a feeling that if I mentioned anything else
about being involved in murder investigations that
I would find myself in handcuffs being stuffed into
the back of his police car.

"Please start from the beginning, Ms. Reed."

I explained how I had left the course early and

every detail I could remember about finding Billy in the steam room. When I finished the detective nodded to Kenny. "You got all that?"

"Yes, sir." Kenny held up the notebook. "I've got it all, sir."

"All right, you're free to go, Ms. Reed, but don't go far. I'm quite confident that we'll have follow-up questions for you."

"One more thing," I said.

He scowled.

"It's about Billy."

"What about him?"

"He was acting weird this morning before our workout."

"Weird?"

"Yeah, he had some kind of physical event. He clutched his chest at one point and almost fell over."

"And?"

"Well, shouldn't you write that down?" I asked Kenny. "He looked like he was having a heart attack or something."

"Are you a licensed physician, Ms. Reed?"

"No, but . . ."

"Thank you. That will be all for now." He pointed to the stairs.

"Okay, it just seems kind of important," I said under my breath.

"I'll be the judge of that, Ms. Reed."

What had I done to get on the detective's bad side? I climbed up the stairs. My entire body felt weak. I wasn't sure if it was the cold, exertion, or due to the fact that I'd found Billy's body. When I was almost to the top step I heard footsteps behind me. I turned to see Kenny sprinting up the stairs behind me.

"Hey," he whispered. "Don't let Detective Bridger get to you. He's been a nightmare ever since he got promoted last week."

"Detective Bridger. He didn't even tell me his name."

"I know." Kenny glanced behind us as we crested the stairs. "This is his first official case. I think it's kind of gone to his head."

"Okay. Thanks for letting me know."

"No problem. I don't know how he got promoted. Everyone thinks he's kind of slow."

"Why are you telling me this?"

"I felt bad for you. It sounds like you had some good observations." He showed me his notebook. "Don't worry, I wrote down everything you said, even the part about the bandana."

"Thanks." I smiled.

"It's no big deal."

"I appreciate it." I held out my hand. "I'm Meg, by the way, but I guess you already know that."

He took my hand and then tapped his notebook. "Mary Margaret Reed, to be exact."

"That's me."

He winked. "Nice to meet you, Mary Margaret Reed."

"You can call me Meg."

"But Mary Margaret Reed sounds so much cuter. Kind of retro. In a cool way, you know."

Was he flirting with me? I'm terrible when it comes to reading signals. Jill is constantly telling me that men flirt with me all the time. I think it's just her way of trying to make me feel better.

"My mother calls me that. You're going to make me think I'm in trouble or something."

"Maybe you are." Kenny grinned down at me. "I have to go grab the next witness. Detective Bridger wants to interview everyone who had access to the locker room before he lets anyone leave. Hope to see you again, Mary Margaret Reed."

"Thanks. You too." I waved as Kenny took long strides down the hall where the rest of my teammates had gathered.

He was tall and cute, despite the crew cut. Was I loopy from stress? Maybe I was just imagining it, but it did seem like Kenny was flirting with me.

My steps felt lighter as I walked to the end of the hallway.

"What's going on?" Kelsey grabbed my arm. "How did you get access downstairs? I have to get down there. Right now. I have a live shot in ten minutes. I'm first on the scene. And there's no way that I'm letting that fake from *Wake Up Portland* steal my exclusive."

"Chill." I held up both hands. I found it more than slightly ironic that Kelsey referred to one of her competitors as fake. She reminded me of a Barbie doll with her miniature waist, augmented chest, and stage makeup. I guessed that she was about my age, but honestly it was impossible to tell with all her layers of makeup. She could be concealing years of sun damage under her thick concealer.

"I want down there. No, I need down there. How did you do it?"

"I didn't do anything. I found Billy's body."

Her face shifted. "So it's true? Billy's dead. This changes everything." She paced back and forth in front of the radiator. Her yam-colored ponytail swung from side to side like a tiger's tail. She reminded me of a tiger about to pounce. "How long has he been dead? How did it happen? When did you find him? Did he collapse? Were you there when it happened?"

I held up my hands in surrender. "Seriously, you need to chill." *You're one to talk, Meg,* I said to myself. Did I sound like Kelsey? Is that why Detective Bridger had been so short with me? I hoped not. Kelsey was out of control.

"Meg, you are a journalist. You know how this works. This is going to be the lead story of the day and I'm on the scene. This story is mine. You have to tell me what you know."

Suddenly, I was a journalist. Kelsey hadn't wanted anything to do with me since we started training. She made it evident that she had an exclusive story for her "serious" journalism gig and was content to let me have all of her scraps. Now that I was in the know, how quickly she changed her tone.

"You're going to have to talk to the police, Kelsey. *You* know that from working in the field. I can't be your source, and I've been cautioned by the police not to say anything about the case. This is an active investigation."

"Whatever. Thanks for being difficult. I guess I'll find another way down there." She walked away in a huff.

Jenny sat against the wall with her knees folded

to her chest. Her Mind Over Mudder bandana was knotted around her wrist. It looked like it was cutting off circulation to her arm. I slid down the wall to join her. "How's it going?"

"I'm freezing, aren't you?" She curled in a tighter ball.

"I am, but I'm also running on adrenaline, so I don't think I'm really feeling anything at the moment."

"Tell me about it." Jenny leaned closer and twisted the bandana. "Tim said that you found Billy. Is he really dead?"

"I'm afraid so."

"Was it awful, finding his body?" Her hand was starting to turn purple.

"Yeah, it was pretty awful." I pointed to her wrist. "Your bandana looks kind of tight. You might want to loosen it."

"What?" She looked at me and then at the bandana. "Oh, this isn't mine. I found it over by the stairs."

"You have to take that to the police, right now!" I shouted and sat up straighter.

"Don't freak out." She untied the tourniquet. "What's the big deal?"

"There was a bandana in the locker room . . ." I trailed off, not wanting to see the image of Billy's body in my head again, and also because I wondered how Jenny had gotten the bandana.

She tossed it on the floor. "Don't worry. I'll give it to police." Then she reached over and put her hand on my arm. "Do you need anything? Finding

Billy must have been horrible. You look pretty jumpy."

I nodded. "A hot cup of coffee would be nice." I tried to smile. "Or better yet, a thick, creamy mocha with extra whipped cream." Was she trying to placate me or was she genuinely concerned?

"Meg, did you know that sugar is ten times more addictive than cocaine?"

"That cannot be true." I shook my head and peeled dried mud from my forearm. The restored hardwood floors were going to need a good scrubbing. It looked like we'd done the mud run inside.

"It is." She nodded vehemently. "Dylan told me. He did a nutritional analysis of my eating habits when I started training. You'll never believe how much sugar I was eating. It was terrible."

"There's nothing terrible about sugar."

"But there is. Dylan had me go on a sugar fast. It was terrible for the first two days. I had the shakes and the sweats. It was like detoxing. But by the third day I started feeling better and now I don't even crave it. You should try it."

"No, thanks. I like my sugar, and the minute they let us go this morning I'm driving straight to the coffee shop and ordering the biggest mocha they have on the menu."

"You're such a kidder, Meg."

"Oh, I'm not kidding. Finding a dead body means there's definitely a mocha in my future this morning. I'm not ashamed to admit that mochas make me feel better."

"But they're so bad for you."

"I don't care. I'm getting one."

Jenny shook her head. "Okay, fair enough. I didn't find a body this morning. Have a mocha, but you really should go talk to Dylan. I'm telling you it will change your life."

I wanted to tell her that I'd had my own life-changing moment in the basement this morning, but I knew that Jenny was trying to be helpful. Sugar probably was ten times as addictive as cocaine. At the moment I didn't care. What I did care about was what happened to Billy, and as much as I liked Jenny and couldn't imagine that she could have killed him, I was going to make sure that Detective Bridger and Kenny knew about the bandana.

Chapter 12

Detective Bridger released us about an hour later. My stuff was in the locker room. I couldn't leave without my keys, so I was going to have to suck it up and face the murder scene again. The hallway and doors to the locker room had been roped off with yellow caution tape. Kenny stood in front of the tape with a clipboard in his hands. All of our gym bags and clothes had been placed in a long line.

"We have your personal items for you," Kenny said. "When I call your name, come get your things and then you're free to go. As Detective Bridger told you, don't go far. We'll be following up if we need anything else from you."

Kelsey pushed to the front of the pack. Her cameraman followed. "Do you have a statement to make?"

"This isn't a press conference, miss."

She wasn't deterred. "How was Billy killed? Have

you found the murder weapon? Do you have any suspects?"

Kenny tapped the badge on his chest. "You're going to have to ask Detective Bridger these questions and he's in the middle of his investigation right now." He scanned the clipboard. "Tim Baxter."

Tim stepped forward.

"Go ahead and get your personal effects," Kenny said.

"I already have my bag." Tim patted the gym bag I'd seen him with earlier.

Kenny looked confused for a minute. Then he made a note on his clipboard. "Okay, go ahead. We'll be in touch."

Tim lumbered up the stairs. He had to have been the person who knocked me down this morning. He didn't have his gym bag with him on our run. He must have been in the locker room before me. The question was, did he kill Billy? Is that why he raced out in such a hurry? I had forgotten to mention the bag to Detective Bridger. I would have to make sure to tell him.

"Mary Margaret Reed," Kenny called out my name, caught my eye, and winked. "Grab your stuff and you can go."

I found my bag in the pile. As I walked toward the staircase, I stopped and told Kenny about the bandana. He made a note and whispered, "We'll definitely be in touch," as I continued on. I got the sense he wasn't talking about Billy's murder.

Without waiting for further instructions, I shuffled up the stairs. Every muscle in my body ached. I wanted out of the barracks—now. My

phone buzzed and vibrated with a steady stream of
alerts as I stepped outside. Social media was blowing up with news of Billy's murder. Texts from Greg,
Jill, and Matt flashed on my screen. How had word
gotten out so fast?

One glance at the news vans blocking the road-
way answered my question. Kelsey Kain. Reporters
were camped out in front of the barracks, trying to
get the tightest shot of the police action inside.
Kelsey's "exclusive" breaking news wasn't so exclusive anymore.

I headed down the hill toward my car with my face
focused on my phone. Hopefully, that would send
a message that I wasn't available for an interview.

The first text was from Greg: Heard the news. You
good?

Jill's was next: TWITTER IS GOING NUTS. DEATH
AT THE BARRACKS! ARE YOU THERE?!?

The last text was from Matt. Jill just called. Call as
soon as you can.

Matt and I hadn't spoken for almost three weeks.
He took off on a mysterious errand before I left for
New York. Seeing his name on my phone made my
heart rate quicken. I didn't know where things
stood between us. We had kissed for the first time
in Hood River when I was on assignment for a wind
surfing competition. Then he left without a word.
Well, that's not exactly true. He did deliver flowers
to my front door. But then he took off. I couldn't
help but wonder if our kiss had freaked him out.

Jill told me that I was overthinking things.
"You're totally blowing this out of proportion. Matt
adores you, trust me."

That was the problem. I adored him too. We'd been friends since college and Matt loved Pops as much as me. We met in journalism class where Matt would save me a seat every day with a silver stick of gum. When Pops came to speak as a guest lecturer Matt freaked out that I was *the* Charlie Reed's daughter. He'd been following Pops' work for years, and was especially impressed with Pops' in-depth and thoughtful coverage of Oregon's meth epidemic. It was Pops who helped get Matt his job at *The O.* I didn't want to do anything to jeopardize our friendship, and yet I couldn't ignore my growing feelings for him. Don't they say you should never date your best friend? I hoped we hadn't ruined our friendship.

My phone buzzed again. Greg's face flashed on the screen.

"Hey," I answered.

"Meg Reed, I'm halfway around the world in a conference room in Japan and my cell phone is buzzing with messages from *Northwest Extreme.* Apparently there's been an accident at the fort. Please tell me you are *not* at the barracks."

"I am."

"Damn." Greg paused. "What am I going to do with you?"

"I don't know. Honestly, I don't know what I'm going to do with myself."

"Are you good?"

"I'm fine. Shaken up, but fine."

"Look, you need to drop this story. It's not worth it."

"No way!" I surprised myself with my reaction.

"Please don't take me off the story. I have to finish this one. I really do. It's more than the story. It's personal."

I could hear Greg sigh on the other end of the line. "Listen, I'm about to head into a meeting. Let me think this through. I'll text you when I get back to my hotel later tonight."

"Okay. But I promise I can handle this. I'm not going to do anything stupid. I've learned from my past."

Greg chuckled. "Right. Famous last words. Be safe."

He hung up before I could say anything else. In fairness I couldn't blame Greg. I hadn't made the best choices in the past. It's not like it was entirely my fault, though. Mud, Sweat, and Beers was my chance to prove myself. To prove to Greg, the team at *Northwest Extreme,* and most importantly myself that I had changed. He couldn't take that away from me now.

What a nightmare, I thought as I unlocked the car and threw my bag in the back. I was physically a disaster and in desperate need of a shower. But first, I was in need of something even more important. A visit with Gam.

I hopped into the driver's seat and made a U-turn. It was kind of ridiculous to drive to Gam's. Her condo was on the other side of the footbridge. Normally, I'd relish in a short walk, but no way were my legs making it any farther than my car at the moment.

Gam's condo is like a retreat on the waterfront. Her porch looks out onto the Columbia River with a majestic view of Mt. Hood and its foothills in the distance. Most of her neighbors' decks are outfitted with Adirondack chairs and sun umbrellas in subdued colors designed to blend in with the natural background. Not Gam's. Gam's deck was impossible to miss. Bright red hummingbird feeders hung from six-foot-tall potted plants and trees. A water fountain with rotating LED lights trickled in rhythm with the river below. Wind chimes, Buddha statues, colorful glass balls, potted herbs, and fragrant flowers took up the remaining space on her deck.

I found a parking space across the street from her condo and checked the time. It wasn't even nine yet. How was that possible? I felt like I'd been awake for days. Gam usually opens Love and Light, her new age bookstore, around ten on the weekends. The shop is as eclectic as her condo. It's more than a bookstore. She teaches classes and workshops, does private healing sessions with clients, and offers it as a safe haven for anyone seeking a moment of pause in an otherwise hectic day. Gam thrives on little to no sleep. She spends the early-morning hours baking homemade treats for Love and Light. Customers come in looking for a book or healing crystal and leave with Gam's heavenly cookies and comforting touch.

Gam answered the door before I even had a chance to knock. "Margaret, come in. I had a feeling that something was going on with you." She grabbed my hands and appraised my appearance with her wise brown eyes.

Tears streamed down my face. Gam has that effect on me. Without saying a word, she wrapped me in a hug and pulled the door shut behind us.

The relief of being at Gam's overcame me. I sobbed on her shoulder. She placed her hand on my back. It radiated heat like an electric blanket. I sniffed.

"There, is that a bit better?" Gam asked, removing her hand from my back.

I nodded, but I didn't trust myself to speak yet. Salty tears ran down my throat,

"Shall we go have a seat outside in the sun and have a little chat?" Gam motioned to the sliding glass doors. "I made a double batch of zucchini bread this morning. I had a feeling I was going to have company. What a pleasant surprise to discover that my company is you."

"Thanks, Gam." I wiped my nose on my muddy arm.

"You go sit. I'll be right out with some warm bread and tea."

I agreed. On my way outside I couldn't help but notice stacks of moving boxes propped in front of her couch. Gam and Sheriff Daniels had been talking about moving in together. But I had thought it was just that—talk. Gam was actually packing. That was more than talk.

I wanted her to be happy, but things were moving fast between them. Plus, if I was being completely honest with myself, I wasn't sure I wanted Gam to move away. I loved Gam's condo. This was where I came when I needed to think. What would I do with her in Gresham and living with Sheriff Daniels? It wasn't as if Gresham was far. It was only a fifteen- or twenty-minute drive, but even small moves can lead to big changes. I didn't want Gam to change.

Gam had lived alone since I was a kid. I never

considered that she might be lonely. She used to say that she and my grandfather had a special kind of romance that would be hard to duplicate. I guess that I never imagined that she might find romance again, especially with the gruff sheriff.

I plopped into a lounge chair and tilted my face to the sun. The heat felt good. Gam scooted out with a heaping plate of sliced bread slathered with butter and a steaming mug of cinnamon herbal tea. "Drink this, it will warm you up inside and out." She handed me the ceramic mug. Gam used to be an artist. I remember going to her pottery studio when I was younger. She'd give me a handful of wet clay and let me practice on her wheel. I would always end up covered in clay up to my elbows, which didn't please Mother. My bedroom used to house a shelf of my custom pottery made at Gam's studio— lopsided bowls and cups without handles. I wasn't particularly skilled at the art, but I was proud of my collection of fired earthenware.

"Is this one of yours?" I asked, cradling the mug in both hands. It reminded me of a sandy beach. Gam had swirled natural brown and beige dyes into the clay giving it the feeling of movement.

"It is. It's not very good. Look at how the handle curves in there." She pointed to the mug.

"What are you talking about? This is perfect. This is the kind of piece that hipsters would spend a fortune on at the farmer's market."

Gam laughed. "Keep it. I have about a thousand of them in the cupboard above the fridge. In fact, I'm on a house-cleaning kick at the moment. I don't know if you noticed, but I've been going through every cupboard and drawer. There's a stack of things I set aside for you. Do you have a waffle iron?"

I grinned. "Gam, I'm twenty-four and single. What do you think?"

"Well, you do now!" She sat next to me. "Enough talk about decluttering. Tell me what's happened."

Everything spilled out. I told her about Billy's murder and how I discovered him in the steam room. She listened intently. After I finished, she handed me a paper napkin and two slices of zucchini bread. "You need to eat something."

I took a bite of the bread. It was moist and slightly spicy. I devoured the first piece and then the second. Gam handed me a third.

"No, I shouldn't." I waved her off. "Billy wanted me on a strict training diet that I haven't exactly been following."

"Eat, Margaret." She placed the napkin in my hand. "You don't need to diet. You're perfect just the way you are."

"Billy didn't think so."

"It sounds as if Billy had other less-than-optimal challenges, doesn't it? Eat."

She waited for me to finish the third slice of bread. An osprey circled above us. We watched as it glided effortlessly across the river and landed on a piling. Gam's wind chimes reverberated in a calming melody. I drank it all in.

"Why does this keep happening to me, Gam?" I asked after I popped the last bite of bread into my mouth.

"Things happen. That's life. It's how we react to what happens that matters."

"I know, but don't you think it's kind of weird that I keep getting in these kinds of situations?"

Gam's face became dewy. She stared at an aloe plant on a glass tile table. I knew that she was "checking in," as she likes to say with her guides. "They're telling me to ask you if you've ever considered that you're finding these situations because you're equipped to handle them better than most people. You have a deep, deep sense of self and inner strength. You need to remember to tap into it, and ask your guides for help."

"What?" I nearly spit out my tea. "I don't think I'm very equipped, Gam. Should we talk about some of the major mistakes that I've made in the past?"

"Mistakes are opportunities for learning. Instead of focusing on what you've done wrong, what if you shifted that and focused on what you've learned?"

Gam had a way of spinning any situation to make it seem positive. I appreciated her perspective, but I also knew that she was trying to make me feel better. I finished my tea. "So what's the scoop with you and Sheriff Daniels?"

A smile spread across Gam's face. She did not look her age. At seventy-four she could easily pass for fifty-something. Gam's a testament to the idea that age is purely a state of mind. Her state of mind was fresh and new. She wore her hair in a modern cut and dyed it black. There wasn't a stray gray hair on her head. She never left the house without "painting her face" as she called it. That really meant applying a thin layer of foundation over her supple skin, lining her eyes with black liner, and lipstick. Gam made aging look like fun.

"That's one of the reasons I've been on such a cleansing kick. I'm trying to move out some of my old things to make room for the new."

"Are you still considering moving in with him?"

"I am. Can you believe it?" Her dark eyes sparkled, making her appear even more youthful.

Returning her smile, I didn't say anything. Surprisingly, she didn't pick up on my hesitancy. That wasn't like Gam.

"He's in central Oregon this week for a statewide training. I'm missing him. I never thought I would say that again." The sun hit her from behind. She practically glowed. "We talked about moving in when he returns. I have so much to do this week. In fact, you wouldn't happen to have some free time to help me take all the boxes I've packed down to the donation center, would you?"

"Of course. I'll help however you need."

Gam reached over and squeezed my knee. "You are the best!"

"*You're* the best. You've helped me so much. I'll gladly return the favor."

Gam's phone rang inside. "I better scoot and get that. Do you want to come to the shop with me?"

"No, I have to go home and take a shower." I pointed to the dried mud on my arms. "Thanks for the tea and bread. I'll check in later."

I let myself out as she answered the phone. I had a feeling it was Sheriff Daniels from the way she danced around the kitchen. I sighed as I walked to the car. Hopefully I was just being selfish, but I couldn't shake the feeling that Gam moving in with the sheriff was a bad idea.

Chapter 13

I showered for an eternity when I got home, letting mud run down my legs and pool in the bottom of the tub. At least it was Saturday. I planned to make a giant pot of coffee and curl up on the couch for the remainder of the morning.

The blister on the back of my left heel popped. Blood dripped down my foot as I toweled myself dry. I bandaged my feet and limped to the kitchen to make coffee. Gam sent me home with a box of things she didn't want any longer including her vintage waffle iron. There was little chance I would use it anytime soon, but I propped it up on the counter. Hipsters would approve. Very Portlandia.

Armed with the biggest cup of coffee I could lift, I padded to the couch and pulled out my phone. *Northwest Extreme*'s social media response continued to be strong. I posted another round of photos from the morning session and a condolence message about Billy, and responded to as many comments as I could without my fingers going numb.

I'm not usually a TV kind of girl. Blame it on my

generation. We have more access with one quick touch on our phones than the old reporter's database at *The O*. The server room that used to house those computers took up an entire floor. Looking for a distraction, though, I turned on the TV, and to my delight the classic movie channel was playing *How to Marry a Millionaire*. They don't make movies the way they used to. Marilyn Monroe, Betty Grable, and Lauren Bacall all in one film? And the dresses. Oh, the dresses.

It was impossible not to have my mood lifted watching the elaborate orchestral opening number. It reminded me of a flash mob proposal that had been making its rounds on the Internet. A Portlander had proposed to his fiancée with a dance production involving his friends and family members that would have made Fred Astaire proud. Maybe the flash mob was my generation's musical. I could live with that. There's something quite romantic and sentimental about strangers breaking out in spontaneous song. I smiled at the thought.

The caffeine pulsed through my veins. I was slowly starting to feel normal again. Slowly. Of course there was the small problem of daily doubles. We were all supposed to be back at the barracks at six for the evening session. With Billy dead did that change anything? I hadn't bothered to ask Dylan in all the chaos this morning. In fact, come to think of it, I didn't remember seeing Dylan anywhere around.

My phone buzzed and alerted me that I had received a private message on Facebook. I refilled my coffee and clicked on the message. It was from Tim Baxter: *Sorry about this morning. Crazy. Can you meet for a beer before daily doubles? I need to talk to you about something.*

I shot back a message right away: *Sure. Where?*

Tim didn't respond. I drummed my fingers on the coffee table while I watched my Facebook page, waiting for a red message alert to appear. What did Tim want to tell me? Could it have something to do with Billy's murder?

I stopped drumming my fingers. *Think, Meg. Don't just jump in here. You're working on being more thoughtful and centered in your approach.* Should I meet Tim, or should I call the police? Kenny had given me his number. The smart thing to do would be to check in with him first.

I shot him a text explaining that I had some information that might be important for his case. Then I sent Matt a text. We had planned to meet at the food carts for lunch. Matt would know what to do.

Still on for lunch?

Matt replied right away. Yep. Meet you in thirty?

Thirty minutes was ample time to drive from my bungalow in NoPo (North Portland) to the food cart pod downtown. Of course, given my gimpy state, I figured I should probably get moving.

I changed into a knee-length black skirt and a pink hoodie. I dusted my cheeks with powder and applied a shimmery pink lip gloss. My stomach churned with hunger and nerves as I drove to meet Matt.

Matt and I hadn't gone this long without seeing each other since we met in college. Usually we had

weekly happy hour and connected for lunch, but
he had left unexpectedly when we got back from
our trip in Hood River and I left for New York. I
hoped things wouldn't be weird between us. Maybe
I should have invited Jill to join us. Having her
around as a buffer might ease any lingering tension
between us.

Too late now, Meg, I told myself as I steered toward
the waterfront. Matt and I were meeting at Portland's most historic pod of food carts just a few
blocks up from the Willamette River. Food carts are
as prolific as pubs in Portland. They're a staple in
every neighborhood from the east side to the west.
You name it, and you can find it at a Portland food
cart. Portland gives new meaning to street food.
Vendors offer everything from pure vegan plant-
based grub to Malaysian and Indian fusion. Each
pod of carts is as diverse as their fare. Mobile units
range from sleek aluminum trailers and trucks to
refurbished funky buses to wooden bike carts.
Some offer beer gardens and picnic tables with
colorful lights strung between trees.

Recently a battle had been brewing between
food cart and restaurant owners. Brick and mortar
restaurants didn't like the fact that food carts had
taken over a lot of turf. There was no evidence that
the craze was slowing, so traditional restaurateurs
were probably right to worry.

My route downtown took me past KPDX's headquarters. The news station was located in a swanky
twelve-story building across the street from the
waterfront. I stopped in front of the building to
let a group of cyclists pass. To my surprise Kelsey
Kain stood near the revolving glass doors to the

building. She looked like she had come straight from Mind Over Mudder. She was covered in mud. Her normally perky red locks were tied in a pony-tail with stray hairs flying free. She glanced to the sidewalk and then to the doors behind her. Her left leg bounced and she kept darting her head from side to side.

I wanted to wait and see what she was doing, but the light changed. I proceeded on toward the food carts, but at the last minute hung a quick right and circled around the block. My curiosity had the best of me. This time I pulled into a parking space across the street that gave me a clear view of Kelsey from a safe distance.

She glanced at her watch and paced nervously. She must be waiting for someone.

I waited and watched her for about five minutes. I was just about to start the car and give up my sur-veillance when a man in a black suit crossed the street and walked over to Kelsey.

He approached Kelsey and handed her some-thing. She stuffed whatever he had given her into her pocket. Without saying a word to the man she hurried into the building. The man scanned the sidewalk, then turned and strolled off toward the waterfront.

What was that all about?

I didn't recognize the man. He reminded me of an FBI agent from the movies with his black suit and black sunglasses. What was he doing with Kelsey? Could their meeting have something to do with Billy's murder?

Meg, stop! I flicked myself on the wrist. You just promised yourself you weren't going to do this and

now you're acting like you're on some kind of
Kelsey Kain stakeout. In the past I may have had a
tendency to get myself into troublesome situations,
like following a potential murder suspect up a
deserted trail, or confronting a killer in blizzard
conditions on the slopes. I had learned my lesson
and was resolved to make wiser and more internally
guided decisions, as Gam would say.

What was wrong with me? First I'd been spooked
by nonexistent ghosts, now I was stalking Kelsey.

I sighed, started the car, and continued on to
meet Matt. Parking downtown can be challenging,
especially on a sunny summer afternoon. The
streets were packed with tourists carrying pink
boxes of Voodoo doughnuts and wearing Portlandia T-shirts. I found street parking a few blocks
from the food cart pod. The smell of grilling onions
and curry infused the air. My hands trembled. I
wasn't sure if it was from drinking too much coffee
or the fact that I'd be seeing Matt any minute.

"Megs!" Matt called from the crowd. "Over here!"

I spotted him standing near a gyro cart. "Here
goes nothing," I said to myself as I weaved through
sweaty tourists.

"You chopped your hair," Matt said with wide
eyes as he scooped me into a hug. He's much taller
than me at six feet. He hunched down and cradled
me in his arms.

My heart rate pounded in my neck. I hoped he
couldn't feel it.

I felt him inhale as if drinking me in. People
passing by became like shadows. I could have stayed
in Matt's arms for the remainder of the day, but
after a second he released me and ruffled my new

pixie cut. "You look great. I love the hair. It fits you, Megs."

"Thanks." I put my hand on the back of my neck. "It's pretty short."

"So are you. It works, right?" He winked. His naturally light hair looked as if it had been kissed by the sun. He must have spent time outside in Bend.

"I never thought of it like that. A short cut for a shorty. Yeah, that's true."

"What are you in the mood for?" Matt looped his arm through mine. His charcoal T-shirt had the outline of a spaceship and read: I'M NOT SAYING IT'S ALIENS, BUT IT'S ALIENS. Matt has an extensive collection of geeky T-shirts. It's a good thing he works for *The O* in Portland. I couldn't imagine his shirt would fly working for the *New York Times*.

Another surge of adrenaline rushed through me. *Keep it together, Meg.*

"Food!" I yelled.

"Okay, that I think we can do. What's your pleasure, miss?" He waved his arm toward the collection of carts. "Something Asian-inspired? Mexican? Good old American?"

Everything smelled good. It was impossible to pick. "How about Mexican," I said, pointing to a cart on the far side of the parking lot. "It has the shortest line."

"Short lines work for me." Matt pulled me in the direction of the cart.

The cart was crafted out of corrugated metal siding with tiki torches anchoring both sides. Strings of chili lights dangled in front of the window. I read the menu board and decided on carne asada tacos with green salsa. Matt opted for a chicken burrito, and we both ordered the drink special of the day—mango lemonade. They packaged our orders in a to-go bag and handed it to Matt through the window. He thanked them and led me away from the crowd.

"Do you want to go find a bench down on the waterfront?"

"Sure." I kept my tone light as I tagged along after him. There was so much I wanted to say, but I didn't know where to start.

"Are you limping?" Matt asked.

"Uh, just a little."

"A little?" He wrinkled his brow. "What happened?"

"It's no big deal," I replied, trying to downplay how much pain I was in. "I have a few little blisters from training, that's all."

"Ha!" he laughed. "Yeah right. Megs, come on, it's me. I happen to know that there's no such thing as a 'little' blister when it comes to you."

I lifted my foot to display the bandages on my heels. "Okay, maybe you're right. I might have wrecked my feet."

"Geez, Megs. Those look terrible. Why didn't you tell me? We could have eaten by the carts."

"No, I want to eat by the river. It'll be much nicer. Plus, that's why I wore flip-flops. At least nothing is rubbing against my heels."

Matt shook his head. "What am I going to do with you?"

"Take me to lunch?" I grinned.

Chapter 14

We found a bench on the waterfront path. Children ran through the nearby Salmon Street Springs Fountain. A jet boat flew through the river down below, peeling out in wild circles and sending spray four feet in the air. The grassy area was a sea of colorful blankets where couples picnicked under shady trees.

"Is this good?" Matt asked.

"Perfect." I plopped onto the bench, grateful to sit again.

Matt unwrapped our lunch and handed me a taco. "So what's new, Megs?"

"What's new?" I said with a mouthful of taco. "Shouldn't you be the one to answer that?"

Matt punched a straw into one of the lemonades and placed it on the bench next to me. "I want to hear what's going on with you first. And I think you should start with what happened this morning."

I knew that he was right. There was no chance of me pulling any information out of him about where he'd disappeared to until I came clean about my muddy murder. "It was awful." I shuddered.

Matt reached his arm around my shoulder and squeezed it tight. "I'm sure it was."

I told him about training with Mind Over Mudder and how tough Billy had been. "You don't think someone killed him because they were fed up with his intense training style, do you?"

"That seems like a stretch," Matt replied. He took a bite of burrito but kept his arm around my shoulder. It felt good there. Natural.

"There's this business guy, Tim Baxter," I said. "Billy was the toughest on him. I'm sure I saw him in the barracks this morning."

"What do you mean?"

I explained about Tim running into me and then seeing him with his bag outside. "He sent me a private Facebook message. He said he has something important to tell me. He wants to meet me for a beer before our training session tonight. Do you think I should meet him? Or is that totally stupid?"

Matt finished his burrito and considered my question. "You said you told the police officer, right?"

"Right."

"Where does he want to meet you?"

I shrugged. "A pub or something."

"Somewhere public. That's good. If you go, you should definitely meet him somewhere with a lot of people."

"That's what I was thinking."

"And he didn't mention why he wanted to talk to

you? Do you think you're reading it wrong? Could it have something to do with your feature?"

"Maybe." I hadn't considered that. Leave it to Matt to think through possible scenarios not involving a crazed killer trying to stalk me. I laughed. "You know what? You're probably right. I'm sure that I'm jumping to conclusions. Like he would confess to me. Honestly, I hadn't even considered that he might want to talk to me about my story. Duh."

Matt removed his arm from my shoulder, crumpled up our wrappers, and tossed them in the bag. "I didn't say that. He might, but he might want to talk about your feature."

"Yeah, he asked me a couple days ago about *Northwest Extreme.* That's probably it."

"You still need to be careful and make sure you loop the police in, got it?"

"Got it."

A toddler zoomed past us on a three-wheeled trike. His mom jogged after him, calling for him to slow down. "She's going to get a good workout in today," Matt said, watching her sprint to try to catch up.

"That's for sure. That's what I felt like with Billy around. Only he was always looming behind us, waiting to take one of us down if we weren't fast enough."

"Was he really that bad?"

"Probably not, but it felt like it on our morning runs." I paused. "I don't know what's going to happen now. Maybe they'll have to cancel our training, especially since Dylan, Billy's business partner, is the opposite of a drill sergeant. If he tried to yell at us to run faster I think everyone would just laugh."

Matt offered me a piece of gum from the bulging pack in his shorts pocket. I declined.

"How's *The O*?" I asked. I figured it was best to start with something less emotionally charged, like work, instead of diving into why Matt took off.

He popped two sticks of gum into his mouth and twisted the silver wrappers together. "It's okay."

"Just okay?" Matt loved working at *The O*. He sounded dejected.

"Yeah."

"Matt, what's going on?"

"Nothing." He looked at his feet. His black low-top Converse shoes looked brand new.

"Wait a second, that's not fair. You made me spill. Now it's your turn. That's how this whole friendship thing works. We tell each other our problems."

Matt met my eyes. He held my gaze. My heart thumped in an unsteady rhythm. "Is that what we are? Are we friends?"

I swallowed. This was uncharted territory. I could tell Matt had shifted his tone, but I wasn't ready for this kind of intensity. I punched him in the shoulder. "Of course we're friends. Besties actually."

He gave me a small smile and looked at his feet again.

"Matt," I said, reaching out and touching his arm. "What's going on?"

"I'm thinking about leaving *The O*." He stared at the ground.

"What? But you love *The O*. Why would you leave? It's your dream job."

"Not anymore. It's not what it used to be, Megs. It's really different."

"I don't understand. What do you mean it's different?"

Matt tossed the crumbled bag into a nearby garbage can. He made a swooshing motion with his arm. "I've still got it. Nothing but net."

"You're acting weird. What's going on at *The O*?"

"It's bad. We had a staff meeting yesterday and the editor in chief announced that we're vacating our building. We're downsizing. Another ten to fifteen percent of the team is being cut."

"Oh wow, I'm sorry. The same thing is happening at *Northwest Extreme*. Greg's thinking about selling to a Japanese investment firm. I sort of thought that we were going to be fine. It seems like the economy has rebounded."

Matt shook his head. "It's not the economy. It's the media environment. Traditional print hasn't figured out how to compete in the digital era."

I knew exactly what he meant. The push for breaking news was at an all-time frenzy. Everything we had learned in our journalism ethics class had been lost in the world of instant and immediate gratification. Any ordinary person with a cell phone could create breaking news on Twitter. It didn't matter if they fact-checked or considered the source. News had become instantaneous, like the old adage of shoot first and ask questions later. Pops would have hated the current newsroom climate.

"Are you on the chopping block?" I asked Matt.

"No, luckily technology is one of the only beats actually doing well."

"That's good."

"I guess, but it's more than that. The paper is pushing us to write sensational headlines. It's all about clickbait. Doing anything we can to try to get readers to bite on a story. It's crazy. We're going to start getting paid based on the number of clicks on our stories. We're creating this insanity. Instead of a well-thought-out and researched story they want us to churn out crap with ridiculous headlines."

"Really? *The O*?"

"Megs, I'm telling you, it's nothing like when your dad was there. Things have changed."

"And no one is standing up and saying anything?"

"What can they say? They don't want to lose their jobs. I don't have it anywhere near as bad as the breaking news guys. The pressure on that department is crazy."

"What kind of headlines are they asking you to write? I don't get it. You're covering technology. How are you supposed to come up with a click-worthy headline for a new piece of software?"

"Good question. My editor sent me a list of examples. He actually suggested that I should be as vague and ambiguous as possible. Clickbait is taking over the Internet. I know you've seen this kind of stuff online, like: MAN TRIES NEW SOFTWARE THAT CHANGES HIS LIFE. YOU WON'T BELIEVE WHAT HAPPENS NEXT."

"I hate those! I saw one the other day on Facebook and stupidly clicked on a story supposedly about a revolutionary new phone everyone was talking about. It was super lame."

"Exactly. It's annoying. And it's not journalism. Readers hate it. They click through on the deceptive headlines and then get mad and leave the page. I don't understand how publishers think clickbait is going to grow our readership or revenue. It's bogus."

"What are you going to do?"

"I don't know," he said, meeting my gaze. His face revealed that *The O* had already won. Matt looked beaten.

"Are you really thinking of leaving?"

"I'm not sure. It's not going to be better anywhere else. I think my best bet might be to leave journalism altogether. Tech is starting to look pretty appealing."

"Leave journalism! But you love writing."

"Not like this I don't."

"Where would you go? I mean, are you thinking Silicon Valley—like working for one of the huge tech companies like Google or something?"

Matt stared at the water. "Something."

"Wait, what are you trying to tell me?"

"I'm thinking of leaving Portland, Megs."

Chapter 15

Matt was thinking of leaving Portland? My stomach dropped. First Jill. Now Matt. I couldn't handle the thought of one of them leaving, let alone both of them.

"Megs?" Matt poked my knee. "You're not saying anything."

"I know, because I'm stunned. I can't imagine you leaving Portland."

"I can't either." He grabbed my hand. "Listen, I don't want to leave, but I'm not sure that I have a choice. There's nothing here for me."

Ouch. My body stiffened. There was *nothing* here for him? What about me? What about our friendship?

I pulled my hand away.

"Don't be mad." Matt's voice had a pleading tone. "You know as well as I do that Portland isn't exactly ripe with job opportunities right now unless you want to wait tables at a pub or be a barista."

He had a point. Portland had become known as the place millennials came to retire. Attracted to the city's vibrant pub and coffee scene, bountiful outdoor recreation opportunities, and laid-back culture, Portland's population had rapidly expanded in the past five years. The influx of young people moving to the city had created a serious housing and job shortage.

"That's it," I said.

"What? You want me to be a barista? I know that you have a serious coffee addiction, Megs, but come on."

"No! A pub. You could open a pub. It's perfect! Think about it, you love to home-brew and your beer is amazing. It's better than a lot of the big microbreweries around."

Matt laughed. "I appreciate your vote of confidence and I'm glad that you like my beer, but there's no way I could open a pub."

"Why not?"

"Megs, be serious. I'm twenty-four. I just started home-brewing. I have no business background or cash. Do you have any idea how expensive it is to start a brewery?"

"It can't be that bad," I protested. "You could find a cute little space and just do four or five taps."

"I love how naïve you can be sometimes."

I punched him in the shoulder. "I'm not naïve. I'm optimistic and positive."

"That's true. And naïve." He ruffled my hair.

I glared at him. "You have no faith in yourself. Gam would not be impressed."

"Megs, I'm not being negative. I'm a realist. Buying the brewing equipment alone would probably cost a hundred thousand dollars. Do you have that kind of cash? Because I don't."

"It can't be that expensive."

Matt nodded. "Yeah, it can. That's probably a low estimate. Think about the stainless-steel tanks alone. They must cost twenty-five or thirty grand a piece."

"Really?"

"Really. I'm not starting a pub." His face softened. "I love brewing, but I don't want that kind of responsibility. Can you imagine having to manage staff and worry about all the dudes who would drink way too much?"

"Fine, but there has to be something else you can do here. What about starting your own technology blog? Forget *The O*. Do your own thing. You're super tech savvy and starting a blog wouldn't cost any money. I mean, maybe twenty bucks to register the domain, but you could do the design. That wouldn't be expensive."

"Again, I appreciate your enthusiasm. You're right, it wouldn't be like starting my own brewery, but it would still be a major risk. How would I make money? I'd have to quit, and I have this thing called rent that my landlord makes me pay every month."

"You could run ads."

"I could, but how many ads would it take to cover my rent? And how long would it take to build the numbers I would need to sell ad space?"

I didn't answer him. Matt had an excuse for all of my suggestions. It was almost like he wanted to leave. He was right, but I couldn't be rational.

"So that's it? You're leaving?"

"Maybe."

"Where are you going to interview? Silicon Valley?"

"Well." Matt paused. I could tell he was holding something back.

"What? What are you not telling me?"

"You know how I left a few weeks ago."

I frowned. "Yeah."

"I went to Bend." He inhaled.

"Okay. What's in Bend?"

"My new job."

"What? You already have a new job?"

"Yeah." He reached to the ground and pulled his phone out of his laptop bag. Scrolling through it, he found what he was looking for and handed it to me. "Bend is booming right now. There are a ton of new tech companies that have been priced out of Silicon Valley moving into Bend. I interviewed with this great new start-up, Blazen. They're a green energy tech company. Their motto is 'Blazen into the future.'"

I scanned through the company's Web page. Blazen manufactured green energy products, everything from LED lighting to solar panels for both commercial and residential clients. According to their "About Us" page they claimed to be committed to supporting manufacturing efforts in the States. It sounded like a great company and a great match for Matt. Why did it have to be in Bend?

"The owners are good guys. They have heart. They really care about the environment and figuring out ways to make technology greener."

"It sounds great." I wondered if Matt picked up on my lack of enthusiasm.

"Plus the benefits are amazing. They're offering profit sharing and a signing bonus. This is the real deal, Megs."

"That's great. You deserve it." He did. I wanted to be happy for him. And I was, sort of.

"Don't look so sad, Megs." Matt scooted closer to me. "I haven't said yes yet. They gave me the week to think about it."

"What are you thinking?" I could feel heat radiating from his body. It made it difficult to stay mad at him.

"Bend's not that far. It's only a three-and-a-half-hour drive. I bet you can convince Greg to send you on assignment, right? It's an outdoor lover's mecca. Think of all the features you could write—whitewater rafting on the Deschutes, heli-skiing on Mt. Bachelor, rappelling in the lava caves."

"Wait a sec. You've been complaining about me working for *Northwest Extreme* and Greg for months, but now suddenly you're cool with it?" Matt had repeatedly voiced his concern about me working for the adventure publication, not only because he was worried that I might injure myself on assignment, but also because he had uncovered information about Greg. When I first met Greg I thought that bumping into him had been purely by chance—divine intervention as Gam would say, but Matt learned that wasn't entirely true. My encounter with my sexy boss had nothing to do with chance. Greg had been asked to hire me at *Northwest Extreme* to keep me safe, or at least that's what he told me. I thought I believed him, but Greg was so secretive and aloof that a seed of doubt lingered. Matt had only fed that doubt with his insistence that Greg was dangerous. It had been a point of contention between us.

"That's not exactly fair, Megs."

"It's true, though."

"You know, actually, that's something I wanted to talk to you about. I may have been wrong about Greg."

"Wrong how?" My foot tapped on the sidewalk. I could feel the nervous energy starting to build.

Matt paused. He seemed to be considering his words carefully. "I didn't go to Bend only because of the interview. I had something else I wanted to follow up on."

"And?"

"And it has to do with Charlie's murder. The thing is, I'm more confused than ever. I'm waiting to hear back from a lead I met out there. As soon as I do, I promise I'll fill you in, but I don't want to get your hopes up until I know more."

"What does that have to do with Greg?"

"I'm not sure. Honestly." He caught my eye. "Don't look at me like that. I don't know yet. I'm hoping this source is going to make everything clear."

"Why would you even say anything to me if you're going to be vague about it now? That's not cool." This lunch date was not going according to plan. I clenched my jaw. It was time for me to go before I said something I might regret. But in fairness, Matt was to blame. Why would he bring up Pops' murder and then tell me there was nothing to tell?

"Sorry, I know that you're mad. I get it. You deserve to be mad. I'm not playing games with you and I'm not withholding information to make you crazy. I want the best for you, Megs. You have to know that."

I stood. "You have a funny way of showing it."

Matt grabbed my hand. "Don't go like this. Don't leave mad."

"I'm not mad," I lied. "I'll talk to you later." I tried to storm away, but my muscles were so tight from the morning run that I'm sure I looked like an idiot. I didn't even care. Matt was leaving and I was going to be stuck in Portland without my two best friends.

Chapter 16

Questions swirled in my head. This was usually when I would take a long walk and try to quiet the noise in my brain, but even a leisurely stroll on the waterfront sounded painful. I had a couple hours to kill before meeting Tim for a pint. I decided to get an iced coffee and find a spot on the grassy hill near the river to park myself.

Ordering coffee in Portland's sometime pretentious coffee culture almost requires a specialized degree. Most of the high-end artisan coffee bars located downtown cater to that culture. In part because it's become such a thing with tourists.

In my NE Portland neighborhood, most coffee shops were hangout spots for neighbors. Local musicians, artists, and writers will kick back with a cup of cold brew for the afternoon. But downtown and the Pearl are a different story. The coffee scene was sleeker and snarkier. Tourists had come to expect a side of abuse with their morning cup of Joe.

I found a shop on the corner—Blue—with tinted windows and sterile white ceramic countertops. It reminded me of a clean room in a lab. There was sparse seating and a standing bar against the far wall. No writers were camped out. No musicians strummed on guitar strings. The space was void of color and character. At the counter there was a long glass case with six white ceramic bowls filled with coffee beans.

A guy about my age dressed in black from head to toe waited for me to order. I glanced at the windowed wall behind him and the glass case for a menu or some sort of signage. There wasn't any. He scowled and adjusted the knit beanie on his head. "Do you know what you want?"

"Do you have a menu?"

Pointing to the ceramic bowls, he said, "Choose your beans."

"My beans? I was hoping for an iced mocha."

He scoffed. "We sell coffee here."

"Right, coffee—as in an iced mocha."

"No," he shook his head. "Did you read the sign out front?"

"Blue?"

He sighed loudly and changed his cadence of speech, as if he was talking to a toddler. "We are a fresh roasted coffee bar. We sell coffee. Period."

I wasn't going to take his abuse. It could have been due to my disappointing lunch with Matt, too, but this hipster coffee snob was a jerk. "A mocha is coffee," I retorted.

"If that's the kind of *coffee* you're looking for, I suggest you walk two blocks that way to Star*sucks.*" He pointed outside.

"I don't want to go to Starbucks. I just want an iced mocha. Since when is a mocha not a coffee?"

"Since always. You must be new to Portland."

If I hadn't been so sore I might have jumped over the glass case and punched him. "Um, no. I don't think so. I've lived in Portland my entire life. How long have *you* been in Portland?"

I had a pretty good guess that he hadn't been in Portland long. Since I'd returned home after graduating from college things had changed dramatically—mainly in the form of hipsters who had gentrified some of the city's poorest neighborhoods. The irony was that young affluent hipsters, who shopped at thrift stores to score vintage finds and ate only organic artisanal foods, had created a housing crisis. Lower-income and at-risk families had been priced out of neighborhoods as twenty-somethings pushed in and bought up cheap old buildings and historical apartments. Rents skyrocketed and long-term residents found themselves priced out of the market. It was a serious problem and something that Pops would have covered for *The O.*

"Two years," the barista said with a scowl.

"Exactly." I gave him a smug smile.

"Are you going to order something or what?"

"Yeah, I'm going to go order an iced mocha at a real coffeehouse." I returned his scowl and walked out of the shop.

How pretentious. I fumed as I crossed the street, trying to find a new coffee spot. I must not have been paying attention to where I was going because I walked right into someone.

"Mary Margaret Reed, what are you doing here?" Kenny stood with his arms on his hips staring down at me.

"Hey! What are you doing here?"

"I work right there." Kenny motioned to the five-story police building across the street.

"Right," I said; then I paused. "But you're a Vancouver police officer. What are you doing in Portland?"

"Working on the case."

"Oh." That didn't clear anything up.

"You look confused." Kenny winked. "Detective Bridger worked for the Portland Police Department for twelve years. He was hired by Vancouver two weeks ago. I think I mentioned this is his first official case with the city. He still has a number of contacts in Portland and asked me to consult with his mentor on a few things related to the investigation."

"Ah, I see."

"You didn't tell me what you're doing here?"

"I was trying to get an iced mocha." I glared in the direction of Blue. "But apparently that's not real coffee."

"What? I love mochas."

"Right?"

He grinned. "You ordered a mocha at Blue? That's a death wish. They are serious coffee snobs."

"Yeah, I kind of figured that out. I wanted to punch that conceited barista in the face."

Kenny glanced inside and then chuckled. "That's not a barista. He's a bro-ista."

"A bro-ista?"

"Yeah, hashtag it. It's a thing, you know—scruffy facial hair, skinny jeans, chain wallets, self-important attitudes. Portland's crawling with them. That's why I'm glad I work in Vancouver, although they're coming north. Watch out!" He put his hand on his holster. "Maybe I'll have to ask Detective Bridger if I can start a hipster stakeout. Catch them coming over the bridge and send them back to Portland."

I couldn't help but laugh.

Kenny adjusted his holster. "Come on, let me buy you a mocha. I know a great place just a couple blocks away, and they put extra whipped cream on top."

"You are speaking my language."

He put his arm around my shoulder. "I like a girl who's not afraid to admit that she drinks mochas. So many women I know order nonfat lattes. Why?"

"Beats me. I'm all about the mocha."

"That could be a song or something." Kenny broke into dance moves. "All about the mocha." He was goofy. I liked him.

We continued on. "If you want a true hipster story you'll love this," he said. "My brother works for an ad agency here in Portland and last week one of his coworkers called in sick, not because he was sick but because his chicken was sick."

"What?" I stopped and put my hands on my forehead. "His *chicken* was sick? No. No way."

"Yep." Kenny nodded.

"How can you even tell if a chicken is sick?"

"No idea." Kenny beamed. "But we got a good laugh out of it at the department. We all decided that a sick chicken is dinner."

"Now that is sick." We both laughed.

"I'm glad I ran into you," I said as we walked past a group of tourists holding Pepto-Bismol pink Voodoo Doughnut boxes. They were gathered near a barricaded sidewalk where a scene for the smash-hit TV series *Grimm* was being filmed. In addition to being a hub for hipsters, Portland had become a prime location for television and film productions. We'd become accustomed to film crews taking over busy streets and backcountry trails. "Did you get my message?" I said to Kenny as one of the tourists squealed and waved frantically to a cast member.

"No, I haven't had a chance to check. It's been a hectic morning—well, afternoon—there's so much paperwork involved in a murder case. I've been buried in it."

"That's a bad pun."

Kenny looked confused for a minute. "Oh yeah. Ouch. That is a bad pun." He thought for a second. "Scratch that. I've been . . . busy. Better?"

"Better." I smiled.

"What did you want to tell me?"

"It's about Tim Baxter."

"Tim Baxter. Business dude. Left in a hurry, right?"

"He's the one."

We arrived at the coffee shop. Kenny held the door open for me. "After you, miss."

"Thanks." I surveyed the space. Much better. A collection of photography for sale lined the walls. People sat at wooden tables chatting and noshing on pastries. An artisan slab of old growth wood hung near the front counter. It displayed the menu and drink specials. Today's read: DOUBLE CHOCOLATE MOCHA WITH HOUSE-MADE WHIPPED CREAM. ICED OR HOT.

Kenny pointed to the second line. "Look, iced mochas!"

"You are a lifesaver."

"I know. I get that all the time." He shrugged and ran his hands over his blue police uniform.

I laughed. "I bet you do."

We ordered our mochas and found a table near the front. Kenny turned down his walkie-talkie. "What about Tim Baxter."

"I think he might have killed Billy."

"Whoa. Where is that coming from?" His brown eyes widened. I couldn't help contrasting him to the sullen barista at Blue. Kenny's dark crew cut and clean-shaven face were polar opposite to the trend of shaggy beards and unwashed hair. It was refreshing.

I told him about Tim running into me and how he had his gym bag outside. Kenny listened, swirling his iced coffee the entire time.

"You observed a lot this morning," he said when I finished.

"It's sort of my thing. I'm a reporter. It's my job to pay attention to details and listen."

"You make a great witness." He looked impressed.

"Thanks." I wasn't used to getting praise from the police. Usually Sheriff Daniels told me to stay out of his case.

"I'll look into it," Kenny said. "We're going to do another round of questioning later today and tomorrow."

"What if Tim hid the bandana in his gym bag? Maybe that's why he ran out of the locker room so fast—he was trying to get rid of the evidence, but he dropped it and Jenny found it."

"How is a bandana evidence?"

"It could be the murder weapon."

"Sorry, I'm not quite following."

"I told your boss that there was a bandana around Billy's neck when I found him. By the time you got on the scene the bandana wasn't there. Maybe Tim strangled him, then went back to the scene after I found Billy and stuffed the bandana in his gym bag. It could have fallen out when he ran upstairs. Jenny had a bandana and when I asked her about it she said it wasn't hers."

Kenny sucked on an ice cube. "Hmm. That's right, I remember you mentioning that at the scene. We don't have the coroner's report yet. We should be getting that soon. Until we have an official cause of death it's too soon to jump to any conclusions."

I took a sip of the chocolaty drink. "There's more. Tim sent me a private message on Facebook this morning. He wants to meet me for a beer before our evening training session. Do you think I should?"

"Why does he want to meet you?"

I shrugged. "I don't know. He said he had something important to tell me."

"Where would you meet him?"

"At a pub."

Kenny crunched the ice cube. It made my teeth hurt. "Actually, that's not a bad idea. He might be more willing to reveal something to you. He probably doesn't perceive you as a threat."

"Are you saying that I don't look threatening?" Was I flirting with him?

"Oh, you're a threat all right, but a completely different kind of threat." He winked. "All that pink is threat enough for me."

"Hey, I happen to love pink."

"I can tell," he said, shaking his head. "I think even the worst witness would be able to pick up that fact."

I furrowed my brow.

"Sorry, Mary Margaret Reed. What if I call you Pinkie?"

I scowled.

"No?" He grinned. "Cool, back to the case. If you're up for meeting Tim, I'll tag along and hang out nearby. If you're meeting him at a public pub in the middle of the day you shouldn't be in any danger."

"That's exactly what Matt said."

"Who's Matt?"

"My friend."

"Oh. Your *friend.*"

"No, really he's a good friend."

Kenny smiled. "Glad to hear it. I guess he won't mind if I ask you out once we've wrapped this investigation, then?"

My cheeks burned with heat. "You're going to ask me out?"

"As long as you don't turn out to be a killer." He picked up our glasses and walked them over to a bin by the counter.

The Universe had uncanny timing sometimes. Only a little while ago I had learned that Matt was seriously considering leaving Portland and now I had a potential new date. I wasn't sure if that was a good thing or a bad thing.

Chapter 17

Kenny followed me to Hopworks where Tim suggested we meet. The organic brewery was located on the Eastside of town. Matt is a big fan of Hopworks not only because of their awesome selection of beers, but because all of their pubs have bike themes. At their North Portland pub there are two stationary bikes where beer lovers can pedal while sipping on a pint or waiting for a table. Pedaling generates electricity and helps offset the carbon footprint that you're using while having a pint—yet another example of a quintessential green philosophy that Portland is famous for.

"Remember, if you feel weird about anything, I'll be at the bar. Tell Tim you have to go to the bathroom and come get me."

"Got it."

I left Kenny at the bar. He stood out from the hipster crowd, wearing flannel shirts and skinny jeans, in his blue police uniform. The Hopworks vibe didn't seem like a match for Tim either. I was surprised that he had suggested it.

A waitress stopped me as I tried to peer around the half wall that separated the bar from the dining room, which was primarily occupied with families. Most pubs in Portland cater to children, offering a casual atmosphere and kid fare like chicken strips and fries with ranch dressing. Hopworks was the pinnacle of child-friendly pubs. They created special menus and play areas for youngsters. Parents could kick back with pints while their toddlers played with pizza dough and cookie cutters and drove toy cars around on colorful play mats on the floor.

"Did you need a table?" the waitress asked.

"I'm meeting someone. Can I see if he's here?"

"Knock yourself out." She moved to let me pass.

Tim was seated in a booth at the very back of the restaurant, directly across from the kids' play zone. Toddlers hopped up on root beer colored with chalk on the walls and threw blocks at each other. Oh joy. I prefer my pubs kid-free.

"Hey," I said, scooting into the booth. "Nice location. Quiet."

"It was the only available table." He stared at a kid covered in blue chalk. "At least we won't know anyone here."

"I didn't figure this was your jam."

"My jam?" Tim looked confused. He wasn't wearing his suit, but he maintained a slightly arrogant posture. His collared shirt was halfway unbuttoned, revealing a roll of fat under his neck.

"You know, your jam, like your thing."

"I'm afraid I don't speak twenty."

"I was trying to be funny."

"Okay." He slid a menu across the table. "What do you want? It's on me."

"Thanks." I took the menu. "What do I owe the pleasure of being treated to a beer?"

"You can eat if you want to. I already ordered appetizers."

"But what about daily doubles? Isn't eating going to make you sick when we have to run, especially through the mud."

Tim waved me off. "I haven't even heard that training is on. It's likely the police are going to want to preserve the crime scene."

The waitress delivered a dark beer with foam spilling from the top to our table. She had to step over a preschooler about to hurl a wad of pizza dough at his brother. Tim grabbed the beer from her and took a giant swig.

"Can I get you something?" she asked.

"I'll take a Rise Up Red."

"Good choice." She gave me a nod of approval. Poor woman. She deserved battle pay working here, I thought as one of the kids let out an ear-piercing scream. Why had Tim picked this section?

Tim wiped foam from his mouth. "Do you want food?"

"No, thanks," I replied to the waitress. "Just the Red." I wasn't taking any chance and couldn't believe that Tim was drinking a heavy porter at this time of day, especially because as far as we knew we would be running in a few hours. I had a feeling I wouldn't even finish my beer.

"Thanks for agreeing to meet me."

"Not a problem. What's going on?"

Tim clutched his beer glass and chugged half of it down in three large gulps.

"Thirsty?"

"You have no idea. My wife has me on a diet unfit for rabbits. I've been hungry for three weeks."

"It sounds like she's watching out for you."

Tim downed the rest of his pint right as the waitress returned with my beer and a huge platter of appetizers. "I'll have another one of these." Tim handed her his empty glass.

She caught my eye and gave me a look of pity as she walked away to refill Tim's beer. I took a sip of my Rise Up Red. It had a nice hoppy flavor and a beautiful mahogany color. The appetizers looked delicious. There were chicken wings, hummus with veggies and hot pita bread, and a pile of wedge-cut fries covered with gravy and cheese. It was a heart attack on a plate. No wonder Tim hadn't lost any weight.

"You're not kidding about being hungry. Are you going to eat all of that?"

Tim pushed the platter closer to me. "No, I'll share. Help yourself."

"That's okay, I'm not really hungry."

He heaped gravy fries onto a fork. "You're lucky you don't have someone at home nagging you. My wife keeps complaining about my weight. She thinks I'm not going to be around to see our kids graduate college. I keep trying to explain that she's going to get her wish if she keeps forcing me to train with Mind Over Mudder."

"Tell me about it. It's been intense."

"Intense?" Tim said with a mouthful of fries. "It's been torture."

I waited while he chewed. "What do you think is going to happen now that Billy's dead? Do you think Dylan will keep it going?"

"God, I hope not. Billy's death was my ticket out of that insanity."

I winced. Did Tim really mean that? Could he have killed Billy out of sheer physical exhaustion?

"I didn't mean it like that," Tim continued. "Don't look so shocked. It wasn't a secret that I didn't like Billy, but it's terrible that he's dead. I meant that I'm hoping Dylan will be too scattered to worry about pushing our little group on, and I can forget about this stupid mud run once and for all."

"If you hate it that much, why don't you quit?" I took another sip of my beer.

"I told you my wife won't let me."

"But you're an adult."

"You should meet my wife. She doesn't take no for an answer. It's 'Yes, dear' or the doghouse for me."

"She sounds a bit like my mother."

"Too bad for you."

The waitress dropped off Tim's second beer, which he proceeded to drink as fast as he could.

"Okay, if your wife won't let you quit, then why don't you put in a small amount of effort and not worry about it?"

"That's what I tried to do, but my wife got to Billy."

"What?"

"She signed me up for Mind Over Mudder. She went straight to Billy and told him to watch me like a hawk. We've been married for almost twenty years, she knows me too well. If it hadn't been for Billy constantly riding me, I would have found a way to opt out. I run a huge company where I'm the boss. I'm fed up with Billy trying to boss me around."

I considered his words for a minute. Billy had seemed to be all over Tim in a way that he wasn't on the rest of us. Maybe there was some truth to what Tim was saying. The question was, could Tim have snapped?

Tim spread a thick layer of hummus on a slice of pita bread. "You're probably wondering why I asked you here."

"I am."

He glanced around the pub. None of the preschoolers playing with blocks on the floor gave us a second look, but nevertheless Tim leaned across the booth and dropped his voice. "I know you saw me this morning."

I gulped. How should I answer that? I took a sip of beer to try and stall.

Tim shoved three olives in his mouth. "I saw you talking to Kelsey. Did she say anything?"

"Anything about what? I'm confused."

He surveyed the room again. "I was there this morning in the locker room."

"You saw Billy's body?"

"No." He sat back. "Billy was alive when I left."

"I don't understand. What does this have to do with me and Kelsey?"

"I have to know what you, and more importantly what Kelsey saw."

"Nothing. I didn't see anything. I didn't see Kelsey. I got run down in the hallway—I think by you." I waited for a response.

Tim scratched his head. "Yeah, sorry about that."

"Look, I'm not following any of this. You ran me over. You were in the locker room right before I found Billy's body. I think I need to go to the police."

Tim reached over and grabbed my wrist. I jerked it away. "No, please don't. Let me explain. You're sure Kelsey wasn't there?"

I gave him a hard look. "In the locker room, no she wasn't there. No one was there."

"All right. All right. Here's the thing. I snuck into the locker room this morning."

My eyes must have given away my distrust.

"Not that like. I needed to get my bag. It had some important things in it. After the debacle in the mud I couldn't take it anymore. I decided that I was willing to face the wrath of my wife. Billy went too far this time, so when the group got to the waterfront I looped back over the bridge."

"What about Billy? I thought he was your shadow."

"He usually was, but he took off. He didn't even run over the footbridge with us."

"Really?" How had I missed that when I was hiding in the orchard?

"Yeah, it was strange. He started around the turn at the orchard and then he called to Jenny to lead the pack. I don't know where he went, but he wasn't with us. I ran with the group up the footbridge. You can see everything from up there. Billy wasn't anywhere around, so I took that as my chance to get back to the locker room before everyone else."

I didn't tell him that I had a similar experience hiding behind an apple tree.

"When I got back to the locker room, I didn't waste any time. I grabbed my bag and was about to leave when I heard voices."

"Whose voices?"

"Billy and someone else."

"Who? Kelsey?"

"I don't know. Their voices were muffled, but it sounded like a man. I didn't want to stick around to find out. I couldn't let Billy see me. I started to go, but my bag caught on the bench. Everything inside spilled out."

"What's the deal with that? You were acting weird with your bag this morning. Did you have a bomb stashed in it or something?"

Tim nearly choked on his beer. "A bomb? Hardly. That bag does contain my secret stash, though."

"Stash?" Was Tim talking about drugs?

He smiled. "Candy."

"Candy!" I shouted.

"Keep your voice down."

I whispered, "Candy? You had a secret stash of candy. That's what was in the bag."

"Yes, I hid it in my locker. I need something right after we finish our runs."

"Wait, wait, let's get back to Billy. You heard him arguing with someone and then you dropped your bag on the floor. What happened after that?"

"Whoever Billy was fighting with left. I didn't see who it was because I was on the floor trying to get all my candy before Billy caught me."

"Did he catch you?"

"No, he came out right as I stuffed the last Hershey bar into my bag."

"What happened then?"

"Not much. It surprised me. I thought he would be all over me for doing a shorter run, but he didn't say anything. He wasn't in good shape."

"What do you mean?"

"He was clutching his chest. Like he did during warm-ups. He said something about taking a steam and went back to the steam room. I didn't stick around. I grabbed the rest of my stuff. Then I ran into you."

"And you didn't see anyone else?"

"No."

My mind tried to keep up with everything I had just learned. I hadn't been alone in the barracks this morning. Tim and someone else had been there too. I wasn't sure if I believed Tim's story. Would he really flip out about candy? Then I thought about Jill. My bestie has the most intense addiction to candy of anyone I know. She might kill for a Snickers bar if she was desperate enough.

"Why did you want to tell me this?" I asked. "And what does this have to do with Kelsey?"

The platter of appetizers was almost empty. Tim was obviously a stress eater. "I saw Kelsey talking to you earlier. I thought she might have video footage of me with my contraband."

"I don't think so. She wasn't there, at least not as far as I know. She was trying to get a shot for the morning show and she wanted to know what I'd seen."

"That's a relief." Tim sighed.

"Did you tell all of this to the police?"

"Not yet. I was worried that it wouldn't look good for me."

"It doesn't, but if you don't tell them now it's only going to get worse."

He popped the last olive on the plate into his mouth. "You're right. I'm supposed to meet Detective Bridger later. I'll tell him about the candy and everything."

"If you don't, I have to." I felt proud of the way I said that with conviction and maturity.

"I will. I feel better knowing that Kelsey wasn't talking to you about me. I could see the headline—PORTLAND BUSINESSMAN BINGING ON CHOCOLATE. Can you imagine how viral that footage would go?"

He had a point.

"You don't think they'll say anything to my wife, do you?"

"I don't know. I'm not a detective, but I can't imagine why that would come up. It's not a crime to love candy, is it?"

Tim reached into his back pocket, pulled out his wallet, and left two twenties on the table. "I have to go. Hopefully I won't see you soon for our nighttime torture. Maybe we'll get lucky and Dylan will call the whole thing off. Thanks for listening. By the way, that would make a great T-shirt slogan—IT'S NOT A CRIME TO LOVE CANDY."

He patted me on the shoulder and left.

That was a strange and unexpected conversation. Tim had been hoarding candy. That's why he ran me down and was clutching his bag like it contained a bomb. Or was he lying? Maybe he invited me out for a beer to see what I knew. If that was the case, I hoped that I'd played it cool. Tim had either just cleared himself as a suspect or solidified that he was the most likely candidate for murder. I wasn't sure, but I knew one thing—I was telling Kenny every single detail of what I had just learned.

Chapter 18

As promised, Kenny was waiting at the bar for me. I squeezed into the empty stool next to him.

"So how did your first investigation go, Mary Margaret?"

"You know you can stop with the Mary Margaret thing anytime. My friends call me Meg."

"But Mary Margaret is so fun, and so are you." He gave me a quick look-over. "And I like watching you squirm when I say Mary Margaret."

I rolled my eyes.

"Do you want a beer?"

"No, thanks. I couldn't finish the one Tim bought me." I glanced at the television behind the bar. "I might have to run five miles in an hour. I'll have a beer after I finish my run. That is if I even finish my run. Speaking of that, do you know if everything's still on with Mind Over Mudder?"

"As far as I know. You won't have access to the barracks depending on whether or not they're still collecting evidence from the crime scene, but you should be able to run outside."

"Drat." I frowned. "I was hoping you would say that it was canceled."

Kenny chuckled. "You are one interesting girl, Mary Margaret."

I fanned my face. "Do go on." Why was I flirting this much?

He shifted on his bar stool. "You also have a way of getting me off topic. What did Tim want?"

I shared everything that I had learned from Tim. Kenny took notes, stopping every once in a while to ask for clarification. "Candy? You can't be serious. He told you that he was hiding candy."

"Weird, right?"

"Right." Kenny's skepticism validated my concerns about the legitimacy of Tim's story.

"What happens now?" I asked.

"We bring him back in for questioning."

"What about me? Should I steer clear of him tonight?"

"I wouldn't worry about it. We'll be monitoring his movements. I would bet he was fishing for information from you. Trying to gauge what you saw."

"That's what I thought."

"Your instincts are good." Kenny stood. "I have to get back. I'll check in with you later. Thanks for your help, Mary Margaret."

I watched him walk out of the bar. Had he really thanked me for my help? That was a first. Unfortunately, I didn't have time to revel in my new status. I was due for our evening session at the barracks in a half an hour. I had enough time to swing by my place to grab my things and head up to the "Couve," hipster slang for Vancouver.

A text buzzed on my phone as I threw my stuff in

the back of my Subaru. It was from Jill. **Movie night? Be to your place at 8. Must hear how you're doing.**

Shoot. I'd completely forgotten about our Italian dinner and movie date. I had planned to spend the afternoon making an Italian feast for Jill. She was going to have to settle for takeout pizza. I knew she wouldn't care.

My stomach gurgled from the beer and my nerves as I pulled into a parking space across from Fort Vancouver. What was I doing here? This was a mistake. Every muscle in my body screamed at me to turn around.

No, Meg. You made a commitment to yourself. You're going to see this through.

I grabbed my bag before I could change my mind and started up the hill.

"Hey, Meg!" Jenny called out behind me. She reminded me of a cheerleader as she bounced up the hill in a matching lime green tracksuit.

"Hi." I stopped and waited for her to catch up.

"How are you doing?" She jogged in place. "Can you believe that Billy's dead? It hasn't sunk in yet. I feel like we were just here and now we're back, but everything is different."

"It is." I walked while she kept pace by jogging in small circles.

"I feel terrible for you, though. I was telling my husband about it this afternoon. Finding Billy's body." She stopped and put her hand over her stomach in a gagging motion. "I would have thrown up."

"It was pretty bad."

We crested the hill. The building housing Mind Over Mudder was completely roped off with yellow police tape. A uniformed officer stood on guard near the front door. Two police cars and a van were parked halfway onto the grass.

"I guess we'll be changing outside," Jenny said.

"Looks like it."

Dylan waved when he spotted us. "Come on over." He wore a loose-fitting hemp shirt that caught in the slight wind and a pair of Birkenstocks. Obviously, he wasn't going to take over Billy's role. "Thanks for coming, everyone. I know you're all as shaken up as I am about everything that's happened."

A murmur worked its way through the group.

"Billy had great passion for our work. He would be pleased to see that you've all shown up tonight. I know it can't be easy for you. It's not for me, and I also know that you have a lot of questions. I do, too, and I'll try to tell you everything that I know so far, but first I think it's important to take a few minutes to remember Billy." He folded his arms in front of his chest in a Namaste pose. "Join me for a moment of silence."

We all closed our eyes and breathed in a soft rhythm. The only sound invading the quiet came from two crows squawking in the trees. It felt good to be silent. There's something powerful and almost palpable about sharing silence with someone else. I focused on my breath, allowing air to completely fill my lungs and releasing it slowly through my nose. It was almost as if I was releasing the memory of finding Billy with each breath.

After a few minutes Dylan cleared his throat. "Thank you for that." He bowed. His voice caught a little as he continued. "I'm sure you're all like me—having a hard time understanding how something so awful could occur. I don't know who could have done something so brutal, but I do know that Billy would have wanted you to continue on. He and I talked at length about the reward he felt at watching our clients transform. You've all already begun that transformation and I think that the best way we can honor Billy is to continue."

Tim lumbered over. "Sorry I'm late."

Dylan bowed. "Namaste, my brother. Don't sweat it. I was just talking about how Billy would have wanted you to go on, and I was going to ask for a volunteer. I'm going to have to start the process of hiring a new trainer, but it's going to take a little while. You know the route by now, I'm hoping one of you will step up and help out while we're in limbo."

Jenny's hand shot in the air. "I'll help."

Dylan put his hand over his heart and nodded at her. "Thank you. I feel that, I really do."

"No problem. I told my husband this afternoon that I might want to become a trainer. I can't believe those words are coming out of my mouth. A few weeks ago I would have laughed if anyone said that, but being part of this team has changed me—inside and out. I want to help."

"We should talk later," Dylan said.

Jenny nodded. "I'd love to."

I wondered momentarily if she could have killed Billy to get his job. She was pretty quick to volunteer. There was still the question of the missing bandana. What if Jenny had killed Billy and intentionally held on to the bandana—hiding it in plain sight? That could be a brilliant move. Then I shook off the thought. A stay-at-home mom turned murderer? That would certainly make headlines.

"The police are still working inside, so you're not going to be able to use the locker rooms tonight. I know that Billy's training schedule had you in the mud again tonight, but in light of the circumstances you should skip that and do your run." He pointed to brown paper sacks with the Mind Over Mudder logo stamped on them sitting on the grass nearby. "I was able to get your supplements. I know many of you are running low, so feel free to grab your bag before you leave. I labeled each bag with your names."

Tim raised his hand. "When are we going to get back in the locker room?"

"I'm not sure," Dylan replied. "The police said it all depends. It could be later tonight or tomorrow, or it might not be for a few days. The good news is that the weather report looks good. It's supposed to be dry and sunny. You've got a week until Mud, Sweat, and Beers. We'll stay the course and make sure you all cross the finish line next weekend. Billy would have loved that."

"There's no chance of getting in there tonight?" Tim asked. His baggy, nylon running shorts and oversized Mind Over Mudder T-shirt made him look even bigger.

"I don't think so. You can ask the police officer on duty. Why?"

"It's fine. I forgot a few papers I need to look over this weekend. I was hoping to save myself a trip to the office."

Tim was acting weird. What did he really want in

the locker room? He told me that he had his bag. Was he worried that he'd forgotten a piece of evidence behind? I planned to keep my distance from him and stick near Jenny.

"Any other questions?" Dylan asked.

Kelsey Kain stepped forward. "What have the police told you?" She made her KPDX tracksuit look stylish. Who could do that?

"Not much."

"Have you spoken with them?" she pressed on.

"I have."

"Do they have a suspect? A theory? Anything?" Her voice sounded strained. "Anything. I need something."

Dylan shook his head. "Not that they've told me."

Kelsey sighed. "How am I supposed to get a story if they're not talking?"

"Is that a rhetorical question?" Dylan asked.

She stared at the police officer blocking the front door. I could tell she was trying to figure out a way in.

"Any other questions?"

No one spoke.

"In that case, I'll have you follow Jenny. I'll be waiting here when you return with your supplements. Have fun and be safe out there." He bowed again. "Namaste, Billy."

Jenny directed us up the hill to a flat grassy section of the park to stretch. I enjoyed the stretching portion of our workout routine. Flexibility and balance have never been my thing. When I started two weeks ago I could barely reach my toes, now I was able to bend over in one fluid motion and the tips of my fingertips actually brushed the grass.

"Let's take the long loop tonight," Jenny said, reaching her arm behind her neck and grabbing her elbow. "I know you're all sore, so we can go slower but get a longer run in. Tomorrow we can work on sprints."

Slower sounded good, but longer sounded terrible. It looked like my other teammates agreed. A round of protests sounded. Jenny stood firm. "We all said we're doing this for Billy. Trust me, Billy would have had us running stairs, sprints, and the longer loop. You're getting off easy."

"Someone's power has gone to her head," Kelsey muttered next to me.

"You think so?" I asked.

"Look at her. Miss stay-at-home mom has decided to go commander on us."

Jenny did appear to be enjoying her new position. I couldn't argue with that, but I didn't want Kelsey to know that. "Hey, were you at the barracks this morning?" I asked, changing the subject.

She glared at me. "Yes, we were *all* at the barracks." How did she manage to get her lips to sparkle? It must be expensive gloss.

"No, I mean when everyone was on the run."

"Why would I have been in the barracks then?"

"I don't know. I just thought I saw you," I lied.

She rolled her eyes. Her lids were coated in a striated layer of blue eyeshadow. "You didn't see me. I was doing my job—reporting—are you familiar with that?"

"What's that supposed to mean?"

"I think you know exactly what I mean. I'm not going to compete with a wannabe journalist for this story. This is my story. All mine. Got it?"

"Got it. We're not competing, Kelsey. Like I said, we work for two entirely different outlets."

"Every journalist is competing for a story. Always."

"Okay." I raised my hands in truce. "Can I ask you one more thing?"

"What?" She folded her arms across her chest.

"I just happened to be downtown this afternoon and I thought I saw you talking to someone outside KPDX's headquarters."

"I talk to a lot of people. I'm a reporter."

"I know, but this guy looked different."

"For someone who isn't competing with me, you seem to be very aware of my movements." She turned and sprinted toward Officer's Row before I could say anything else.

Kelsey hadn't liked me from day one, but this was getting ridiculous. Billy's murder had turned her into a crazed reporter. I thought about what Matt had told me about *The O* paying their journalists for writing the best sensational headlines. Maybe Kelsey was in the same position. Writing for *Northwest Extreme* was looking better and better by the minute. I just hoped my newfound appreciation for my job wasn't about to come to an end.

Chapter 19

Jenny took her newfound leadership role seriously. Aside from the fact that she didn't have Billy's whistle and looked nothing like him, she ran the workout exactly like him. Only her syrupy voice and T-shirt reading, ONE TOUGHER MUDDER with a picture of a mom running through the mud with a baby on each arm, gave away that something was different. So much for a slower pace. Jenny pushed us just as hard—if not harder—than Billy.

"Come on, you guys! Remember, we're doing this for Billy," she would continually call over her shoulder as we ran past the college and looped down toward Fort Vancouver.

I think I reached a new level of pain. Running hurt so much I almost couldn't even feel it anymore. It was like I was having some sort of out-of-body experience. I'd have to remember to ask Gam about that later. Jenny stayed in the front of the pack. I lost sight of her after the first mile, content to jog at a snail's pace. When I made it back to the barracks I noticed that she and Dylan were involved in a serious conversation. They stood under a giant oak tree talking with their heads close together. When one of my teammates approached them, Dylan startled. He recovered quickly, whispering something in Jenny's ear and then joining my teammate to find his bag of vitamin supplements.

I wondered what they were talking about. Had Dylan offered Billy's job to Jenny? That would be great for her, but I couldn't imagine him hiring someone without any formal training.

Let it go, Meg, I told myself as I limped to my car. It was almost eight. I ordered Jill's favorite pizza—tomato and basil sauce with artichoke hearts, olives, feta, and marinated chicken—from the delivery shop near my house. Then I texted her to tell her to be at my place in thirty minutes. That would give me enough time to hop in the shower and pull on a pair of sweats.

On cue, the doorbell rang thirty minutes later. I ran my fingers through my wet hair as I opened it. "Are you feeling Italian?" Jill said in a perfect fake accent. She held a bottle of Italian wine and a blue and brown box that looked suspiciously like it might contain chocolate.

"Is that what I think it is?" I let her in and pointed to the box.

"If we're going Italian for the evening, we need Italian chocolates, right?" She handed me the box and hung a thin cashmere wrap on the hook by the door. Jill's version of casual Saturday movie night attire was much more glamorous than mine. I had pulled on a pair of well-worn pink sweats with holes in the knees and a gray hoodie that I'd had since my freshman year of college. Jill wore sleek yoga pants, a long V-neck silk T-shirt, and the cashmere wrap. If I hadn't known her for practically my entire life I would have been intimidated by her effortless beauty.

"Pizza should be here any minute," I said.

Jill walked into the kitchen and found my wine opener in the first drawer. She's the only person who ever uses it. "Meg, are you going to try a glass of this gorgeous Chianti for me?"

"Only for you." I handed her two wineglasses. My kitchen isn't well stocked with stemware. I had scored the wineglasses at a rummage sale earlier in the summer. They came in a set of four. Each glass had a different rose etched on it. I'm not a wine fan, but I fell in love with the vintage glasses and knew exactly where I would display them—on the original filigree cabinet near the picture window in my kitchen.

"Have you ever used these?" Jill asked as she poured Italian wine into each glass.

"Nope, I was saving them for a special occasion. Like this."

"Liar." Jill handed me a glass. "If you don't like it, I won't be offended, but give it a try. It's one of my favorite wines and is really smooth and drinkable."

I followed Jill's lead and swirled the wine in my glass. The light caught the carving in the glass at the perfect angle, making it almost shimmer. "It's beautiful," I said.

Jill frowned. "You haven't tried it yet."

"I know, but the color is really unique. It's almost magenta. Can you see the purple?"

"Try it."

I took a sip of the wine fully expecting to hate it. A rich, fruity flavor hit my palate. I tasted blackberries and a hint of smoke. To my surprise the wine slid down my throat. Jill was right; it was smooth and drinkable. "Wow. This is amazing. I like it. I really do."

Jill gave me a smug grin. "I knew that you would. I'm going to make a wine lover out of you after all."

The doorbell rang.

"Pizza's here!" we shouted in unison and raced each other to the front door. Don't ask. It's our thing.

Jill made it to the door first and composed herself before opening it. She posed with her wineglass in one hand and swung the door open. "Oh, do come in," she said to the delivery guy, and winked at me.

He gulped and held the pizza box up. "Uh, here's your pizza, miss. It'll be twenty bucks."

I gave Jill a hip bump and pushed her out of the way. "This one is on me." I handed the guy a twenty and a couple extra bucks for a tip.

"No," Jill started to protest, but I snatched the pizza and shut the door before she could stop me.

"You didn't have to pay. We could have gone halfsies."

"No way! This is your celebration, and you already brought wine and chocolate, which is totally breaking the bestie rule."

"What bestie rule?" Jill sat on the couch.

I placed the pizza on the coffee table and grabbed a stack of napkins and the bottle of wine from the kitchen. "The rule that says when your bestie invites you over for a celebration, you just show up."

Jill raised her wineglass. "Cheers to that! Thanks for the pizza."

"Thanks for the wine." I sat next to her. "Fill me in on what you're thinking while I get the movie set up. Do you want to watch *Roman Holiday*?"

"Are you kidding?" Jill opened the pizza box. Fragrant steam erupted from the pizza. "This smells like Rome," she said, taking a slice.

"Exactly. It goes with our theme."

"You're the best, Meg."

"Right back at ya." I reached for a piece. I was so hungry that I probably could have eaten the entire pizza if Jill wasn't around. "So what's the scoop?" I asked, blowing on the gooey slice of pizza. "Have you told your parents yet?"

Jill shook her head. "Not yet. I want to be sure that I'm going to do it before I talk to them. Then it's a matter of finding the perfect time to try and break it to them."

"You realize there's never going to be a perfect time?"

"Yeah," Jill sighed. "I know."

"But you're going to do it, right?"

"I think so." Jill bit into her slice.

"You think so? Jill, you have to do this. It's a once-in-a-lifetime opportunity." I knew I shouldn't be saying anything. This wasn't my decision to make, but I couldn't help it. I didn't want to see Jill pass up her dream.

"I know. I'm leaning toward saying yes, but I have a few things I need to think through first." She picked an olive from her slice of pizza and popped it in her mouth. "This is awesome."

"And it pairs perfectly with your vino." I took a sip of my wine.

"What about you?" Jill asked. "You have to fill me in on everything that happened today." I knew that was code for not wanting to talk more about the scholarship. That was fine. I was used to doing this dance with Jill. If pushed too hard, she would shut down completely, so I changed the subject and filled her in on Billy's death, running into Kenny, meeting Tim for a beer, and the overall weirdness of the rest of my Mind Over Mudder teammates.

Jill took a second slice and considered everything I had said. "That's intense."

"Exactly."

"So are you saying you think that Tim could have killed Billy?"

I nodded. "I think so. I don't buy his story. Kenny, the police officer I met, thinks that maybe Tim was trying to figure out what I knew."

"That could be," Jill said. She twisted her hair up into a ponytail. "We should approach this like Miss Marple."

"That's always your solution."

"I know, but think about it. The most obvious suspect is rarely the killer. Think of how boring Agatha Christie's books would have been if it was always the person you suspected from the first chapter. Totally lame."

"Totally lame." I nodded in agreement. Jill hit me with a pillow from the couch.

"Don't make fun of Dame Agatha. She knew her stuff."

"Never." I threw my hands up in surrender. "I was agreeing with you."

Jill has read every Agatha Christie book at least twice, if not more. I don't understand how she does it. To me the fun in a mystery is puzzling out who did it, but Jill claims that each time she reads Dame Agatha she discovers something new.

"Anyway, as I was saying," Jill continued in an exaggerated tone. "Tim is too obvious. What about Kelsey? You said she's cutthroat about getting a story? Or Dylan? What do you know about him? Maybe he and Billy were having financial trouble."

"Maybe. It seems like Mind Over Mudder is thriving. I know there's already a waiting list for the next training session."

"What about the stay-at-home mom? What do you know about her?"

I told her about Jenny running the workout earlier.

"Maybe she's desperate for a job. Does she seem like a killer to you?" Jill poured more wine into both of our glasses.

"I don't know. What does a killer look like?"

"Excellent point." Jill scrunched her wrinkle- and blemish-free face. "What's the deal with these supplements that everyone is taking? That seems weird."

"Yeah." I sat up a little. "Actually, I think you're right about that. You know me, I hate taking aspirin. I think I'm one of the only people not taking the 'super supplements,' as Dylan calls them. He tried to sell me on them when I started, but I said no."

"What's in them? Are you sure they're even legal?" Jill asked. "One of the partners at my firm has been working with the FDA on a case here in

Oregon where a natural health food chain has been selling substances banned by the FDA. It's a big business."

"You think that a natural substance could be illegal?"

"Of course. Just because it's 'natural' doesn't mean that it's good for you. That's why we have the FDA to regulate what's safe and not safe. Natural products, even vitamins you take every day, can have terrible side effects if ingested in the wrong combination or in high doses."

"Good point."

"You should try to get ahold of some of the supplements."

"You think I should take them?"

"No!" Jill shook her head. "Of course not. Just pretend. Tell Dylan that you changed your mind and that you want to try the supplements. They should have all the ingredients listed on the label. That's federal law. If you can get a bottle, I can give it to the lawyer at my firm. He'll know if anything on the ingredients list is illegal."

"Great idea."

"Meg, I don't watch endless hours of Poirot and Miss Marple for nothing."

I laughed. "Are you finished?" I nodded to the almost-empty pizza box.

"Yep."

I topped off Jill's wine, took the pizza box to the kitchen, and returned with the fancy box of chocolates. "Movie time?"

"For sure."

Jill and I spent the next two hours in the romantic black and white world of Gregory Peck and

Audrey Hepburn's Rome. There aren't many movies that rate as high as *Roman Holiday* in my book, but I had a hard time concentrating on the iconic comedy. Jill had raised a valid concern. First thing tomorrow I was going to get my hands on a bottle of Mind Over Mudder's magic supplements.

Chapter 20

My alarm sounded early the next morning—too early. I fumbled with my eyes closed trying to find the snooze button. What time was it? I opened one eye. It couldn't be time to get up already, could it? The sky outside was still dark. I must have set my alarm for the wrong time. I grabbed the clock to turn it off. It flashed 5:30 over and over again. Damn. I had to get up.

My body felt like I'd been run over by a garbage truck. I yanked off the covers and stretched my arms toward the ceiling. They got halfway up before they flopped back onto my cotton sheets. Coffee. I needed coffee—stat.

Reaching both legs toward the floor, I pushed myself to standing. Every muscle in my body tightened in response. Pain seared from my spine to my toes. This was going to be a rough morning.

I padded straight to the kitchen and dumped beans into my coffee grinder. The smell of the pulsing beans made me smile. If nothing else, at least I had coffee. I shook the grounds into the coffeemaker, filled it with cold tap water, and hit the button for the darkest brew possible. Billy had cautioned us not to drink anything but water before our morning workouts. I hadn't heeded his advice when he was alive, and I certainly wasn't going to heed it now that he was dead.

That's an awful thought, Meg, I chided myself as I hobbled back to my bedroom to get dressed. I blamed my snarky attitude on lack of caffeine. Pops got me hooked on java when I was a freshman in high school.

He used to start his mornings with a full pot of coffee and the newspaper. Pops was an early riser. Mother liked her beauty sleep, so most mornings it was Pops and me at our old farmhouse kitchen table. I would make myself a bowl of cold cereal and join him at the table. Pops would hand me the comics. One morning when I was fourteen he looked up from the World News section. In those days the paper was an inch thick and it covered in-depth and thought-provoking pieces from all corners of the globe. His glasses rested on the tip of his nose. "Maggie," he said, nodding to the pot of coffee resting on a hot pad in the center of the round table. "Go get yourself a cup from the cup-board."

"Okay, why?"

"You'll see, sweet one."

I returned with one of Gam's ceramic mugs. Pops removed his reading glasses and rested the newspaper on the table. He reached for the pot of coffee and poured the hot brew into my mug. "Consider this your initiation into adulthood. I know how much you love the morning paper, and no paper should be read without a cup of my exceptional brew."

"But I'm only fourteen, Pops."

"There's no age limit on when you can drink coffee. You happen to be one of the smartest fourteen-year-olds I know. It's time. Drink up."

I took the coffee from him. It smelled pretty good, but the taste, not so much. I gave it a tiny sip and stuck my tongue out. "Yuck. It's bitter."

Pops threw his head back and laughed. "You'll get used to it. It will put hair on your chest."

"I don't want hair on my chest."

This made him laugh even harder. "Good point, Maggie," he said after he recovered from his fit of laughter. "Grab some cream and sugar. That might help."

I added three tablespoons of sugar and a healthy dose of cream to my mug. I still wasn't sure I liked the taste, but I felt grown up and sophisticated drinking my coffee and reading the paper in unison with Pops. From that morning on, Pops had a mug, a pitcher of cream, and a bowl of sugar waiting for me on the kitchen table. I never really did learn to love the taste of black coffee, but I loved my mornings with Pops. Some mornings we'd read each section in silence. Some mornings we would have lively discussions about politics and whatever other topic Pops was fired up about at the time—like requiring the city to put in bike lanes downtown or expanding Portland's curbside recycling program. It didn't matter what we talked about. That was our sacred time. I missed everything about him from his newsprint-stained fingers to his jovial laugh. More than anything, I missed our coffee ritual.

* * *

My coffee beeped, jarring me back into the
present. I laced up my kicks and poured myself a
giant cup. If I had to be up before the sun on a
Sunday, I wasn't skipping my morning cup of Joe.
Gam had been trying to convert me to healthy
green tea or veggie smoothies. She'd taken up juic-
ing a few years ago and swore her daily blend of
yams, prunes, beets, strawberries, and kale kept her
skin supple and young. It could be true. Gam
looked great for her age. She looked great for
someone ten or twenty years younger, but I
couldn't stomach cold, pureed, veggie sludge in the
morning. It was all coffee for me.

I downed my coffee, grabbed my gym bag, and
headed to the car. Hadn't I just done this drive a
few hours ago? It felt like déjà vu as I crossed the In-
terstate Bridge into Washington State. I wondered
if Jenny would be keeping her temporary role as
trainer in chief, or if Dylan had managed to find a
professional overnight. My first goal was to survive
the workout. My second goal was to find time to
talk to Dylan alone and put Jill's master plan into
place.

When I arrived it was clear that the police had
finished their investigation. The caution tape
had been removed from the barracks' front doors,
and there was no sign of an officer on patrol.

As I made my way toward the building, a sense of
familiar dread washed over me. Less than twenty-four
hours ago I'd discovered Billy's body here. I couldn't
shake the image from my head.

Squaring my shoulders and mustering up as much confidence as I could, I climbed the stairs to the barracks.

Please let someone else be here, I thought.

Thankfully, my wish was immediately granted. I heard the sound of voices—multiple voices— downstairs. I walked down the hallway, trying to focus on my breathing and pushing all thoughts of Billy from my mind.

"Meg, you made it," Jenny greeted me from the base of the stairway. She looked like she'd had a vat of coffee this morning. Her skin glowed a cheery red as she bounced from side to side in a pre-run warm-up.

"Sure did," I mumbled, and dragged myself down the stairway. "I'm thrilled that we're back at it bright and early."

Jenny clearly missed the sarcasm in my voice. "I know! Isn't it so fun?" She grinned. "I was telling everyone that our hard work is starting to pay off. I can feel the results in my waistline and my energy level. It's so motivating."

"Right, motivating." It took everything in me not to roll my eyes.

Dylan came out of the locker room. He was wearing another loose-fitting hemp shirt and his Birkenstocks. "Morning, everyone." He bowed in a Namaste pose.

Everyone returned his bow.

"Jenny and I met last night and came up with a plan to get you all through these last few days of training."

That's what you get for jumping to conclusions, Meg,

I thought to myself as Dylan spoke. I had thought they were talking about Billy's murder or conspiring when I spotted them under the tree last night, but they were just coming up with a workout plan.

"We thought we'd try to incorporate some yoga stretching and breathing into your morning routine," Dylan continued. Jenny bounced on her toes. "Billy and I had talked about a more balanced approach, but sadly he died before we had a chance to incorporate some of my techniques. If you all want to proceed up to the lawn, I'll show you some yoga poses and then Jenny will take it from there."

Jenny clapped. "That's right! I'm going to be your gal for the next week. Can you believe it?"

A few of my teammates offered halfhearted congratulations. No one was awake or in the mood to cheer with her this early.

"Dylan made it official last night. I know I'm not Billy, but you all know how committed I am to the team, and I don't just want to finish Mud, Sweat, and Beers next weekend. I plan to win it!"

I scanned the hallway. Kelsey Kain wasn't here yet. That wasn't like her. She was usually one of the first people on-site, probably because she didn't want to miss out on a potential scoop.

"Billy's training book has the week all spelled out for us. We're going to hit it hard for the next few days and then taper off to give our bodies a couple days of rest and repair before the race," Jenny explained. "I'm going to follow Billy's protocol to the letter. You know what they say, 'If it ain't broke, don't fix it.' And Dylan has agreed to teach us yoga, which really should give us an edge. I'm so excited about this and can't wait to race with you all in less than a week."

Jenny's eagerness would have been slightly annoying at this ridiculous hour regardless, but in light of Billy's death it seemed strange and in poor taste. It raised my suspicion even more.

"Follow me," she said as she bounded up the stairs.

We all trudged after her. Tim caught up to me. "Is she on something?"

"What?" I stopped to tie my shoelace.

"Jenny. She's jacked up. You think she's on speed?"

"Do you?"

He shrugged. "That, or she shoots up caffeine in the morning. Who is that excited about exercising at six on a Sunday morning?"

"My thoughts exactly. I mean, not on the shooting up caffeine or speed, but you're right. She's way too energetic for me."

Tim held the door open for me as we stepped outside. "I think she's got help. What did they call speed in the 1970s, 'Mother's Little Helper.'"

"Are you serious?"

He pointed to the grass. Dylan's stance matched the towering evergreens in the distance. He stood on one foot with the other bent over his knee, and clasped his hands together, stretching toward the sky. Jenny, on the other hand, continued to bounce from foot to foot, like she couldn't stand still. "You tell me," Tim said, and walked away.

Dylan directed us in the tree pose, encouraging everyone to close our eyes and center our breathing. Gam would love this, I thought as I moved my arms above my head. Instead of closing my eyes, I kept close watch on Jenny. She raced through Dylan's fluid moves in a matter of seconds and went back to jogging in place.

Was Tim right? I liked Jenny. She'd been my training ally for the last two weeks, but ever since Billy was killed, something had changed. I wasn't sure what that meant, but I was sure that she was steadily creeping up my suspect list.

Chapter 21

Dylan's yoga stretches felt shockingly good. My body opened up and the tightness in my muscles seemed to dissipate as he took us through a sequence of poses. Maybe there was something to this yoga craze after all.

However, the looseness in my body quickly disappeared as Jenny shouted at us to follow her up the hill. *Five more days, Meg. Five more days and this will all be over.* Then I could go back to my normal Sunday routine of coffee, the newspaper, and my comfortable couch.

I had to think of a good excuse to ask Dylan for the supplements. I'd been so against them that I thought it might be too obvious if I said that I'd changed my mind. Jenny waved from a few hundred feet up the hill. "Hurry up! Come on, everyone in the back. We don't want to lose you."

I knew she was talking about me. Her transformation continued to stun me. A couple weeks ago her legs had been like Jell-O when we jogged this same route. This morning they looked firm and muscular in her tight black running capris. If I hadn't witnessed her dramatic weight loss I wouldn't have believed it. Maybe that was it. I could tell Dylan that I was so inspired by Jenny that I wanted to give his supplements a shot. Hopefully he'd buy it.

Kelsey Kain flew past me up the hill. Where had she come from?

I didn't bother trying to catch up. It was futile. My short legs didn't have anything left in them. My goal was just to survive the next five days. The pack disappeared around the corner as I crested the hill and crossed the street. With no one nearby, I slowed to a walk. Jenny's goal might be to win Mud, Sweat, and Beers, but mine was just to finish. Anything better than last place would be gravy.

Sure, that might be a lousy attitude, but I was past the point of caring. I should have been motivated by the fact that everyone else on my training team was crushing it, but I was too tired and distracted by Billy's murder to care anymore.

My lungs stopped burning as I walked past the historical Marshall House down Officer's Row. The rising sun filtered through the tree canopy. It was going to be a beautiful day. Too bad I had to come back and do this all again later. It was the perfect Sunday to pull out a beach chair and a paperback and read on the sandy banks of the Columbia River.

A team of bikers whizzed past on the street. They wore an assortment of bright spandex and racing helmets. They moved with such speed that the tree branches shook in their wake.

I wondered what Matt was doing right now. Probably sleeping. I didn't like the way things ended between us yesterday. I didn't like anything about what was—or wasn't—going on between us. Had that been why I was flirting so much with Kenny?

"Meg, you are one muddled mess," I said aloud.

At that minute, I caught movement in my peripheral vision. I couldn't explain it, but it felt like I was being watched. The tiny blond hairs on my forearms stood erect. A shiver ran down my spine. I stopped in mid-stride and turned around slowly.

There was no one behind me.

I turned the other way.

Nothing.

Then I looked toward the mansions lining the street. Standing in the corner window was the creepy old woman I'd seen yesterday. I jumped back and threw my hand over my heart. She stared straight at me, holding the lace curtains in one hand.

Maybe she wasn't looking at me. Maybe there was someone behind me. I moved my head in a slow half circle in each direction. No, I was alone. She was staring at me.

I returned my gaze to the window.

She was gone. The lace curtains shielded my view.

Was I just imagining things? More than one person has given me feedback that I can have a tendency to let my imagination run wild, but she had been staring at me. I was sure. The question was why?

I almost considered walking up and knocking on her front door, but my nerves got the best of me. What if she was a ghost? Maybe she wasn't a figment of my imagination, maybe she was one of the many ghosts thought to roam the old houses. She was certainly old enough to be a ghost. And creepy enough, I thought.

Time to run.

I sprinted onward, not paying any attention to my burning feet. Fortunately, the rest of the team had gotten stuck waiting for a stoplight. I caught up with them and stayed in the middle of the pack for the remainder of the run.

The old woman left me with an unsettled feeling. It was almost like she had a message for me. That, or she was a ghost. If she was in the window tonight, I was resolved to confront her. Our daily double was scheduled for five. It wasn't like it was the middle of the night or anything. I didn't have anything to lose, right?

Once we made it back to the barracks and finished our cooldown, Jenny explained that we'd be working out in the mud tonight. "Bring a change of clothes," she said, still jogging in place. "We're going to get muddy tonight. It's going to be a blast. See you all in a few hours."

She headed up the hill again. Was she insane?

I shook my head as I watched her go, then went inside. Everyone else made a beeline for the locker room. The water heater wasn't very strong, so whoever ended up showering last was usually stuck with cold water. Billy told us it was better for us anyway. I disagreed. I like my showers hot—scalding hot.

While everyone raced for the showers, I walked down the hallway to the office. The door was shut. I knocked twice on the glass-paned window.

"Come in," Dylan called.

I pushed open the door to find Dylan organizing bottles of supplements.

"Meg, what can I do for you?" He twisted a bottle so that its label was facing out.

"I was hoping to talk to you for a couple minutes."

"Of course." Dylan left a box of supplements on the shelf and sat down at the table. I was tempted to try to grab a bottle without him noticing, but if he caught me that would be even more obvious. "Still working on your story?" he asked.

"It's coming together," I replied, and sat down across from him. "Although I'm kind of stuck now. With Billy and everything that's happened, I'm not sure exactly how to proceed. I think I'm going to have to take a new angle."

"That's very astute for someone so young."

"I'm not that young."

Dylan bowed and clasped his hands in front of his chest. "Ah, but youth as they say is wasted on the young. When you get to be my age, you'll understand how very young you are."

Was that an insult? I wasn't sure how to take his comment, so I plowed ahead with my plan. "Speaking of young, Jenny looks great. Really great. I can't believe how much weight she's lost. She looks ten years younger and we're not even done with training yet."

"She's worked very hard," Dylan said.

"It shows, and actually that's why I wanted to talk to you. Jenny mentioned that she's taking a special supplement you created for her."

Dylan shook his head. "No, she's taking our standard vitamin weight-loss regimen."

"Well, it's working. I was wondering if I could give it a try. I mean, her results are so amazing. She's like a different person."

"You should have the same vitamins in your packet. Haven't you been taking them?"

"No, well, I mean kind of. To tell you the truth, I'm not exactly a fan of taking anything so I kind of tossed them."

"Tossed them?"

I scrunched my nose. "I threw them away."

"Oh." Dylan frowned. Then he pointed to the shelf that he'd been organizing. "You can grab another bottle, but I'll have to charge you for them. A bottle is thirty dollars."

"Thirty?"

"Yes, these are high-quality vitamins, procured from the highest quality organic plants."

"Right." I grabbed a bottle off the shelf. "And this is what Jenny is taking?"

"Isn't that what I already said?" Dylan snapped.

"Yeah, I just wanted to make sure. She looks so great and has so much energy. I would love it if I could have the same kind of results."

Dylan studied me for a minute. His normally serene guru-like vibe had shifted. "You're what? Twenty-something and you are in great shape. If you had results like Jenny's you would be in the hospital. And here's a warning for you. I had a discussion with Jenny last night about overdoing it."

"What do you mean?"

"Have you noticed how much she's running? Billy and I had very different opinions on overexercising."

"You think Jenny's overexercising?"

Dylan looked solemn. "I'm sure she is. That's what I told her last night. She can't keep up this pace. Billy might have been able to, but he was a rarity. I don't want our clients to push themselves to the brink of exhaustion, or worse; I want them to find balance. Jenny is out of balance, and her results are because she won't stop running. I wouldn't want to claim that any of my supplements would do that. My supplements are designed to help restore and repair tired muscles. Billy knew that."

"Did you guys disagree a lot? It seems like you are polar opposites."

Dylan nodded. "We were. That's how we achieved balance."

He had a point, but it also must have been difficult to manage a business with such very different attitudes and goals.

"Was there anything else you needed?" His eyes lingered on his office door. I got the sense that our conversation was over. "I have a bunch of work to get caught up on, and I still need to hire a new trainer."

"What about Jenny? I thought she said that she was going to take over the training role."

"That's only a temporary solution. I made that very clear to Jenny. It's important to be transparent in business. She knows that I'm in the process of hiring someone to replace Billy." He sighed. "It's going to be hard to do. Billy was the best at what he did, but I have to focus on the future of Mind Over Mudder. Jenny's not qualified to run that side of the business."

"Right." I held up the bottle of supplements. "So how do I pay you for these? Can I give you my credit card?"

Dylan ran my credit card and offered me a bag. "Meg, don't get trapped into worrying about outer beauty. Trust me, I was a chubby kid growing up and it's taken years to learn that beauty is on the inside." He paused and made the Namaste sign with his hands. "That is one of the many things that Billy and I disagreed about."

I thanked him and left. As I walked down the hallway to the locker room, I wondered what he meant by that last comment and why he'd been so insistent that Jenny wasn't taking a special supplement and that her weight loss was due to running too much. It made sense. But Jenny told me Dylan gave her a combination of vitamins and herbs designed specifically to shed pounds. Why would she have lied about that? And had she lied about taking over for Billy? I wasn't sure, but a new plan was forming in my mind. If I could get ahold of Jenny's bottle of supplements, I could give both bottles to Jill and then maybe we could figure out who wasn't telling the truth.

Chapter 22

By the time I showered, all of the hot water had been used up. I did a quick rinse and shampoo in the frigid water and headed straight to the steam room to warm up. That might have been a mistake. A nauseous feeling assaulted my body as steam poured from the small wooden chamber. I shivered, but not just from the cold. This is where I'd found Billy's body.

Forget it. I wrapped a towel around me and went back to the dressing area. Warming up wasn't worth it. I would have rather frozen all day than go back into the steam room. I dried off, got dressed, and blew my hair dry. Then I ran some lip gloss over my lips and spiked my semidry hair with my fingers.

I guess the pro of being up, showered, and awake this early on a Sunday was that I had the entire day ahead of me. Before I did anything else, I knew that I needed coffee—more coffee. There was a cute coffee shop next door to Gam's store. I could grab a mocha and chai tea latte and surprise Gam with a morning treat. A visit with Gam was exactly what I needed, not only for a shot of her healing energy, but also to talk through everything that I had learned. Gam was one of the best listeners I knew. Usually, thanks to her gently probing questions, any problem would become clear after an hour with Gam. Gam claimed it was the guidance of the Universe. I'm sure that was partly true, but I also knew that it had something to do with her unique ability to stay fully present, very quiet, and yet still ask the perfect question to lead me to "my truth" as she would say.

The locker room was empty. Everyone else had already showered and taken off. Everyone except for one person. I spotted Jenny's gym bag on the bench as I packed up my sweaty clothes and wet towel. She must still be running. Dylan was right. She was addicted to exercise.

This was my chance. I had to see if Jenny had her supplement in her bag. That way I could give Jill both bottles to compare. My heart beat faster as I poked my head out the door and scanned the hallway to make sure no one was around. There was no sign of Jenny or any of my teammates.

Do it now, Meg. Do it before you lose your courage.

My fingers fumbled with the zipper to Jenny's bag. I kept checking behind me, feeling like a criminal. *You are a criminal, Meg, you're breaking into someone else's property. But for a good cause,* I told myself.

The main section of Jenny's bag contained all the usual items—a towel, brush, shampoo, lotion, and a change of clothes. No supplements.

I zipped it shut as quickly as I could and paused. Were those footsteps in the hallway?

This is stupid, Meg.

I held my breath and waited. There was no sound of movement in the hallway or stairs. I should have just left, but I couldn't help myself. I unzipped the side pocket of Jenny's bag. For a minute I thought I'd found them. My hand ran over a small plastic bottle. Jackpot!

When I pulled it out I realized it was just a bottle of anti-inflammatory medication. No wonder Jenny had these, I thought. With how much she was running she was probably downing the entire bottle before breakfast.

Next I found a tube of Chap Stick and an expensive bottle of sunscreen.

I returned everything to the side pocket and stopped to check and make sure that I was still alone. My heart thumped in my chest. You would have thought I was robbing a bank. Have I mentioned that usually I'm not exactly a rule follower?

Just as I was about to give up the search, I felt another zipper on the inside of the pocket. A secret pouch. With one eye on the door, I unzipped the pouch and pulled out a small red bottle. This was it!

My heart pounded.

Now what?

The bottle was completely unmarked. There was no label, logo, or any information about what it contained. It was simply a red pill bottle. I shook it. It sounded pretty full.

I tried to twist open the cap. It wouldn't budge.

Something sounded in the hallway. I almost dropped the bottle on the floor.

Oh no, had Jenny returned?

I froze.

Footsteps echoed in the hallway above me.

Think fast, Meg.

I pushed the top of the cap with the palm of my hand and twisted with all my strength. The cap came off.

My hands trembled as I shook one of the supplements from the bottle into it and hurried to get the cap back on.

The footsteps were on the stairs now.

Hurry, Meg.

I shoved the bottle back into the secret pocket, but the zipper stuck. It wouldn't zip.

This was bad, really bad. If Jenny caught me going through her stuff she would be so mad. And if she was the killer . . . *Don't think about that, Meg.*

I gave up on the zipper and shut the side pocket.

At that moment the locker room doors swung open and Jenny stepped inside.

I scooted away from her bag and grabbed mine. "Hey, Jenny," I said, looping the strap over my shoulder and moving toward the door. "The showers are all yours. I'm the last one here." I hoped that my voice didn't sound as forced to her as it did in my head.

Her eyes lingered on her bag for a second.

Oh no. I held my breath.

She glanced back at me. "You're kind of slow this morning."

"Yeah." I clutched the pill in my hand. "I took a really long shower."

"They weren't cold?" she asked. Was she staring at my clenched fist?

"No, not at all," I lied. "A bunch of people must have decided to shower at home. Mine was great."

Jenny gave me a quizzical look. "Really? But they're always cold after two people have showered."

Time to get out of here, Meg.

I shrugged. "I don't know. I must have had good luck this morning. I've got to run. See you later."

I didn't wait for Jenny to respond. That was close. Too close. And not my wisest choice as of late. Hadn't I just promised myself that I wasn't going to do stupid things like this?

This time I ran up the stairs. I didn't want to risk Jenny opening her bag and realizing that the secret pocket was unzipped. Hopefully, she'd think that she had forgotten to zip it. And hopefully I had put everything back in the right place.

Despite the fact that breaking into a potential suspect's bag and stealing from her probably wasn't something I should have done, I had a major piece of evidence in my hands—literally. As soon as I said hi to Gam, I was going to drop the supplements off with Jill. But first, I needed a celebratory mocha.

Chapter 23

I wrapped Jenny's supplement in a napkin and hid it in my glove box before driving to the coffee shop. It should be safe there while Gam and I had coffee. It was too early to stop by Jill's anyway.

Bikes jammed the racks and were propped against the side of the coffee shop as I pulled into a free space on the street. I wondered if this was the same group of bikers I had passed earlier. They had taken over all the outdoor tables with their biking gear. I continued inside. There were only a handful of customers reading newspapers and working on laptops.

"Good morning," a woman wearing a pink apron with roses on it called from behind the counter. "What can I get you?"

"I love your apron," I said. "Pink's my favorite color."

She smiled. "Thanks, it was my mother's. I see that you're a fan of pink, too. Nice shirt."

I'd forgotten that my shirt was pink. In my rush to swipe Jenny's supplements, I had pulled on my clothes. This shirt was a new favorite. I'd found it at one of Portland's many vintage stores. It was made of thin cotton with capped sleeves, delicate shimmery pink buttons, and was darted in at the waist. I had paired it with black capris and pink flip-flops.

"Would you like to hear our specials?" the woman asked.

"Sure."

"Today I'm featuring a blended cocoa-moo."

"What's that?" I asked.

"It's a mocha blended with coconut. I can serve it straight over ice, too, but I really recommend blending it. It makes all the flavors come together well."

"Chocolate and coconut. I'm sold."

"You'll love it." She pointed to a row of plastic cups on the counter. "What size?"

"The biggest size you have."

She held up a large cup. "Will this do?"

"Perfect."

"Can I get you anything else? My delivery guy brought in some fresh pastries this morning. If you want to take a look at the case."

I deserved a pastry after a five-mile run, right?

"I think I will," I said, walking toward the pastry case. "Can I also get a chai tea latte?"

"Sure. Do you want that hot, iced, or I can blend it?"

"Blend it!" Gam usually drank her chai teas hot, but I had a feeling she would get a kick out of trying something new. She's always up for an adventure. I surveyed the pastry case. Everything looked delicious. My stomach growled in response. I decided on a chocolate éclair and a blueberry Danish.

The woman packaged my pastries in a box to go and handed me my blended drinks. I paid her and promised to let her know what I thought of the cocoa-moo the next time I came in.

Gam would definitely be awake. I couldn't wait to surprise her. As I left the coffee shop, the bike club was getting their gear together to continue their ride. I started to cross the street toward the river-front path, when I noticed the front door open at Love and Light.

Why was Gam at the shop this early?

I held our drinks in one hand and the pastry box in the other. "Gam! What are you doing here so early?" I called as I stepped inside.

The bookshop is an eclectic mix of gemstones, salt lamps, chimes, waterfalls, books, card decks, and jewelry. A self-serve tea station sat near the door. Gam encourages her customers to sip tea as they browse her many offerings. In the back of the store there is a private room where Gam does individual healing and Reiki sessions. The space is welcoming and calming.

However, something felt off this morning.

"Gam?" I called again. "Are you here?"

The door to the back room opened and Mother walked out.

"Mother. What are you doing here?" I couldn't believe my eyes. Mother isn't exactly a fan of Gam's alternative work. She never came to the shop.

"Mary Margaret, what a nice surprise." She walked toward me on three-inch black heels. Her "casual" Sunday attire was a pencil skirt with a blouse and matching scarf and pearls. She kissed me on the cheek. Then she pulled back and studied my appearance. "What did you do to your hair?"

"I cut it." I clenched my teeth in anticipation of her response.

"It frames your face well." She turned my cheek from side to side and assessed my profile. "I like it."

What? Mother never liked anything I did. Certainly not my hairstyles.

She touched my neck. "You're wearing the locket." Her voice lost some of its poise.

"Oh yeah." I tugged at the locket. Mother had given it to me before I left for New York. Believe it or not I loved it. Somehow Mother had managed to find a piece of jewelry we could agree on. When I was growing up she tried to dress me in pearls and designer costume necklaces. I prefer simple vintage pieces. The locket from Mother was exactly that, a delicate antique silver chain with a vintage typewriter. I'd worn it every day since she'd given it to me. Not only did I adore the locket, but it felt like a symbol of my evolving relationship with Mother.

"Stop tugging at it, Mary Margaret. You'll break it." Mother batted my hand away.

That was pretty much how it went with Mother. The moment of closeness was lost. "Where's Gam?" I asked.

"She's not here."

"I can see that. Where is she?"

Mother pursed her lips. "What do you have there?"

"Pastries and a chai for Gam."

"Pastries? Mary Margaret Reed, how many times

have I told you that sweets will linger on your hips for decades?"

"Mother, please don't start. It's early. Where's Gam?"

She scowled at the pastry box. "She's out of town."

"Out of town? But I just saw her yesterday. She didn't say anything about going out of town." I walked to the cash register and placed the pastry box on the counter. "Do you want her chai?"

Mother shook her head. "No."

I shrugged and set the chai next to the pastries. Then I took a giant sip of my cocoa-moo from the straw, intentionally trying to make a loud slurping sound.

Mother scoffed.

"What? I'm drinking?" Fine. So maybe sometimes when I'm around Mother I have a tendency to revert back to childish behavior, but I swear it wasn't entirely my fault. Mother brought out the worst in me.

"Where did Gam go?" I asked.

"Bend." Mother repositioned a rack of greeting cards. "With that sheriff of hers."

"Gam went to Bend with Sheriff Daniels? Why didn't she say anything about it yesterday?"

"I'm not your grandmother's keeper. She's a grown woman. She makes her own choices."

"Right, but it's not like Gam to take off without saying anything." I slurped more of my coffee. It was delicious, slightly sweet with a tropical flavor. I was going to have to go back for another before I went home.

"She told me." Mother looked smug. "She asked me to look over the store."

"You don't even like the store."

"I don't?" She twisted the silver tennis bracelet on her wrist.

"Well, do you? You're never here, and you're always complaining about Gam's healing work." I waved my arm toward a display of incense. "You hate the smell of half of the stuff in here."

"According to whom?"

"Um, everyone."

Mother readjusted her scarf. "Mary Margaret, I don't know where you get these ideas sometimes."

I dropped it. I knew if I said anything else it would start a fight, and I'd been trying very hard not to fight with my mother. "What is she doing in Bend? I thought Sheriff Daniels was working."

"He is. He invited her to come stay with him. He's doing some sort of mock disaster training. I encouraged her to go."

"You did? I didn't think you liked Sheriff Daniels."

"I don't. I don't trust him. That's exactly why I told her she should go." Mother's eyes were clear and focused. "I even offered to take care of the shop while she's away."

This wasn't like Mother. I needed sustenance to process what she was saying. I opened the pastry box and ripped off a hunk of blueberry Danish. She watched me and frowned in disapproval.

"Mary Margaret, don't chew with your mouth open," she scolded.

"I'm not." I forced my lips together and chewed in an exaggerated cow-like motion. She and Gam definitely shared the same genetic line. Mother's olive toned skin was supple and smooth. Her dark hair didn't hold a trace of gray. I wasn't sure if that was due to the fact that she colored it, like Gam, or good genes.

"You're intentionally trying to antagonize me." Mother ran her perfectly manicured finger along the top of a bookcase. "Your grandmother needs to dust. Where does she keep her cleaning supplies?"

"Gam hasn't dusted?" I couldn't believe it. Gam was notorious for "ammonia moments" as I liked to tease. Unlike some of her peers in the new age community, Gam was a neat freak. She was obsessive when it came to cleaning, taking the old adage that "Cleanliness is next to godliness" to heart. At least once every few months she would launch into an ammonia moment where she scrubbed every counter, cupboard, and baseboard with bleach and water.

Mother held up her index finger. She was right. The tip of her finger was coated in dust. "Look at this." She pointed to the trail she'd left on top of the bookcase. "Something is going on with your grandmother."

"I think you might be right."

"It's that sheriff. He's got her under some kind of spell."

"A spell? I think you're under some kind of spell. You're helping at Gam's shop and talking about spells. My head is about to explode."

"Don't be so dramatic," Mother scoffed.

I ripped off another hunk of blueberry Danish and drank my mocha shake.

Mother picked up the blended chai tea. "Maybe I'll give this a taste. My mouth is quite dry with all the dust in here."

"Why did you tell Gam to go with Sheriff Daniels if you don't think he's right for her?"

"Oh, he's not right for her. That's a fact." Mother took a sip of the chai. "This is delicious. Do I even want to know the calorie count?"

"No." I rolled my eyes. I couldn't believe she was actually drinking it. "Just enjoy it."

She sucked on the straw. I thought I almost saw a smile tug at her cheeks as she drank, but I was probably imagining things. "I advised your grandmother to go on this outing to Bend because I think the more time she spends with the sheriff for longer periods, the better. Did you know that he's a hunter? Can you imagine your grandmother living with a hunter?"

"No, I didn't know that Sheriff Daniels hunts. I mean, I guess that doesn't really surprise me, but does Gam know that?"

"She hasn't said anything to me."

I took another drink of my mocha too fast. A brain freeze spread across my forehead. "I still don't understand your plan."

Mother sighed. She rested the chai on the countertop and walked behind the cash register. "Your grandmother has a tendency to leap before she thinks sometimes."

I winced. My forehead stung from the icy drink. "She does?" I had the opposite impression of Gam. Gam had always appeared to be mindful and thoughtful about her decisions. Of course, Mother and I disagree on pretty much everything, so Gam shouldn't be anything new.

"I know that you and your grandmother have a very special relationship, and I'm glad that you do." She opened drawers and cupboards in search of something. "But you're also old enough to understand that she's human, and she's made her fair share of mistakes over the years."

Gam had made mistakes? Please.

"Like what?"

"Where does she keep her cleaning supplies?" Mother sounded exasperated as she emptied a drawer.

"Maybe in the back." I pointed to the private room.

"Probably. Come with me." Mother left the drawer on the counter and walked to the back of the store.

"What kind of mistakes has Gam made?" I asked, tagging along after her.

"Where do you want me to start?" Mother flipped on the light switch.

"Seriously?"

"Never mind." She flung open a freestanding cabinet and found a Costco-sized bottle of Pledge and a dry rag. "Take these. Go dust."

I took them while she unwound the cord on the vacuum.

"Why are you standing there watching me?"

"Because I want to know more about Gam and why you think she's making a mistake with the sheriff. You're right, I haven't been acting very mature lately, especially with you, Mom."

I never called her mom.

Her eyes flinched for a brief second, but she continued to twist the cord in a perfect circle around her wrist.

"I'm trying, okay. I don't know why it's always been so hard with us. It's like we speak two different languages or something."

"We both speak English, Mary Margaret." Mother pushed the vacuum out into the shop.

I followed after her. "That's not what I mean."

She moved a potted fern and plugged the vacuum into an outlet on the wall.

"You know I've been thinking about our relationship a lot lately, and I'm wondering if part of it is because of Pops."

"What about your father?"

"I mean, Pops and I were always so close. We had so many things in common—writing, swimming, morning coffee. I guess he was always a buffer between us. I didn't need to come to you with my problems because Pops was always there."

Mother's eyes misted. She squared her jaw and looked away. "I'm well aware of how close you and your father were."

This wasn't coming out how I intended it. I was trying to build a bridge between us, but I seemed to be making it worse. "I didn't mean it like that."

She ignored me and started vacuuming. So much for trying to mend things. I took the can of Pledge and dust rag to the front of the shop and started dusting every cabinet and bookshelf. Mother vacuumed with a purpose. I tried not to chuckle as she zoomed the vacuum past me in her high heels.

Soon Love and Light was sparkling and smelling of lemon Pledge. Mother shut off the vacuum and started organizing the cash drawer.

"Do you think Gam is really going to move in with Sheriff Daniels?" I asked, dumping my empty coffee cup in the trash can. Hopefully, keeping the focus on Gam would be a better tactic for communicating with Mother.

"I wouldn't put it past her."

"What should we do?"

"Nothing. That's what I was trying to explain earlier. Your grandmother is thinking with her heart. Sending her out to Bend to spend the next few days with the sheriff in his natural habitat should hopefully open her eyes a little."

"But I thought he was working? Doing training or something?"

"He is. It's a statewide emergency disaster training."

"How will that open Gam up to seeing another side of the sheriff?"

Mother gave me a smug look. "He'll be surrounded by his fellow hunters and burly police types. Your grandmother has been so caught up in his sexy cowboy boots that she hasn't taken time to reflect on the fact that he's actually a *cowboy*."

"Oh my gosh—you're right."

"I know that I'm right. They are a terrible match. Your grandmother needs to recognize that fact."

"And you think a week in Bend will help?"

"Without a doubt."

I considered what she said. Was I siding with Mother? That was a first.

"I can tell that you don't trust me. I'm not trying to sabotage her happiness."

"No, no, I didn't think you were."

She rolled her eyes. "Anyway, my point is that not only are they a bad match, but I don't trust him."

"I know. Why? You said that Pops didn't trust him either? I thought they were friends." Despite the fact that Mother and I weren't exactly close, she had been trying to get me to talk about Pops for months now. I hadn't appreciated her approach. She had a tendency to stop by my place unannounced, drop a piece of news that would send me reeling, and then get angry when I wasn't ready to discuss it. Lately I'd been wondering if I should have been more open to what she had to say.

"Hmpf. Friends? No." She stacked twenty-dollar bills in a crisp pile. "They were not friends."

"But Sheriff Daniels made it seem like he had helped Pops with a bunch of his investigations."

"I'm sure that's what he wanted you to believe."

My head throbbed. Trying to have a normal conversation with my mother was nearly impossible. She didn't give much and she certainly didn't bend when it came to our relationship. Why wouldn't she just come out and say whatever she was trying to say?

"Mary Margaret, don't get that faraway look in your eyes. I know that you're not naïve. I don't know why you insist on acting like it sometimes."

"How am I acting like I'm naïve? I don't know what you're getting at, and I don't know what to believe. When I first met Sheriff Daniels he seemed really sincere about Pops and sad that he'd lost a friend. Now you're telling me that they were never friends."

"They weren't. Your father tried to tell the sheriff what was happening right under his nose, and he refused to do anything about it."

"Are you talking about the Meth Madness story?"

"Of course I'm talking about the Meth Madness story."

My heart sank to my knees. A sick feeling came over me. "Are you saying that Sheriff Daniels was somehow involved in the Meth Madness story?"

"I'm saying more than that. I'm saying that he knew that meth was being funneled through his town, and when your father confronted him about it, he did nothing." She placed the stack of twenties back into the cash register and shut it. Then she picked up her Coach purse and started toward the door. "I have to run to the bank. There's not enough change in the register."

"Wait," I said. "I have so many more questions. If the sheriff knew that drugs were being funneled right past him and he did nothing about it, are you suggesting that he had something to do with Pops' death too?"

Mother waited at the door. She tapped her diamond-encrusted watch.

That was her not so subtle cue that it was time for me to go too. I walked toward the door. "Don't you think it's weird that he and I met? And that he's dating Gam? That can't be a coincidence, can it?"

Mother pursed her lips together. "That's the

smart girl I raised. It sounds like you have some thinking to do." She held the door open for me.

We walked outside. She locked up the shop. I started to ask her more, but she tapped her watch again. "I have to run, Mary Margaret. We'll talk later." With that she turned and walked away on her heels leaving me more confused than ever.

Chapter 24

I wasn't sure what to think. Part of me thought Mother didn't like Sheriff Daniels because his cowboy boots and faded jeans wouldn't fit in with her country club friends. Then again, Mother had never volunteered to help in Gam's shop. Never. She must be concerned if she was willing to skip her Sunday brunch with the ladies from the club.

When I got home I was going to pull out a box of Pops' old newspaper clippings and notes that I'd saved. I'd probably been through the box a hundred times, but maybe this time I would see something with new eyes. Sheriff Daniels had been quoted in a number of the articles. Could I have missed something about his involvement in the Meth Madness investigation? Could our first meeting have been a setup?

But how? I thought back to my first assignment for *Northwest Extreme*. Greg had sent me to Angel's Rest in the Columbia River Gorge to cover an adventure race. When one of the contestants fell from the top of Angel's Rest, Sheriff Daniels arrived on the scene. There's no way that could have been anything other than a coincidence. Could it?

A sick feeling assaulted my stomach. What if the sheriff had been involved in Pops' death? What was Greg's involvement? I remember Pops saying something offhand before he died about trusting no one. I had thought he was being funny, but now his words loomed heavy in my mind. Usually at times like this I turned to Gam for guidance. I couldn't do that. I was going to have to figure this one out on my own.

Matt and Jill would help. We'd find a way to figure this out, right?

Speaking of Jill, I had to text her about the supplements. I dug through my gym bag in search of my phone. It wasn't there. I checked all the pockets—twice.

Oh no. I must have left it in the locker room when I was going through Jenny's bag. Right on par for my morning. Oh well, I couldn't get much done without my phone, so I steered the car in the direction of the barracks.

Another thought crossed my mind. I hoped Jill hadn't sent me a text about getting ahold of a bottle of supplements. Text messages signal with the sound of an old-fashioned typewriter returning on my phone. What if Jenny heard it beep and read Jill's message?

I stepped on the gas. At the barracks there was no sign of any of my other teammates, but there were plenty of people out for early-morning jogs, bike rides, and strolls. This was a much more reasonable hour to be up and moving on a Sunday. Waving to a sweet elderly couple pushing a dog in a baby stroller, I jogged toward Mind Over Mudder's headquarters. I hoped the doors were still unlocked.

I reached for the handle and it turned in one quick motion. That was good.

The hallway and stairway were deserted. I hurried into the locker room but stopped in mid-stride when I spotted Jenny popping pills like candy in front of the mirror.

"Jenny, I . . . I . . ." I couldn't think of what to say. My reflection in the mirror looked dumbfounded.

Jenny's hand shook. She dropped the bottle on the counter. White capsules scattered on the floor. "Meg, what are you doing here?"

I dropped to my knees and scooped the capsules into a pile. "I forgot my phone. You haven't seen it, have you?"

"No." She took the capsules I had picked up and dropped them into the red pill bottle. "This isn't what it looks like."

"What is it, then?" I asked, and sat down on one of the benches. "Are you okay, Jenny? That looked like a lot of pills you just swallowed. Aren't these supposed to be taken in moderation?"

Jenny sighed. For a minute I thought she might cry, but instead she shook two more pills into her hands and popped them into her mouth.

I winced. "Is it okay to take that many? I mean, aren't you just supposed to take one?"

"It's no big deal. Don't look at me like that. It's not like I'm taking drugs or anything. These are natural supplements."

"You took like ten! Nothing—even if those really are natural—is good for you in that kind of dosage."

"Meg, I didn't take ten. Five maybe. It's not a big deal. Stop looking at me like I'm shooting up heroin or something. It's just hCG."

I didn't want to debate the fact that I had indeed seen her take ten. "What's hCG?"

Jenny handed me the bottle. As if that would explain anything. "It's a naturally occurring substance that speeds up your metabolism and enhances weight loss and, as you've seen, it's working." She tapped her narrowing waist.

"You look great, Jenny. You really do, but I'm concerned about you." I placed my hand on her knee. "You have two young kids at home depending on you. You don't want to do something stupid to your body. Think about your kids."

She rolled her eyes and stood up. "Now you sound like Billy."

"Billy?'

"Yeah, my God. He drove me crazy with his constant lectures about my body being my temple. He told me he was going to kick me off the team if I kept using them. Please. That man ran so hard and so fast, you think he wasn't getting a boost with something too? No way. I know he was taking supplements too. Probably steroids. You can't get a body like his without help."

"Wait, you think Billy was taking steroids? But you just said that these supplements—hCG—were natural."

"They are." Jenny studied herself in the mirror. She smoothed her hair down with one hand. "Look it up. I swear it's no big deal. hCG is sold everywhere.

I wouldn't do anything to harm myself. That's what I told Billy, but he refused to believe me."

"You told Billy this?"

"Yeah, he and I got in a fight right before he died. He caught me taking a few pills and demanded to know where I got them. I didn't tell him, and he freaked out on me. I told him that he couldn't kick me off. You know what my husband said last night?"

I shook my head.

"He said he had the woman he married back. How amazing is that? Billy was envious."

"Envious?"

"Yeah, I could continue to kill myself with his workouts and never see results like this."

"Why wouldn't you tell him who gave you the supplements? If they're not a big deal, then what's the big deal about telling him where you got them?"

"I promised that I wouldn't."

"Who, Dylan?"

Jenny looked surprised. "That's what Billy asked too."

"Was it Dylan?"

Jenny got quiet.

"Jenny, listen, this could be important. This could have something to do with Billy's murder."

She looked at her feet.

"Please, Jenny. You have to tell me. Who gave you the hCG?"

"It doesn't have anything to do with Billy's death. I know that much for sure."

"How?"

"Because Dylan didn't give them to me. Kelsey did."

Chapter 25

"Kelsey Kain? Kelsey Kain gave you weight-loss supplements?" I asked Jenny.

"Yeah. Why are you acting like that?"

"Why did Kelsey give you hCG, and why did she ask you not to say anything?"

"Kelsey saw me crying in the locker room after our first workout. I think she felt sorry for me. She asked me a bunch of questions about my weight-loss routine and what Dylan had given me. Then she asked me if I wanted to try a couple of her supplements. She's been taking them for a while now, and she hasn't had any weird side effects or anything."

So that's why Kelsey was so thin and fast. She was taking hCG. I thought about the man who handed her that packet outside the news station yesterday. Maybe he was Kelsey's source. Whom else was she giving hCG to? And why hadn't she asked me if I wanted to try it. Not that I would have said yes. But I was kind of offended that she hadn't at least offered.

"Is she charging you for them?" I asked.

Jenny shook her head. "No, of course not. She gave me a few to be nice. Told me to track my progress and results." Jenny walked over to her gym bag and unzipped it. She pulled out a spiral notebook. "In fact, I give her an update every few days with my weight loss."

I thumbed through the notebook. Jenny had lost twenty pounds in two weeks. "Why did Kelsey want to know your progress?" None of this made sense. No wonder Billy had been upset.

"She didn't tell me—she asked me to keep this kind of quiet. She didn't want Billy to find out."

"Don't you think that's strange?"

"No, why?"

"It's kind of a red flag, Jenny. I mean, why would Kelsey give you a drug for free and ask you not to say anything? It sounds like she was trying to get you hooked and then once you had developed a habit she'd start making you pay." I didn't add that by the way Jenny was popping hCG she probably already had made it a habit.

"I'm not hooked, and Kelsey was helping out a friend. I'm thrilled with what she's done for me." She snatched the notebook back from me, grabbed her bag, and headed for the door without another word.

Kelsey was giving Jenny weight-loss drugs? I didn't care what Jenny said. As far as I was concerned they were drugs. I couldn't wait to get my stash to Jill.

I found my cell phone in the locker I'd used earlier. **Are you up?** I texted Jill. **Have the goods. Will come by now.**

Jill texted back right away with a thumbs-up emoji.

The drive to Jill's apartment in the Pearl District was a breeze. There was no traffic and my mind was so spun up on everything I'd learned about Jenny and Kelsey, so much that I'm surprised I kept the car in the center of the lane. Despite my exhausted muscles, I took the stairs to Jill's penthouse condo. I hate elevators (or any small, enclosed space) more than I hated the burning feeling in my calves and the piercing pain on the back of my heels.

Jill was waiting with a pot of French press when I knocked on the door.

"Have I ever told you how much I love you?" I asked as I stepped inside and inhaled the scent of darkly brewed coffee.

"I had a feeling that coffee was going to be a necessity. How much have you already had?" Jill walked to the kitchen and poured a cup for each of us.

"Not much."

"Liar." Jill handed me a steaming mug. "I'm guessing five or six cups."

I laughed and held the cup up in a toast. "Maybe something like that. But—hey—after what I've discovered this morning, that's nothing. You're not going to believe what just happened."

Jill poured a small amount of cream into her coffee and offered it to me.

"No, thanks. I'm going straight black this morning."

"Whoa. This is serious." Jill set the container of cream on the counter and walked to the couch.

"Don't leave me hanging. What happened and where are the supplements?"

I removed the bottle of Mind Over Mudder's supplements and the white capsule that I'd stolen from Jenny's bag. Then I explained to Jill how I'd gotten the capsule and what I'd just learned from Jenny.

"A TV news reporter is dealing on the side?" Jill held her mug in between her hands.

"It seems weird, right?"

Jill blew on her coffee. "Yeah, really weird. There has to be some other explanation."

I told her my theory that Kelsey was trying to get Jenny hooked. Jill didn't look convinced. "Maybe. That's a stretch. If Jenny's been taking the supplements the entire time you've been training it seems like she would have made her pay up by now."

"You're right." I sighed. "Do you think Kelsey was supplying all my teammates with hCG?"

"Has anyone else had dramatic weight loss like Jenny?"

I shook my head and took a sip of my coffee. "No, actually. Not at all. Good point."

"Meg, that's the thing: Weight loss takes a long time. That's probably why Billy confronted Jenny. As a professional trainer he would have known that something wasn't right."

"Do you think she could have killed him because of it?" I didn't even want to consider the possibility that Jenny could have done something so horrific.

Jill scrunched her nose. "No idea, but we can't rule her out." She picked up her coffee cup and walked it over to the kitchen sink. "I'm going to e-mail my colleague about these." She pointed to the supplements on the glass coffee table.

"Thanks. I'm going to see what I can find online about hCG. I'll call Matt too. Maybe he can help."

"Good plan. I have no idea how long it will take to get the samples analyzed. I'll let you know what my friend says. I think you better call your new boyfriend and fill him in on what you've learned too."

"You mean Kenny?"

"Yeah." Jill nodded toward the bottle of pills. "In fact, maybe you should check with him before I hand those off."

"That's not a bad idea." I stood. "You check in with your lawyer friend. I'll check in with Kenny and text you to let you know what he says. If he wants them, is it okay if I send him here?"

"Of course. I don't have anything to hide." Jill gave me a coy smile. "Or do I?"

I gave her a quick kiss on the cheek and took off. Suddenly, I was glad that I had been awake early. I had an agenda for the rest of my day, and I wanted to get started right away.

Chapter 26

Kenny was less than thrilled with my update. "You what? You stole from Jenny?"

"Don't think of it so much as stealing, but borrowing from a friend."

"In the police world that's stealing. There's no way around that."

"I'm worried about her. I think she has a serious addiction problem. She's lost over twenty pounds in two weeks. That can't be healthy."

"I'm glad you're concerned about your friend, but that doesn't justify stealing from her. You've broken the law."

"Sorry."

"Hey, that's on you. I'm not going to turn you in, but I can't take the supplement. We can't use that in court."

"You think it's okay to give it to Jill's friend at the law firm?"

"Go ahead, but any lawyer is going to tell you what I just did. This isn't evidence. It's stolen property."

"What if we learn from the analysis that Jenny has been taking an illegal substance?"

"Then we'll have to use *legal* protocol to investigate."

He had a valid point, and I was glad that I didn't have to hand over my evidence to the police, regardless of whether or not it really was evidence. Before we hung up Kenny asked me if I wanted to meet for a beer later. Was Jill right? Was he into me? I agreed with one caveat—it would depend on whether I was still moving and upright after my second training session later. I promised I would text him when I was done and let him know one way or another.

Then I texted Jill. It's a go. Send them to your friend.

On it! she texted back.

I made myself a peanut butter and jelly sandwich with a jar of Gam's homemade apple butter and booted up my laptop. I intended to learn everything I could about hCG.

The sandwich hit the spot. Creamy peanut butter and Gam's slightly spicy apple butter were the perfect combination. I chewed it slowly while sipping on a cold glass of milk and scoured the Net for information about hCG. It didn't take long to return a lengthy list of search results. hCG was *not* the benign, naturally occurring substance that Jenny had made it out to be. Yes, it was naturally occurring, but it was also banned by the FDA. In fact, I found a recent article in which an FDA spokesperson was quoted as saying that they were actively pursuing people and companies selling the supplement.

Anyone caught selling hCG would be prosecuted and arrested.

I reread the article twice and scribbled notes in my notebook. hCG had some nasty side effects too. The drug had been documented to cause a racing heartbeat, breathing trouble, and even death.

What had Jenny gotten herself into? I wondered if she had any idea how dangerous the supplement could be. I jotted down everything I could find on hCG including a hotline number for anonymously reporting to the FDA.

My heartbeat raced as I read on. I couldn't believe how many articles and stories I found from just within the last few months. If Jenny had taken even two minutes to Google "hCG" she would have known that it wasn't something she should be putting in her body.

I finished my sandwich and sat on the couch trying to decide what to do next. Before I did anything else, I copied all of the research I'd collected on hCG and sent it to my work e-mail account and to Jill.

Then I remembered what Tim had said about seeing Billy in the locker room the morning that he died. Could Billy have been taking hCG too? His symptoms matched—he'd been clutching his chest and struggling to breathe. What if he'd had an adverse reaction to hCG? But he'd been so insistent about clean and healthy living that I couldn't imagine him taking a banned substance.

And how did Kelsey play into this? If she was supplying the hCG, where did she get it? Was she taking it too?

My mind wouldn't quit. I had to do something. I jumped to my feet, took my empty plate and glass to the kitchen, and texted Matt.

Wanna grab a pint?

I scrubbed my plate while I waited. It was probably the cleanest plate in my cupboard. The rhythm of scrubbing the sponge across the plate was the only thing keeping me calm.

My phone dinged with Matt's response. **Sure. Where?**

Public House in fifteen?

See u there.

I closed my laptop, grabbed my phone and keys, and headed for the door. A lunchtime pint sounded fantastic, and I needed to get Matt's input on hCG and on Sheriff Daniels.

Drat. I'd forgotten to go through my box of Pops' newspaper clippings. I would have to do that later.

Oregon Public House, where Matt and I were meeting, had a philosophy that beer could do good things. It was Portland's first volunteer-run pub where all of the proceeds are donated to charity. Each month the pub hosts four or five different charities that help bus tables and deliver burgers. Diners get to choose which charity they want their meal to be donated to. The food is delicious, and it makes me feel good too. A win-win in my opinion.

I made it to the pub first and ordered pints for

Matt and me. I opted for a summer blonde and got Matt a pint of a new nut brown on tap. While I waited for Matt to arrive, I scrolled through the articles I had collected on hCG on my phone. My stomach swirled. I drank a sip of the light and refreshing beer. It didn't help. I felt sick that Jenny was taking something so potentially dangerous. And I couldn't shake the feeling that hCG must have had something to do with Billy's death. I just couldn't figure out what.

"Megs, what's up?" Matt slid in the booth across from me. He was wearing a neon green biking T-shirt with a silhouette of an alien on the front that read: YES, THEY ARE REAL.

"Did you bike here?" I asked.

Matt nodded. "And you got me a pint as a reward. Thanks, Megs." He tapped his glass on mine.

"Thanks for meeting me. I had to talk through what I've learned with someone sane."

"Am I sane?" He pointed to his alien shirt.

I laughed. "The sanest person I know, except maybe Gam, but that's another story . . ." I trailed off.

"Gam's not sane? What? I need to hear that story."

"You will, but first I have to tell you about what happened this morning."

Matt drank his beer and leaned back against the high booth. "I'm all ears."

I told him about Jenny and the supplements. He interrupted twice to tell me it was a stupid idea to steal from her and to ask why I hadn't gone to the police with this information. "The police know," I assured Matt. "They said they can't use the hCG I took from Jenny because I didn't use the proper protocol to obtain it."

"I'll say." Matt gave me a disapproving look.

"I thought you were on my side."

"Megs, I'm always on your side, but you have to use your brain sometimes."

"That's not fair. I was using my brain. Thanks to my quick thinking we have one of Jenny's supplements in our hands."

"But the police can't do anything with it."

"No, that's not necessarily true." I showed him the article on my phone with the FDA hotline. "Here's what I'm thinking; as soon as the lawyer at Jill's firm confirms that it's hCG, then I'll call the hotline. They will investigate."

Matt drank his beer and contemplated what I told him. "That might work."

"You think?"

"It's kind of your only play right now."

"Unless I go to Kelsey."

"Kelsey?" Matt looked confused.

"Oh yeah, I forgot to tell you that part. Kelsey has been supplying Jenny with the hCG."

"Kelsey Kain, the news reporter?"

"Yeah. Can you believe it?"

Matt shook his head. "No, I can't."

"Me either." I sighed and stopped a volunteer waitress walking by. "Can we get an order of fries?"

"Sure. Regular or with bacon and cheese sauce?"

Matt and I both replied, "Bacon and cheese sauce," at the same time.

She wrote down our order and left.

"Bacon and cheese on fries, yeah that's right." Matt grinned.

"I know. Yum."

"Back to Kelsey, though," Matt continued. "What would her motivation for selling illegal growth hormones be? She strikes me as someone with her sights on the anchor desk."

"Me too," I agreed. "I think that's what I've been stuck on. She is consumed with getting the story. She literally pushes anyone out of her way to get a story. I don't see her as an underground drug dealer. It doesn't make sense."

"Do you think she's taking it?"

"Not really. I mean, maybe she's been on it a long time or something and her body has built up a tolerance to it. Jenny is a different person since I met her two weeks ago. Not only because of the drastic weight loss, but she's jumpy and shaky and running in place all the time." I took another drink of my beer. "Now that I think about it, she acts like someone on drugs."

"Let's assume that Kelsey isn't taking hCG. She gave it to Jenny, but as far as we know no one else on the team is taking it. Is that right?"

I nodded. "Yeah, if Jenny is an example of what happens when taking hCG, then my guess is that no one else is taking the supplement because no one has had results like Jenny's. People have lost a few pounds and firmed up, but no one has dropped twenty pounds."

"Okay, so the next logical step is to see if you can talk to Kelsey. If she's aspiring to have a career in illegal drug sales she's doing a pretty lousy job. She's supplying drugs to one person for free. No way."

"No way." I agreed. Matt was right. Jill and I hadn't considered his point that Kelsey had a sole client at this stage. "Well, unless she's selling it somewhere else too. Or Jenny is her first client. Is that an appropriate use of the word *client?*"

Matt grinned. "You're asking the wrong guy. I'm not exactly well-versed in the drug-dealing lingo."

"Thank God for that." I paused. "On that note, taking things to a more serious level . . ."

Matt interrupted me. "There's something more serious than illicit drug deals and murder?"

"When you put it like that, I guess not."

A volunteer wearing a T-shirt that read I LOVE CATS delivered our bacon-and-cheese–smothered fries to the table. They smelled like fried salty deliciousness.

"Let me guess, you're with the Humane Society," Matt said.

The volunteer ran her hand across her shirt. "Did this give it away?"

"Thanks for donating your time." Matt smiled at her. She smiled and winked at him. She was definitely flirting, and Matt appeared to be enjoying it.

Knock it off, Meg. You've been flirting with Kenny for the past two days and made plans to go out for a beer with him tonight. As the waitress walked away I wondered how I would feel if Matt told me he had a date for beers with someone else. Not happy.

Maybe I would keep that to myself for the moment.

Matt scooped a heap of gooey fries. "This is ridic."

"Since when did you start speaking in slang?" I asked, diving into the fries too.

"Since never. But look, this is one circumstance that calls for the use of slang. Come on, Megs, who puts cheese sauce and bacon on fries?"

We didn't speak for a few minutes. Not because

we didn't want to, but we were too busy scarfing down the fries that neither of us paused except to breathe and swallow.

After I had sufficiently gorged myself on the salty, fatty fries, I pushed the plate toward Matt's side of the table. "I want to talk to you about Pops."

"You are getting serious. What's going on?"

"What do you think of Sheriff Daniels?"

"Sheriff Daniels?" Matt wrinkled his brow. "Why do you ask?"

Something shifted in Matt's demeanor. It was subtle, but it was there. His back became slightly stiffer against the wooden wall of the booth. The floor shook underneath my feet from Matt pounding his heel into it. To someone who didn't know Matt the shift would be unnoticeable, but to me it was obvious. Matt was holding something from me.

"Mother doesn't trust him," I said, trying to sound casual but carefully studying his body for a reaction. "She said that Pops didn't either."

"When did you see your Mom?" Matt avoided my eyes.

"Earlier this morning. She was at Gam's shop. Mother, *my mother,* was at Gam's shop, and not just as a customer. She's taking care of the shop while Gam's in Bend with Sheriff Daniels."

"Your grandmother is in Bend?" Matt frowned. His foot tapped harder on the cement floor.

"Yeah, she went to meet the sheriff. I guess he's there for some kind of state training. Mother thought it would be a good idea for them to spend some quality time together."

"Your grandmother is in Bend?" Matt repeated.

"Yes, I just said that. Gam is in Bend. Why?"

Matt bit his bottom lip. "It's nothing."

"It's something. What aren't you telling me?"

He massaged his temples. "Listen, Megs, I'm not sure. Like I told you at lunch yesterday, I'm waiting for a couple of things to come through. I don't know who to trust, and I'm worried that you're going to end up in a dangerous position. I think it's better that you know as little as possible right now."

"Matt," I said, not liking the sound of anger in my voice but unable to hide it either. "You have to stop worrying about me. I'm a big girl. I can handle whatever you're going to tell me."

"I'm not sure you can handle this."

"Try me." I sat forward and rested my elbows on the table.

Matt picked at a soggy fry. "Okay, but this is speculation at this point in time, so I don't want you to flip out. Deal?"

"Deal. Like I ever flip out."

"Right." He smirked. "Never. You're always the model of calm."

"Stop stalling, Matt."

"When I was in Bend I found another source that your dad worked with on the Meth Madness investigation."

"Okay."

"I'm not sure how reliable this source is."

"What do you mean?"

"A lot of your dad's informants were addicts. That population isn't exactly stable. It's hard to find people who will talk to me. Your dad worked for years to build trust within the community. I don't have it. And honestly, some of the people who I'm talking to are users, so who knows how much of what they say is true, and how much of it is part of some kind of trip that they're on."

"What did this informant say?"

"You're not going to like it, Megs." Matt cracked his knuckles. "And this guy was definitely high when I was talking to him."

"Just tell me."

Matt looked pained as he spoke. "He thinks your dad was in on the meth scheme."

"Of course he was in on it. He was working the story."

"No, Megs. I mean, there's some evidence that your dad was actually involved in funneling drugs through the state."

Chapter 27

"Matt, you know as well as I do that Pops was deep undercover for the story. He probably told his source that he was dealing. You know as well as I do that there's no way that can be true. We're talking about Pops—my dad, your mentor. You're saying that you believe that Pops—the most ethical human being I've ever known—was involved in getting meth in the hands of kids throughout Oregon? No way. No way!"

"Megs, this is exactly what I was talking about. I told you not to freak out." Matt leaned forward and reached for my hand. I jerked it away.

"I am freaking out. I'm freaking out because I thought you were helping me with this."

"I am helping you, but I think we have to be open to the reality that your dad was human like the rest of us, maybe something happened. Maybe he didn't have a choice. Maybe someone threatened him—or you and your family. You never know."

"I know." I stood. "I know Pops and he would

never, *never* sell meth. I thought I knew you, too, but I guess I don't."

I walked to the door as fast as I could, ignoring Matt's plea for me to come back to the table. Anger pulsed through my veins. I wanted to hit something—hard. How could Matt consider the possibility that Pops was involved in dealing meth? No way. Absolutely no way.

We hadn't even had a chance to talk about Sheriff Daniels. I couldn't believe this was happening. Why? Why would Matt say something so terrible?

I stormed to the car. Why was I so angry? Matt's words felt like a direct blow. I slumped into the front seat and took a moment to try to steady my breathing and calm down. Images of the last time I saw Pops flooded my mind. It was a month or so before graduation. Jill and I came to Portland for a long weekend. Jill's parents were in the process of buying her a swanky condo in the Pearl District and wanted her to pick out paint colors and flooring before she moved in. We stayed at my parents' farmhouse just outside of the city. Matt, who had graduated the year before us and was interning at *The O*, joined us for dinner.

Pops loved having my friends around. He built a bonfire in the backyard and brought out hot dogs, graham crackers, marshmallows, and bars of chocolate. "Okay, kids, go forage for sticks and we'll have dinner."

"Pops, we're not kids anymore. We're going to be college graduates in a month."

He kissed the top of my head and placed the tray of grilling supplies on the picnic table. "Aw, but sweet Maggie, you'll always be my little girl."

I kissed him back. His cheek was scruffy and he smelled like a campfire. "Your little girl is on her way to becoming a serious journalist. Did you hear, Pops? I have a phone interview with your editor in chief next week. I've been pulling all-nighters for a week to prepare."

"When she should be studying for finals," Jill chimed in.

Pops' face clouded. "When did you get invited to interview?"

"I don't know, a week or so ago? I was surprised when they called because I know things have been kind of strained with you."

Pops had been covering "Meth Madness," a multiple-piece exposé about the state of drug use in Oregon, for three years. When he first broke the story, he'd been labeled a hero by his editor, coworkers, and every other publication in town. Media outlets throughout the Northwest and all across the country jumped on the story. Oregon was suddenly on the map for its growing meth epidemic. Pops' ethics when it came to accuracy and reliable sources were infallible. He was at the height of his career. Then it all came crashing down. The *New York Times* accused *The O* of falsifying statistics and not using credible sources. Pops was placed on leave and went underground. When his editor called to schedule an interview, I was more surprised than anyone.

I waited for him to reply. He busied himself with unwrapping chocolate bars.

"If you don't want me to do the interview, I won't."

Pops broke off the end of a chocolate bar and

put it in his mouth. He smiled at me, but it wasn't a happy smile. "No, Maggie, you go follow your dream. Don't worry about me."

He stoked the fire and launched into a story about a camping trip he took after he graduated from college where he ended up lost in the forest for three days. If I had been paying better attention I would have noticed that Pops' laughter that night was halfhearted. But I didn't. I was wrapped up in planning for graduation, taking off on a road trip, and landing my dream job at *The O.* A few weeks later I would get a call from Mother that brought me to my knees and forever altered my dreams. I never imagined that night would be the last time I would ever see, smell, or touch my dad.

Tears streamed down my cheeks as I relived my last happy memory of Pops. Why hadn't I realized that something was terribly wrong? Why hadn't Pops told me what was going on? Was he in too deep? Was he trying to protect me? Or could Matt be right? Maybe I'd put Pops on a pedestal. What if he wasn't the man I'd always believed he was?

I sobbed uncontrollably, sucking in air and swallowing salty saliva. Pops was dead and I'd made a mess of everything. I hadn't followed my dreams. I'd lied about my skills to land a job that I wasn't even qualified to do. And what would he say about Billy's murder? Would he tell me to stop getting involved, or would he dive in with me?

The sound of someone knocking on my car window startled me. I lurched forward and landed on the steering wheel. The horn blared. I jumped back and placed my hand on my heart.

Matt tapped on the window again. He gave me

his best sad puppy dog frown and was holding a bunch of yellow daisies.

I rolled down the window.

He handed me the daisies. "A token of my remorse."

"Where did you get these?" I wiped my eyes.

Matt looked sheepish. "Over there." He pointed to a vacant lot across the street.

"You stole flowers for me?"

"I was worried that you would take off. I had to think fast."

"Thanks." I rested the flowers on the passenger's seat.

"Megs, listen. That didn't go over the way I intended it to. I'm sorry."

"It's okay." My nose dripped.

Matt reached into his bike messenger bag and handed me a travel size package of tissues.

"Do you stock that thing every day? How are you always so prepared?"

He gave me a salute. "Boy Scouts. It's my badge of honor—to be prepared for any emergency."

"Like crying women?"

He nodded. "Especially crying women. They did an entire workshop on how to deal with tears. Bring it on."

I couldn't help but laugh.

"That's more like it," Matt said, crouching onto his knees. "Megs, really I didn't mean to lay something on you that you weren't ready for, especially given Billy's death and everything that you've been through the past couple days. That wasn't cool. I'm sorry."

"Don't be." I unwrapped the tissues and dabbed

my eyes and nose. "I'm a big girl. I can handle it. I shouldn't have freaked out. You were right—I freaked. It's just that Pops was my life, and it's hard to swallow the possibility that maybe he wasn't who I thought he was. Maybe you're right. Maybe he was involved in Meth Madness at some crazy level I never considered."

"Megs . . ." Matt started to apologize.

"No, really this is good. I'm glad you brought it up. I want to be a full-fledged journalist, and real journalists follow every single lead no matter where it takes them. I want to know the truth about Pops and what happened to him, even if it means that I'm going to have to take him off his pedestal. It's time."

I handed Matt his tissues. "I'm going to take off, but I'm not mad. I'm fine. In fact, I think I'm more fine than I've been since he died. I've been putting blinders up. Mother has been trying to tell me that, Gam has been too. I just haven't paid attention—or probably more like I have intentionally avoided listening. I'm done. I'm ready to do this."

Matt stood. "Are you sure? Do you want me to come with you? You're not going to do something crazy, are you?"

"No, I'm not. I'm going to go back to my place and read through every single note and article that Pops wrote on the Meth Madness story. I know there's something right in front of me that I'm missing, or that I ignored."

"I'll come with you."

"Thanks. Really, but I want to be alone this afternoon. I need some space to think."

"If you're sure?" Matt didn't look sure. He leaned his head into the window frame, as if to get a closer look at me.

"Matt, I swear. I'm good." Without even thinking I tilted my head toward his and planted a kiss on his lips.

What was wrong with me? A few minutes ago I'd been fuming at Matt and now I was kissing him. Maybe instead of driving home I should drive myself straight to the state mental hospital and have my stability evaluated.

Matt grinned. "I guess you are *good*."

I laughed. "I'm going before this gets weirder. I'll text you later."

He stepped away from the car. I watched him watch me drive away in the rearview mirror. I was lucky to have him as a friend. Real friends push each other. Matt was pushing me forward to find the truth. I wasn't sure if I was going to like what I discovered, but I knew it was time to face my future head-on.

Chapter 28

I spent the remainder of the afternoon reading through dusty old news clippings and Pops' journals. His nearly illegible handwriting and undecipherable notes gave me new appreciation for Mother's frustration with him. She used to lament endlessly that he needed a system. When things were going well between them she would bring me to his office for lunch and help organize his files with color-coordinated sticky notes and pens.

Some of my fondest childhood memories were of sharing homemade peanut butter and jelly sandwiches at Pops' desk. What went wrong between them? When did Mother change? Or had Pops changed too?

My fingers darkened from the newsprint as I read story after story about Meth Madness. Pops had been the most thorough journalist I'd ever known. He didn't miss a single detail as he outlined the state of illegal drug usage in Oregon and how meth was being funneled back and forth from Mexico and all the way up to Alaska. The drug had wreaked havoc in big cities and rural communities throughout the state of Oregon and all up and down the West Coast.

It had been a while since I'd read Pops' work. I'd forgotten what an incredible writer he was. His heart came through in each story, and yet he was able to maintain an appropriate level of journalist detachment. If I could be half the reporter he was, I would consider myself a success.

The features made me even more sure that Pops couldn't have been involved in drug trafficking. He must have had some other reason for lying to his sources. The meth epidemic had reached far and wide, and Pops had followed it to every corner of the state, from big cities to tiny farming communities. He interviewed parents who had lost their children to drug addiction and politicians who brushed the problem aside. One state senator was quoted saying, "Meth is a fringe problem." Not according to Pops. The drug was rampant in Oregon, and the number of users was growing daily. It wasn't just kids either. Soccer moms had turned to meth to give them a kick throughout the day. I thought of Jenny. One particularly graphic photo showed side-by-side pictures of a young mom in her early thirties before and after meth. It looked like she had aged twenty years in the period of six months. Her hair was brittle. Her face was pocked with open red sores.

I had to look away.

Pops was trying to highlight the very personal and real effects of the drug. He couldn't have been involved. I wondered if I kept repeating that to myself if I could will it to be true.

While Pops' ability to write a clear and concise story was evident, his notes were another story. I scanned through scribbled sentences on the back of napkins, receipts for coffee, and his monthly calendar. What was the method to his madness?

There was the one major clue that I had found after his death—a meeting he had scheduled with a source he called PDJ on the day that he died. Matt had tracked down PDJ a few months ago. We thought we were finally getting somewhere until PDJ was found dead from a drug overdose a few days later. PDJ held some key to the story, but now that he was dead, too, that was a dead end.

I took a break and made myself an iced coffee. I knew I was way over my caffeine limit for the day, but I could feel that I was so close to a break-through I didn't care.

Pops used to tell me that he would intentionally take notes in a special code so that he didn't put any of his sources in jeopardy. He would have done jail time before revealing a source. With more coffee in hand, I grabbed a notebook and pen and made a chart of every word, letter, or sentence that appeared more than once in Pops' notes.

At first the effort seemed futile, but after about an hour I thought I had cracked the code. Pops made reference to "the hood" five times in his bizarre collection of scrap paper notes. I thought he was being funny, referring to a neighborhood in slang, but after the fourth reference I realized that "the hood" was code for something else.

It hit me as I read an article where Sheriff Daniels was quoted. In every article including the sheriff, Pops

introduced him as, "Hood River County Sheriff . . ."
The hood!

Could that be Pops' code for Sheriff Daniels? I
dropped the newspaper and went back to Pops'
notes.

At the bottom of a stack of receipts I found what
I was looking for. One crumpled receipt for a
coffee and scone from Pops' favorite hippie coffee
shop made my heart pound out of my chest. In
Pops' messy handwriting it read: *THE HOOD, PDJ*.
Next to that he'd written a date two weeks before
he died.

I'd seen that note before, but I always thought he
meant he was meeting PDJ in the hood, but now it
had an entirely new meaning. Sheriff Daniels was
connected to PDJ? Could Pops have learned something about his source and the sheriff that got him
killed?

My hands shook. I felt a sense of panic rising in
the back of my throat. What if Mother was right all
along? What if Pops didn't trust the sheriff? Maybe
he'd been keeping Sheriff Daniels close and quot-
ing him as an authority in the drug trade in order
to try and keep watch on him. I didn't know what
to do next. I sat on the couch with the receipt
clutched in my hands. I had no idea what it meant,
but I knew there was only one person who did—
Sheriff Daniels. What if the man who was currently
dating my grandmother wasn't to be trusted?

Chapter 29

I'm not sure how long I sat on the couch with the receipt. A text from Matt jolted me back into the present. He wanted to know how I was doing and if I had learned anything. I shot him a text back: I'm fine. Major development. Must talk. Have to run tonight. Tomorrow? After work?

He replied right away. Sure. 5:30. Meet at Deschutes?

See you then.

Megs, don't do anything stupid.

Me? Never ;-)

I'm serious.

I won't. See you tomorrow.

My phone beeped, reminding me it was time to get ready for tonight's daily session with Mind Over Mudder. I was actually thankful for the distraction.

Maybe a workout would get some of the nervous energy out of my body.

I changed into my running gear and grabbed my gym bag. Thank goodness that Sheriff Daniels was in Bend. Matt had good reason to tell me not to do anything stupid. If he'd been in town I might have skipped my workout and gone straight to his place to confront him. That would have been an insanely stupid idea.

If Sheriff Daniels was connected to the Meth Madness case in some way other than his official capacity, he could be dangerous. I had to be strategic about my next move. Sleeping on what I had learned would be good for me, as would talking to Matt.

I considered calling Greg. I had to know what he really knew and what his connection to Pops was. The picture of his youthful face smiling as he stood next to Pops in front of one of the desks at *The O* had haunted me since Matt found it. What if he had been asked to protect me from Sheriff Daniels? But by whom? According to Greg someone at *The O* had asked him to watch out for me.

Or what if his whole story was a lie? Maybe he killed Pops. Or maybe Sheriff Daniels had suggested that Greg hire me so that *he* could keep me close.

You have to stop, Meg, I told myself as I neared the exit for the barracks. I needed a short-term plan, and my best plan was to focus on my training session and stop obsessing about the sheriff.

Tim pulled into the parking space next to me when I arrived at the park. "Hey, Meg. You ready for run number two?" he asked.

"Can't wait." I stuck out my tongue. "You?"

"Jenny is on some kind of crazy power trip." He waited for me while I grabbed my bag.

"Yeah, I've noticed." I walked in stride with him up the hill. "Hey, you haven't been taking any special supplements by chance, have you?"

"Supplements, like what?" He took his headphones out of his bag and rested them around his bulky neck.

"I don't know. To promote weight loss."

"Do I look like I'm taking a weight-loss supplement?" Tim rubbed his beer belly.

"Well . . ."

He didn't let me finish. "My wife would love it if I would take a supplement, but not me. I prefer my nutrients to come in the form of real food."

"Me too."

"Why are you asking?" Tim huffed a bit as we trekked up the small hill.

"No reason." I tried to keep my tone light.

"Right. No reason."

I checked around us to make sure Jenny wasn't in earshot. "I heard a rumor that some of our teammates are using supplements to help speed up their weight loss. No one has asked me about taking anything, so I just wondered if anyone had approached you."

"Approached me?" Tim scratched his head. "You make it sound like we have a dealer in our midst."

I coughed. "Sorry. I swallowed a bug. Well, could we?"

"Maybe. You know who I would bet my money on?"

"No." I pretended to have no idea whom Tim could be referring to.

"Jenny. Have you noticed how jumpy she is? She's always running and she's skittish."

"You know, you're right. She is kind of on edge."

"On edge?" Tim rolled his eyes. "More like jacked up. She reminds me of this guy I had to fire last year when I caught him doing lines of coke in the bathroom at my office."

"Really?"

Tim gave me a serious look. "You haven't noticed?"

"I mean, I have, I guess I just didn't picture a stay-at-home mom being a drug user, that's all."

"Everyone uses drugs."

We made it the barracks and parted ways. Drug usage was a recurring theme for me today. I had learned something important, though. Kelsey hadn't offered hCG to Tim. I didn't know what that meant, but it had to mean something. He was a prime candidate for a weight-loss supplement. I couldn't figure out why she had only approached Jenny. I had to be missing something. Another theme for the day.

Inside, Jenny bounced around as she explained that we were going to do "mud work" tonight. I studied her appearance, envisioning the young mom Pops had interviewed about her addiction to meth. Were Jenny's teeth rotting? Was her hair always that stringy? I worried for her at a new level. Jenny had to stop taking hCG before something terrible happened to her.

Kelsey kept to herself. She didn't even acknowledge that Jenny and I were in the locker room. She seemed to be rehearsing in front of the mirror. Her false eyelashes took on a life of their own as she practiced looking stern and serious and posing at different angles.

On our way outside I overheard her ask Dylan if she could have access to the barracks early for the next few days. What was she up to?

After a quick warm-up we were back outside and running up the hill. I jogged alone in happy silence. Well, that's not quite true. I blared music in my ears, trying to drown out the noise in my head. Pine needles the length of my forearm blew down from stately evergreen trees. The breezy evening air quickly became infused with their earthy scent.

As I crested the hill and crossed Evergreen Boulevard I immediately had the sense that I was being watched. I stopped and stared straight ahead. Sure enough, the curtains in the corner apartment were pulled to the side and the creepy old lady was staring straight at me.

I'm not sure if it was due to my new resolve to face my problems and start acting like a responsible, mature, twenty-four-year-old journalist, or if I was delusional, but I clicked off my tunes and walked to her front door. The curtains swung closed. I knocked on the door. Nothing. There was no movement inside. Was she a figment of my imagination and the ghost that everyone claimed to see haunting the barracks?

I knocked again, this time louder.

For a moment I had myself convinced that she really was a ghost. I leaned closer to the door. It was dead quiet inside.

I tried one more time, banging with my fist.

Soft footsteps sounded inside. Either my ghost

was on the move or the woman was coming to the door.

The door swung open. I jumped back in surprise.

"Yes?" The woman held a long cigarette in one wrinkled hand. She wore a pink bathrobe that blended in with the outdated pink shag carpet and rose-colored wallpaper. I'm a fan of pink, but not shabby washed-out pink. The apartment smelled like stale cigarettes. I wondered when was the last time the windows had been opened.

"What do you want?" the woman asked as she puffed on the cigarette.

I tried not to cough or breathe in the smoke. "I'm Meg. I was wondering if we could talk for a minute."

"About what?" her voice sounded crabby.

"I'm with Mind Over Mudder." I pointed to the sidewalk behind me as if that explained anything. "I've noticed you watching us train. I'm a journalist and I thought it might be fun to include some anecdotes from bystanders, and since you've watched our training practices I thought you might be a perfect match for my story." Wow, I was laying it on thick. I couldn't believe the words rolling off the tip of my tongue.

She tapped her cigarette ashes on the porch. "I wasn't watching you."

I craned my neck toward the bay window. "Oh, I thought I saw you watching from right there."

She scowled. "What's this story you're writing?"

"It's about Mind Over Mudder—the training group that I'm part of. We're all competing in a mud race next week."

I expected her to ask for an explanation, but she

didn't. Instead, she stepped to the side to let me in and said, "I know about the mud race."

So she was watching us. I felt slightly vindicated, but I decided it was best to keep that to myself. The little old lady wasn't exactly friendly.

It was difficult to breathe inside. I had to inhale through my nose and constantly fight back the urge to clear my throat. Thick smoke residue coated the walls. The small living room was cluttered with glass ashtrays, figurines of toy poodles, and piles of discolored knitting.

"Do you knit?" I asked, trying to make conversation.

"What does knitting have to do with your mud race?" She sat in a wooden rocking chair next to the bay window. The lace curtains, now closed, were yellowed from smoke.

"Nothing," I replied, glancing at a collection of photos on her mantel. There was one photo of a young pudgy boy in the center of the mantel.

"Put that down," she scolded.

I returned the photo to its place on the dusty mantel and walked over to a floral couch covered in plastic. "Do you mind if I sit?" I asked.

"That's what a couch is for." She tapped a pack of cigarettes and lit a new one.

She's sure chipper, I thought as I took a seat on the cold, sticky plastic. "I didn't get your name," I said.

"I didn't tell you my name."

This was going well.

"How long have you lived here?" I tried a new tactic.

"Longer than you've been alive." She took a drag

of the cigarette and blew smoke in my direction. "I don't like your sharp eyes. What do you want?"

"Well, this is such a great location. I bet you see a lot of action in the park and with so many people walking by, and I was just kind of wondering if you'd seen any of my teammates around." That was a lie. My back stiffened. I couldn't shake the feeling that we weren't alone in the historic space. There was a dark energy in the room that was almost palpable. I half-expected to feel an unseen hand brush across my shoulder.

She inhaled smoke. "Nope, I don't see anything."

I got the sense that she was lying, but why?

"Have you been watching our training?"

"No."

"I wondered if there's anything you could share for my story? Maybe something interesting that you've seen when we've been running by."

"I haven't seen anything."

What was I doing here? This was stupid. The woman was clearly unhappy and didn't want me in her apartment.

I stood. "Sorry to bother you. Thanks for your time." The smoky apartment felt as if it was closing in on me.

She scowled. "You barge into my house for that? For nothing? I thought you wanted a story." Her fingers shook as she tapped her cigarette in a ceramic pink ashtray. "Sit."

I sat down again. There was something about her demeanor that made me follow her command. The plastic crinkled under me. "I did. I do. Sorry. I didn't mean to barge in or bother you."

"You're pretty chatty for a reporter. I thought reporters asked the questions."

"We do. I just didn't think you were into having me here."

"Maybe you should ask a question and we'll find out."

"What do you know about Mind Over Mudder?" I tend to be claustrophobic in tight spaces. The apartment was feeling smaller and smaller by the moment. I pressed my finger and thumb together until they turned white. It was a centering technique that I'd learned from Gam.

"I know a lot about it." Her voice was raspy from the smoke.

"Are you happy to have it in the neighborhood? It's the first business in the barracks' new renovation. How do you feel about that?"

"Fine."

What had I gotten myself into? Was she intentionally antagonizing me?

"Has it brought more people and new faces into the area?"

"You're here, aren't you?"

I laughed. She didn't return my smile.

"Did you hear about what happened to Billy?"

"You mean that crazy military type who liked to blow his whistle at the crack of dawn?"

"Yeah."

"I saw the police here. Heard someone died."

"That's right. Billy was killed."

She inhaled more smoke. "I heard he had it coming to him."

"What?" She caught me off guard. "How did you hear that?"

She nodded to the picture window. "I like to sit on my front porch and watch the birds in the trees. I feed them. They come right up to the railing. I hear things when I'm sitting out there."

"Who did you hear that from? Have you told the police?"

"Why would I do that?"

"It could be important for their investigation."

"A couple runners yapping when they run by, I don't think the police need to be bothered with that kind of gossip." She put out her cigarette in the glass ashtray. "You got any more questions?"

"No." I stood again. "I should probably catch up with my group. Thanks for your time."

"You can see yourself to the door." She pulled another cigarette from the pack.

I hurried to the door, feeling her eyes burn into the back of my neck. That was weird. I was sure that she knew more than she was saying. Something was off about her, but I couldn't figure out what—other than the fact that she was bad-tempered and unsociable. I should have had a firm plan and better questions in my mind before talking to her. *That was a wasted opportunity, Meg,* I scolded myself as I breathed in the fresh air.

The rest of my teammates were long gone. That was good for me. I wasn't in the mood to crawl through the mud. Who needed to practice that anyway? It wasn't as if I was going to develop a great mud technique.

I ran to the end of Officer's Row so that I could

feel like I'd accomplished something; then I looped across the street and back down the hill. I didn't even feel guilty about skipping out on the mud. This had been a long, crazy day. I had made an appearance; everyone knew I was here, now I was going to go home and crash on the couch.

Someone was walking up the hill on the opposite side of the street as I made my way down. I blinked twice as the person came into view.

I would recognize the stance, cowboy boots, and hat anywhere. My heart thumped wildly in my chest. "Sheriff Daniels, what are you doing here?"

Chapter 30

"Ms. Reed." The sheriff tipped his hat to me.

"I thought you were in Bend?"

"Your grandmother wasn't feeling well so we returned early."

"Gam's not feeling well?" Impossible. Gam was the model of health. She never got sick—never.

He twisted a toothpick lodged in the side of his mouth. Sheriff Daniels was rarely without a toothpick. It was like his grown-up version of a security blanket.

"She's fine. Tired and had a headache, that's all."

Gam had a headache? I'd never known Gam to have a headache.

"What are you doing here at the barracks, though?" Had his eyes always been so threatening?

Sheriff Daniels smiled. "Stretching my legs after a long car ride. It's a nice evening for a walk. I thought I'd take a turn before heading back across the river, unless you have a problem with that?"

I knew he was trying to be funny, but things had changed between us. I didn't trust him. I was seeing him in a new light. How did he always seem to show up wherever I was?

"Good to see you," I said, giving him a small wave. "I've got to go catch up with my training team."

He nodded and tipped his hat again. "Enjoy. I'll be seeing you around, Ms. Reed."

Did he mean that in a menacing way? I picked up my pace and ran down the hill to the barracks. I have to admit that I stopped and checked twice to make sure he wasn't watching me. He wasn't. At least not that I could see.

I grabbed my things and raced to my car. I didn't want to bump into anyone from Mind Over Mudder and I wanted to check on Gam. As I drove past the mud pit toward Gam's condo, I saw Tim crawling through the gooey mud and Jenny cheering him on from the grass. She looked like she'd been dipped in chocolate.

Smooth move, Meg, I told myself as I sped by the mud pit, praying internally that no one was looking in my direction. If anyone asked I would tell them I had to check on my grandmother who was ill. That wasn't a lie.

When I arrived at Gam's condo, I could hear the tranquil sound of new age music playing inside. I knocked on the front door. "Gam, it's Meg," I called.

The minute Gam answered I knew something was wrong. She was wearing a purple and teal apron and was covered in flour. Her eyes were puffy and streaked with black mascara. She'd been crying.

"Gam, is everything okay?"

"Margaret, am I ever glad to see your face. Of course you would know to come."

"What's going on, Gam? I thought you were in Bend?"

She pulled me inside and walked to turn down the music. "I felt like baking." She motioned to the kitchen. Every bowl she owned was on the counter. There were bags of flour, sugar, stacks of butter, chocolate chips, raisins, oats, and an assortment of spices.

"Are you baking for the entire condo association?"

"It looks that way, doesn't it?" Gam laughed.

I was glad to see her smile. "I don't think anyone will complain, but yeah—that's a lot of baking you've got going on in there."

She patted the sofa. "Come sit."

"Gam, is something wrong?" I asked, sitting next to her on her non-plastic-covered couch. "You look like you've been crying."

"Margaret, you are so in tune with your intuition." Gam smiled and placed her hand on my knee.

I didn't tell her about running into Sheriff Daniels, or how her streaky mascara gave her away.

"Is it Sheriff Daniels?" I asked.

Gam nodded. She closed her eyes and placed both her hands over her heart. "I'm afraid I haven't been as in tune with my own feelings as I would like to be."

"Did you have a fight or something?"

"No." Gam sighed. She took in a long, slow breath and opened her eyes. They looked a bit brighter, but held an unfamiliar sadness. "Sometimes we only see what we want to see. Have you ever had that happen?"

"Uh, yeah, all the time. In fact, I had that happen today."

"We are in tune spiritually, aren't we?"

"We always are, Gam, but I want to know about *you*. What happened?"

"I opened my eyes."

"What do you mean?"

"I mean that I really saw who Sheriff Daniels is, and I'm not sure he's a match for me."

I thought about what Mother said about Sheriff Daniels being a hunter. "But, Gam, you're always so in tune with your emotions."

She shook her head. "Not this time."

"Do you want to talk about it?"

She leaned her head onto my shoulder. "How did I get so lucky to have such a kind and caring granddaughter?"

I leaned into her. She smelled like cinnamon and lemon Pledge. "Gam, you're always here for me, let me be here for you."

She sat up. "I'd like that, Margaret. I really would. I'll take you up on that offer, but tonight I need to bake and clean." She looked around her condo. "And unpack."

My phone buzzed with a text message. It was Kenny asking if we were still on for a beer. Shoot. I'd completely forgotten about meeting him.

"It sounds like you're busy anyway," Gam said, noting my buzzing phone. "Go, have fun, be young. We'll talk tomorrow."

"Are you sure you don't want company?"

"I'm sure." Gam gave me a hug and pointed me in the direction of the door. "Come by tomorrow. We'll have a chat and by the looks of my kitchen I'll have some cookies to share with you."

I gave her a kiss on the cheek. "I love you, Gam."

"I know you do, Margaret. I love you too." She opened the door. "Scoot. Go!"

I couldn't be sure, but it sounded like she might have started to cry. I hung my head as I walked past Gam's lush collection of potted plants. I was glad that she had a realization about Sheriff Daniels, but I hated seeing her heartbroken.

Chapter 31

I canceled on Kenny. Too much had happened today to process. I drove straight home, pulled on my favorite pink and gray striped Long Jane pajamas made of soft cotton, and crashed. I didn't remember dreaming or even falling asleep on my couch when I woke to the sound of birds chirping outside my window the next morning.

We had a standing all-staff meeting every Monday at *Northwest Extreme*. I wondered if Greg was back from Japan yet, and whether he had any kind of an update on the future of the magazine to share with us. I showered, downed two cups of coffee, and headed for the office.

The drive from my bungalow in NoPo to *Northwest Extreme*'s headquarters on the Willamette River took me through Old Town. The historic district is one of the most iconic sections of the city with the Skidmore Fountain, Chinatown, Saturday Market, and the Shanghai Tunnels. Unlike other areas that had undergone revitalization, Old Town was overrun with Portland's rapidly expanding homeless population. Large congregations of street people camped out in front of missions and shelters. I thought of Pops. Had he wandered these sidewalks while investigating the meth epidemic? Could any of his sources still be alive? I scanned the faces of the men and women huddled together for warmth. My heart ached. A few blocks away Portlanders would be throwing five bucks down for their morning coffee fix. Yet here in Old Town, people were queuing up for a free meal and a chance to shower.

This is the kind of work that Pops was committed to, I thought as I continued along Naito Parkway. He spent his career giving voice to the voiceless. I had to finish what he started. No matter the cost. No matter the outcome. I felt a new sense of resolve and purpose. It was time to get to work.

Work sounded like a welcome reprieve from the chaos of the past few days. My feature on Mind Over Mudder needed some tweaking, and I wanted to check the status of our latest social media campaign. When I arrived at the office, a group e-mail was waiting in my inbox. The all-staff meeting had been postponed for a week. Greg was still in Japan, and would give us a full report when he returned.

I booted up my laptop, plugged in my headphones, and blasted Sinatra. Our latest social campaign was blowing up. I had arranged a giveaway with some of our ad partners. We'd never hosted a giveaway before, and I knew that Greg was going to be thrilled with the response. Hopefully, with solid data in terms of shares, likes, and comments, we could leverage the concept for ad dollars.

The rest of the day was pretty mundane. I chatted with concerned colleagues who were already plastering their résumés around town, researched extra backstory on the history of Fort Vancouver and the barracks for my feature, and responded to all of *Northwest Extreme*'s social media comments and questions. I also arranged a meeting with the ad team, which, sadly, was down to two salespeople. I wanted to talk through our plan for ad sales online. We agreed to pull data and meet later in the week to craft a pitch to present to Greg when he got back. Maybe, just maybe, social media could take the magazine into the future and save some jobs. I couldn't stop thinking about Gam, the sheriff, Jenny, and who might have been motivated to kill Billy.

After work I went straight to Deschutes to meet Matt. To my surprise, Jill was waiting for me at one of the bar tables. "Hey," I said, squeezing past a line of people waiting to order beers at the bar. "I didn't know you were coming."

"Is that a bad thing?" Jill winced.

"Never. I could use time with my two favorite people tonight. It's been a rough couple of days." What I didn't say out loud was that this might be one of our last times together. Deschutes had been our hangout spot since graduation. My eyes welled as I glanced around the pub's warm interior. Framed TVs behind the long bar played a college football preview. Brewers in coveralls were working on the giant copper tanks visible inside the brewery through large windows behind the bar. Hand-carved woodwork and iron chandeliers gave the modern space a rustic vive. A fire burned low at the end of the bar. *Drink this in, Meg*, I told myself. *Everything is changing.*

Jill handed me a pint of amber beer. "Meg, you're a million miles away."

"Huh?"

"Are you okay?" She had abandoned her legal wardrobe in favor of a creamy peasant shirt and skinny jeans. The look suited her.

"I ordered pretzels too. Just like old times." Jill held up her pint glass in a toast.

"Just like old times." I managed a smile and clinked glasses with Jill.

"It might be one of our last. I was thinking about that on the drive over. It's weird, isn't it? Everything's changing." She twisted a strand of hair around her finger.

I took a drink of my beer. "It is weird, but I guess that's life. It's all good things. Did you hear about Matt?"

She ran her finger along the rim of her glass. "The job in Bend?"

I nodded.

"He texted me. He's worried about leaving you."

"I can handle it."

"Of course you can, it's just hard. The three of us have been together since college. I don't think any of us want to break up our little pack."

"But we can't hold each other back either, that's what I told Matt."

"What did you tell Matt?" A deep voice sounded behind me. I spun around, and Matt stood behind me grinning.

"You already got pints, nice!" He gave Jill a thumbs-up as she handed him a beer. "What did you tell me?"

"Nothing that exciting," I replied. "Jill and I were

just talking about how much things are changing with the three of us."

"Way to bring the conversation down," Matt said. "At least let me get a drink in first."

"Any news on the murder investigation?" Jill asked.

I told them about my weird meeting with the creepy old lady and how there was something off about her that I couldn't figure out. "She's probably a ghost."

"Totes." Jill winked.

Then I explained how Tim had confirmed that Jenny was the only one taking hCG.

Jill reached into her leather bag and handed me a file folder. "On that note, this is for you."

"What is it?"

"I gave my colleague at work the supplements. He said he'll let us know as soon as he hears back from the lab, but it shouldn't take very long, maybe a day or two. He's very familiar with hCG and gave me copies of everything he has on it for you."

"Thanks." I thumbed through the file. "This is great. I'll read it over tonight. Then, as soon as we get confirmation, I'll hand everything over to Kenny and call the FDA hotline."

"It sounds like serious stuff, Meg." Jill frowned. "My lawyer friend said people have died taking it."

"I know. I did some preliminary research myself and found the same thing. I'm glad to have some legit research to share with Kenny. Tell your friend thanks."

Our pretzels arrived. We all broke off bites of the hot, doughy bread and dipped them in beer-infused spicy mustard.

"To old times," I said. "And besties." A lump began to form in my throat. I fought it back.

"To besties," Jill said, holding out her pint.

"I can't say 'besties,' but to my favorite friends," Matt said, joining in the toast.

"You guys aren't going to believe this," Jill said after we toasted each other. "I talked to my parents last night. They said they're okay with me going to Italy. I'm still not exactly sure I believe it, but I think they were impressed with how prestigious the program is."

My voice caught in the back of my throat. "Congratulations."

Matt clapped Jill on the back. "That's awesome. You're going to be a world-famous artist, and we'll be able to say we knew you when you would eat a pound of Skittles in one sitting."

"Oh, don't worry. I'm not giving up my Skittles habit." Jill grinned.

"You're doing it, then? It's a go for Italy?" I asked.

Jill's cheeks looked like they hurt from smiling. "It's a go." She squealed. "Can you believe it? I'm going to Italy!"

She gave Matt all the details about the program and extended an invitation for him to come visit her too. "You're coming for sure, right, Meg?"

"For sure," I agreed.

"Whew. I don't think I could do a year completely on my own." She reached across and squeezed my arm. "If I know that you're coming for the holidays, I can make it for the first three months."

"You're going to be so busy with the program and all those dreamy Italian men, you won't have time to be homesick."

"Wait. What dreamy Italian men? No one told me about dreamy men." Matt winked.

I punched him in the arm.

Jill finished her beer. "Sorry to break up the party early, but I have so much to do I can't think straight. Paperwork, packing, finding someone to sublet my place, and about a million shots—why do I need a hepatitis shot to travel to Italy?" She stuck out her tongue. "Good times. Which reminds me, I don't think I'm going to be able to do the run with you, Meg. I've got so much to do."

"That's okay, don't sweat it."

"Good one, sweat it." She winked. "I'm going to take off, but I'll text or call you the minute I hear anything back about the samples."

She gave us both hugs and practically floated out of the bar.

"Someone is happy." Matt waved over a waiter to order another round of beers.

"I know." I tried to smile.

"And you're not?"

"No, I am."

"Megs." He tilted his head to the side. "Come on."

"I'm going to miss her." I sighed and looked up at him. "And you."

The words hung in the air between us. Matt reached for my hand. His hand felt warm and comforting. "Megs, you aren't going to have to miss me. I'm not going that far."

"But you are going?"

"For a couple weeks."

"What do you mean?"

"I thought it would be good to really give Bend a shot before I make a decision one way or the other."

"When are you leaving?"

"Tomorrow."

"What?"

The waiter delivered two cold pints to the table.

"What about work?" I asked.

"That's the thing. That's why I'm leaving tomorrow. There's a technology summit in Bend for the next two weeks. Rumors are swirling that one of the tech giants is thinking of moving in. My editor assigned the story to me. Kind of a crazy twist of fate, huh?"

"Gam would call that divine intervention."

Matt drank his beer. "I sort of thought the same thing. Being on assignment will give me a chance to live in the city for the next couple weeks and really get a feel for whether it's a place I can see myself staying."

"Right."

"Don't look so dejected. I told you that Bend isn't far. Even if I take the job, we can see each other all the time."

"Not like this." I waved my hand toward the crowded bar. "I can't just text you and say meet me for a pint."

"No, but we can see each other on the weekends, and like I said I'm sure you can convince Greg to send you to central Oregon to cover something for the magazine."

"Yeah." I took a drink.

"Let's talk about what you really wanted to talk about." Matt scooted his bar stool closer.

I glanced around the bar. It was humming with lively conversation. Now soccer, also known as Portland's official sport, played on the TVs strategically placed on the walls, so that every table had a prime view.

"You'll never guess who I ran into at the barracks."

"Who?"

"Sheriff Daniels."

Matt frowned and nodded. "I wondered if that's what you were going to say."

"Do you know something about him that you aren't telling me?"

"I never said anything about the sheriff."

"Maybe not officially, but I know that he's tied to whatever you learned in Bend."

"How did you know?"

"Matt, come on, you always tell me that I'm a terrible liar and you can see through me. Right back at you."

He held his hands up in protest. "Okay, but you have to promise that this stays between us. I don't know who to trust, and I know that we're in over our heads on this one."

"Okay, I promise."

Matt stared hard at me. "Megs, I'm serious."

"I am too." I met his gaze.

He sighed. "None of this is confirmed. Like I told you, I'm waiting to hear back on a couple things. In fact, that's one of the reasons I'm glad that I'm going to be in Bend. I can work on this too."

"You just said that it's dangerous."

"It is, but I know what I'm doing."

I raised my brow.

"Trust me. You are the only person I've talked to about this." He pulled a package of gum from his shorts pocket and offered me a piece.

I declined.

He fiddled with the pack. Matt checked behind him and moved so our knees were touching. "I tracked down a friend of PDJ's when I was in Bend. He told me something that may change everything we know."

"What?"

"He said that Sheriff Daniels was on the scene when PDJ died."

"Okay."

"Megs, think about it. Why? Sheriff Daniels' territory is an hour away in Hood River County. Why was he on the scene of a drug overdose in downtown Portland?"

My breath caught in my throat. Matt had just confirmed what I suspected—Sheriff Daniels must have had something to do with Pops' murder.

Chapter 32

"Don't you think it's strange that the sheriff is always hanging around in Portland and Vancouver? Like today. What was he doing at the barracks?"

"He said he dropped Gam off."

"What if that's why he's been dating your grandmother? What if he figured it was an easy way to stay close and watch what you're doing."

My stomach sank. I wondered the same thing.

"Matt, I think I found something that might confirm this."

"What?"

I told him about Pops' notes and old news clippings and how I had pieced together Pops' code.

"Megs, you know what this means?"

"No." I shook my head. It was starting to throb.

"It means the police are involved. Really involved. We can't go to them for help. And we can't let Sheriff Daniels know that we know any of this."

"Got it."

"No, really. This is dangerous stuff. Both your

dad and his source have been killed. I don't want you to be next."

"Like I do?"

"No, but you've got to be careful. Really careful."

"So do you. You're the one who's planning to dig deeper in Bend. What if Sheriff Daniels is working with people out there? What if the disaster training was just a front? Maybe he was really in Bend for other reasons?"

Matt rubbed his neck. "I thought about that. I promise, I'm going to be careful."

I finished the last of my beer and yawned.

"You look tired," Matt said.

"It's been a long day."

"You should get some sleep." He paid the bill and helped me off the stool. "I'll text you tomorrow from Bend."

"Matt, please be safe. I couldn't handle it if anything happened to you."

He wrapped his arm around me and walked me to the door. Once outside he paused and kissed the top of my forehead, letting his lips linger on my skin. I wanted to freeze this moment in time. My heart pounded. My face felt tingly.

After a minute, he released me. "I'll be safe, I promise. You do the same." He kissed my head and walked away.

I watched him unlock his bike before I moved in the direction of my car. Everything was in disarray. I didn't like this feeling. I wanted things to go back to the way they'd been with Matt, Jill, Gams, everyone.

My head felt heavy on the drive home, like it was exhausted from overthinking. There was a nice cool evening breeze. I opened the front windows in my bungalow and plopped on the couch. I had so much to think about.

I replayed every conversation I'd had with Sheriff Daniels. When I first met him at the trailhead to Angel's Rest, I'd been surprised that he knew Pops. What had he said?

Something about me being Charlie Reed's daughter and blowing things out of proportion. He said something about following up on leads in the investigation into Pops' biking accident. He called it an accident, not me.

The details were fuzzy, but I remember him saying something about how there hadn't been any new leads in the case and how it was probably better if I just dropped it and let it go. At the time I thought he was being kind—even worried about me. I thought he was trying to nudge me back into my life, but now I wondered if I'd interpreted his meaning the wrong way. What if he had been trying to give me a subtle warning?

And come to think of it, why was he involved in the investigation? He said it was because Pops was a friend of his. But Pops had been killed outside of Portland—nowhere near Hood River County, Sherriff Daniels' jurisdiction.

Matt was right. Sheriff Daniels was everywhere. I thought about him and Gam. I had been the person who suggested he see Gam. His back had been hurting, so I gave him Gam's card. I never thought he would actually call her. His gruff exterior didn't seem like a match for Gam's alternative healing techniques. But he said that he was desperate for pain relief and that Gam had magic hands.

What if that all had been a ruse? Could Sheriff Daniels have dated Gam just to stay close to me and the investigation into Pops' death? Mother might have been right this entire time. I'd pushed her away and been so angry with her. I never even considered that she might have had Gam's best interest at heart.

I'd been such an idiot. I missed so much.

There was no way I was falling asleep anytime soon, so I padded into the kitchen and made myself a mug of peppermint tea. Gam would be proud of me.

Conversations collided in my mind. How had I been so blind? Mother had tried to warn me, more than once, but I blew her off. I didn't listen. What had she said? That she didn't leave Pops. That Pops left her. To protect her. From what? From whom? Sheriff Daniels?

I almost picked up the phone and called her, but it was late and I wanted to have a clear head when I talked to her. I owed her an apology. A big one.

You have to stop, Meg. I was obsessing and slipping into a slight mania.

I found the file that the lawyer at Jill's firm had given her. A distraction was what I needed.

Jill's friend had included a lengthy stack of research and articles on hCG. I would have to send him a thank-you note. The documents revealed even more details about how dangerous the drug was. There were case notes from over thirty FDA investigations. I read through each one.

My tea turned cold as I scanned each document. I was about to call it a night, when a byline caught my eye. One of the stories in the file was a feature

The O ran four months before about a small herbal shop that lost their business license due to illegally selling hCG. There wasn't anything particularly shocking about the story. The file contained dozens of stories just like this one. The difference was the reporter cited in the story for breaking the case was none other than Kelsey Kain.

Kelsey had broken a story on hCG, yet she was the person supplying Jenny with the drug. I was missing something important.

"Unless . . . Unless," I said out loud, taking the remains of my tea to the kitchen sink. Unless Kelsey had set them up. What if she was so desperate for a story that she had set up the owners? What if she supplied them with hCG and then burst in a week later with her camera crew. Had she done the same thing with Mind Over Mudder? And more importantly, could she have killed Billy for that?

I wasn't sure. I needed sleep. After I shut the windows and locked the front door, I crashed on my bed. First thing tomorrow morning, I was going to confront Kelsey.

Chapter 33

I must have fallen asleep because my alarm was suddenly blaring in my ear. I clicked it off and got dressed in the dark. Against my better judgment, I skipped coffee in order to get to Mind Over Mudder's headquarters before Kelsey. She had arranged for early access to the barracks. Could she be dealing first thing in the morning before anyone else showed up? Maybe she had been running a drug ring out of the locker room. Could Jenny have caught her dealing and gotten looped in? It sounded a bit far-fetched, but stranger things had happened.

The sky threatened rain. Dark gray clouds erupted from the sky. The air felt heavy and thick. It matched my mood. Too many things were in turmoil. I had to get time with Kelsey alone this morning. Billy's murder and whatever was happening with hCG were the only things I felt like I could control. Pops' death and Sheriff Daniels' potential involvement felt too big to tackle at the moment.

Matt was on his way to Bend. He promised that

he would check in later today, and I owed Mother a phone call. My eyes were open now and there was no turning back. But for the moment, I needed to focus on the problem at hand—Kelsey.

When I arrived at the barracks the KPDX news van was parked on the street. Good. She was here. I jogged up the hill without even thinking about it. Jogging had become my routine. I never would have thought I'd be saying that two weeks ago.

Yellow lights glowed from inside the barracks, but there was no sign of anyone outside. Kelsey had to be inside. I opened the front doors and tiptoed down the hallway, stopping twice to listen to see if she was here alone or meeting Jenny.

I couldn't hear anything, so I continued downstairs to the locker room. I started to open the locker room doors when I heard the sound of her voice.

Who was she talking to?

I waited by the doors, trying unsuccessfully to eavesdrop. The doors were too solid and Kelsey was too quiet. I pushed them open, just a crack, and peered inside.

Kelsey stood in front of the lockers with a camera in her hand. She was speaking into the camera. "This is Kelsey Kain, reporting from Mind Over Mudder in Vancouver, Washington."

She clicked the camera off and cleared her throat. Then she paced in front of the lockers for a minute and started recording. "This is Kelsey Kain, reporting from the site of an underground drug trade in Vancouver, Washington."

She shook her head. "No, that's not good." She clicked the camera off and looked in my direction.

I froze.

"Who's there?" she asked.

I considered my options. I could run back upstairs, but Kelsey was fast. Plus, I had come to confront her. This was no time to lose my nerve.

"It's Meg," I said, swinging the door all the way open and stepping into the locker room.

"What are you doing here?" She glared at me. Her scowl left indents in her makeup.

"Getting an early start."

"Right," she scowled. "More like spying on me. Get out. You're not stealing my exclusive this morning. No way."

"Kelsey, I've told you a thousand times that I write for *Northwest Extreme*. We don't cover breaking news or do serious investigative stories. I'm not trying to steal anything from you, but I do want to talk."

"About what?" Her KPDX warm-up jacket was unzipped halfway, revealing her ample cleavage.

I walked closer to her. "About you giving Jenny hCG."

The camera slipped from her fingers. It almost landed on the floor, but she caught it at the last minute with her other hand. "How did you know?"

"She told me."

"I told her not to talk to anyone about it." Kelsey set the camera on the counter.

"She didn't. I got it out of her."

"You got it out of her?"

"I found her popping a bunch of pills." I looked toward the showers and steam room. "Are we the only ones here?"

Kelsey opened a makeup compact and applied a layer of powder to her already shine-free nose.

"Yep, I got here early to work on my story before you rudely interrupted me."

"I didn't mean to barge in, but I have to be honest with you, I'm going to go to the police."

"What?" Kelsey's face turned bright red.

"You've been supplying Jenny with illegal supplements. I don't know why, but I know it's not legal and I'm pretty sure it has something to do with Billy's death. Is this where it's all been going down? Who else are you selling to?"

Kelsey looked incredulous. Her lip crinkled and her overly eye-shadowed eyes bulged. "What are you trying to say? You think that I killed Billy?"

I shrugged. "It makes sense. You've been crazy about getting a lead story. I found an article from *The O* where you broke a story on a mom and pop shop selling hCG. I think I've figured out how you do it. You supply them with the supplement, make them feel secure, and then you bust them, is that right?" I wasn't sure where my confidence was coming from. I probably should have felt more nervous, but after all my training I knew I could hold my own with Kelsey. Plus, all of my teammates would be arriving soon. Kelsey wouldn't risk getting caught. Or would she?

Her eyes narrowed; then she threw her head back in a wild laugh. "You're ridiculous. You think that I staged an elaborate setup and killed Billy. I'm impressed. That's quite the imagination you have. Have you considered writing fiction? I think you have a knack for it."

"Okay, if you didn't do those things, then why don't you tell me what's really going on?"

Kelsey rubbed her temples. "I guess I don't have

much of a choice. I don't want you to mess this up. I've been working on this story for three months."

"Story?"

"Story. Yeah, I'm working with the FDA on investigating businesses in Oregon selling hCG."

"The FDA?" I knew I sounded like an idiot, repeating everything Kelsey said.

She gave me a smug look. "Yes, the FDA. I've been partnering with them and working underground on exposing illegal sales of hCG."

"Is that who I saw you with the other day? The guy in the suit handing you a file at your office. Was he with the FDA?"

Kelsey nodded. "Yes, he's with the FDA."

"I don't understand. Why would you give hCG to Jenny? If you're working with the FDA you must know how serious the supplement is."

"It's nasty stuff," Kelsey said, nodding in agreement.

"How could you put Jenny at risk like that? She has two young kids at home."

"I didn't."

"But you gave her the supplements. She told me and you just confirmed it."

"I didn't confirm anything. I gave her a supplement, but not hCG. I gave her a placebo. A sugar pill."

"What?"

Kelsey sat on the bench. I did too.

"The FDA has been looking into Mind Over Mudder for a while. When they first started the business they were selling hCG straight off their shelves, but when the FDA caught them, they agreed to stop selling the supplement and paid a hefty fine.

Basically they got a slap on the wrist." She paused and looked toward the locker room doors. "Did you hear something?"

We both listened for a minute. I didn't hear anything.

Kelsey continued. "No big deal, Mind Over Mudder was still in business and they dropped hCG, or so the FDA thought. Then they got word from an anonymous source that Mind Over Mudder was still selling the drug."

"How?"

"That's what I've been trying to figure out."

"I still don't understand the connection with Jenny and why you gave her fake supplements."

"Jenny experienced radical weight loss right away. I'm sure you've noticed."

"She's half the size she was when we started." I nodded.

"That doesn't happen naturally. I was assigned to go undercover. To pose like I was doing a fluff piece about training and then try to get ahold of the hCG."

"Okay, that sounds easy enough."

"I thought so, too, but it hasn't been. The FDA suspected that Mind Over Mudder's natural supplement line contains hCG, so I was tasked with getting a bottle of supplements. We sent them straight to the lab to be tested. Everything came back clean."

I thought about how I'd stolen Jenny's pill and sent my bottle to be tested. Maybe Kelsey and I were more like each other than I realized. Maybe it was the journalist in both of us.

"So what did you do?"

"We thought it was a dead end at first. My bottle came back clean, and I couldn't find anything in Dylan's office that looked out of place. We were going to pull the plug on the story, but then I noticed Jenny's drastic results."

"And you gave her sugar?"

"It was the FDA's idea. They thought that if Jenny trusted me, she might confide in me."

"You mean tell you who was really giving her the hCG?"

"Exactly."

"But Jenny thought you were giving her the supplement."

"I know. I realized that after a week or so. I figured out what was going on." She looked at the doors again and put her finger to her lips.

I held my breath.

Kelsey waited another minute longer and then continued. "I think that Mind Over Mudder targets specific clients for hCG use. Jenny was the perfect match—overweight, motivated, desperate."

While Kelsey's description was accurate, it made me feel sorry for Jenny.

"It's a brilliant plan if you think about it. They gave out their main line of supplements that are a collection of healthy vitamins and herbs, but then they have a line of 'special' enhanced supplements they offer to particular clients."

"Enhanced meaning containing hCG?"

"You got it. Jenny's been taking a sugar pill from me and hCG from Mind Over Mudder."

"How do you know?"

"I finally got my hands on a bottle of what she's taking."

"How?"

"You remember how Dylan had bags waiting for all of us outside after Billy died?"

I nodded.

"I swapped bags with Jenny when no one was looking. I handed the supplements over to the FDA. They called late last night to confirm the pills contain hCG. That's why I'm here. I'm breaking the story this morning."

"Do you think this could be tied to Billy's murder?"

She nodded. "I'm sure it is, and I know who killed him."

"Who?"

"Dylan."

Chapter 34

"Dylan!" My voice sounded louder than I intended.

Kelsey waved for me to be quiet. "Don't scream it."

"Sorry." I lowered my voice. "Why do you think Dylan did it?"

"You remember how I said that the FDA received an anonymous tip that Mind Over Mudder was selling hCG?"

I nodded.

"Guess who that tip came from?"

"Billy?"

"You got it. Billy didn't want to have anything to do with hCG. He really was serious about his clean living campaign. When the FDA busted them the first time, it almost broke up their partnership, but Dylan swore that he didn't know that hCG was illegal. Billy trusted him. He shouldn't have."

I swallowed. I knew something about trusting someone I shouldn't have.

"Billy might have acted like a drill sergeant, but he was a smart guy. He figured out pretty quickly what I was up to."

"He did?"

"Yeah. He pulled me aside the morning that he was killed and asked if I was here for a story or *a story*. I told him the truth. He told me that he made the call and he would help in whatever way we needed. Then the next thing I knew he was dead."

"Have you told the police all of this?"

Kelsey looked surprised. "I've told them what they need to know for now."

"We're talking about a murder investigation. The police need to know everything that you've just told me."

"We're also talking about the biggest story I've ever done. Of course I'm going to go to the police—so will the FDA—but not before I break this story *live* on air this morning."

"Kelsey, Billy is dead and Jenny is jacked up on hCG, I think your story can wait. We need to call the police right now."

She looked at her watch. "Do what you want, but I'm live in ten minutes." She jumped to her feet. "Speaking of that, where's my camera crew? I told them to have the dish up and running no later than five forty-five."

I wasn't sure what to do next. Kelsey raced out of the locker room in search of her camera crew. I had to call Kenny. The police needed to get here before Kelsey went live. What if Dylan saw the news? He would bolt.

Cell service was bad in the basement. I had to go outside to get reception. I walked upstairs and headed for the doors. On my way out, I ran straight into Dylan.

"Good morning, Meg," he said with a warm smile.

"Hi," I answered, breathless.

"You're here early."

"We're only a couple days away from the big race. Have to hit it hard, you know."

He folded his arms in front of him and bowed. "I like that spirit and energy."

I smiled and started toward the door.

"Meg," Dylan called. "I think you're going the wrong way. The locker room is behind you." Was I imagining things or had his tone turned cold?

"Right. I knew that." I chuckled, hoping that Dylan didn't share Gam's intuition.

"Hey, hold up." His tone had definitely shifted.

I swallowed and paused, keeping careful control to keep my voice light. "What's up?"

His yoga attitude transformed into something much darker. He knew that I knew.

"I forgot something in my car," I said, pointing with my thumb toward the stairway. "I should go grab it." Where was Kelsey?

"What are you really doing here?" His shadowy eyes stabbed at me.

This was bad. I considered my options as Dylan strolled closer. He looked like it was taking every ounce of his yoga training for him to maintain self-control.

Without thinking or giving him a chance to come any closer, I bolted for the stairs, shouting, "I'll be right back." So much for not being obvious.

Kelsey and her camera crew were setting up the shot in front of the barracks. Thank God I wasn't alone.

I ran as fast as my short legs could carry me to

the nearest tree and punched in Kenny's number. He answered right away.

"Kenny, it's Meg." My breath came in quick short bursts.

"I don't know anyone named Meg. Is this Mary Margaret Reed?"

"Kenny, I don't have time for you to joke around. You have to get to the barracks—right now!"

"Missed me that much last night? I told you I would buy you a beer."

"No, it's not that. It's Dylan. He's the murderer. Kelsey is about to go live with the story. You have to get here now. Otherwise Dylan's going to get a head start."

Kenny's tone turned serious. "Kelsey's going on air?"

"Yes! In five minutes, and I'm pretty sure that Dylan knows. He just cornered me in the basement and I ran upstairs."

"Okay good. Stay near other people. I'm hanging up and calling a squad car right now. Stay put!"

I watched as Kelsey paced in front of the barracks. Where was Dylan? How long would it take for a squad car to arrive? Kelsey's cameraman started counting down with his fingers.

Someone came up behind me and said, "Hey, Meg."

I jumped higher than I'd ever jumped in our training and screamed.

It was Tim.

"Jumpy, aren't we?" He pointed to Kelsey. "What's going on?"

"Kelsey's doing a live report."

"On what?"

I didn't know if I should say anything. Where were the police? Why hadn't they arrived yet? My hands trembled and my legs started to shake.

Tim looked concerned. "You okay?"

"It's Dylan! He killed Billy. Kelsey's uncovered the entire story. She's about to go on air and he's somewhere around here."

"Dylan?"

"Yes, Dylan," I repeated. Nervous energy pulsed through my body. Could Dylan be armed? What if he came after me?

Tim unzipped his bag and grabbed a bulky sweatshirt. "Here, take this." He thrust it at me.

"Thank you." I pulled the sweatshirt over my head; it hung to my knees and my arms were lost halfway down the sleeves, but I didn't care.

"Dylan, huh?" Tim chomped on an energy bar coated in milk chocolate and dark chocolate with a white chocolate drizzle that he had dug out of the bag. He noticed me stare at him. "You look like my wife. What? I'm a stress eater." He patted his gym bag. "Want one? I have more."

"You were serious about having candy and snacks stashed in that, weren't you?"

"Yes." Tim peeled back the wrapper and popped the remaining piece of chocolate bar in his mouth. He opened the bag and revealed a mound of candy bars, chips, and prepackaged cookies. There were enough unhealthy snacks in the bag to feed a small army. "Why? Did you think I was lying?"

"I wasn't sure. I sort of wondered if you were."

Tim tossed me a chocolate crunch bar. "I don't lie about candy. Eat this. You'll feel better."

He was right, between the sugary chocolate, his

warm sweatshirt, and his hefty frame, my anxiety began to calm. I wasn't alone and the police were on their way. *Relax, Maggie.* I heard Pops' voice in my head. Everything will be okay.

"It's good, isn't it?" Tim shoved another chocolate bar into his mouth. "Hey! Isn't that Dylan?" He pointed to the far end of the ramp leading up to the barracks.

Dylan sprinted down the ramp. He looked like a deer in the headlights. Kelsey motioned for her cameraman to pan to Dylan.

Dylan raced through the grass, up the hill toward Officer's Row with Kelsey shouting after him.

Sirens wailed in the distance. Thank goodness, the police were here.

Tim looked to me. "Where does he think he's going?"

"No idea." I shook my head.

Tim's expression changed. "Oh, wait a minute. I know what's happening now. You thought that I killed Billy? What, did you think I had stashed the murder weapon in here?" He patted his bag.

"Kind of." I wrinkled my nose. "Sorry."

"Don't you dare tell my wife. I'd rather have her think I killed someone than know that I've been cheating on her this whole time."

"I've never even met your wife, and cheating?"

He considered this for a minute. "You might meet her at the run. Trust me, she calls candy my other woman; she'll leave me if she finds out. Not a word, understood?"

"Got it." I gave him a half salute. "Why are we talking about this right now? Dylan is getting away."

Tim hesitated. I could tell that he was still trying to decide if I really would keep his secret.

"What are we doing standing here? We're missing out on all the action." I pointed to Evergreen Boulevard where police lights were flashing off the oak trees. "We should head that way."

Tim dropped his bag. We ran up the hill together. I had a feeling it was the first time that either of us was glad for our grueling training. Police sirens wailed. The pulsing blue, red, and white lights reminded me of the annual Fourth of July fireworks celebration at the fort.

"There's Dylan!" I shouted over the sirens as we watched Dylan jump over two short bushes and sprint up the steps to the creepy old lady's front porch.

A police car sped to a stop in the parking lot across the street. Had they seen him?

I watched as the creepy old lady peered out of the curtains and then opened the door for Dylan. Why? She must know him. Or maybe her weirdness had been because *she* was somehow involved in Billy's murder?

Tim pulled me toward the police cars. "Where did he go?"

"That way!" I yelled, pointing behind me.

A swarm of police officers with guns ready sprang from their police cars and swept in a broad formation on both sides of the sidewalk.

"Maybe we should get out of here," Tim said.

"Yeah." I started walking backward. This was a bad idea. Why had I suggested that we run toward a killer? Don't most normal people run *away* from danger?

"What should we do?" I asked Tim as the officers signaled to one another, moving straight toward us with their guns pointed.

"Freeze!" one of the officers shouted. "Put your hands in the air."

"Let's do that," Tim replied, raising both hands.

I followed suit, but my arms swam in Tim's over-sized sweatshirt.

The first team of police officers approached us.

"He went that way," I said, motioning to the creepy old lady's apartment with the sleeve of the sweatshirt.

"Put your hands in the air and do NOT move!" the officer in the front of the pack shouted.

I threw my hands back into position.

"It's okay, I know her," I heard one of them say. Kenny stepped forward. "Mary Margaret Reed, you can put your hands down."

"He's getting away!" I shouted. "He went inside that apartment."

Kenny turned around and signaled to the team. They moved in silent synchronization. Officers barricaded the street. Two stood guard on either end of the barricade. Not that there were any cars to direct at this early hour. Another officer stretched his arms wide and motioned Tim and me back to the grass.

"Move away from the perimeter."

Officers circled the vintage house. A team snuck around the back, another lined the front lawn.

"Damn, they aren't messing around," Tim said.

Kenny approached us. "What do you know about the suspect? Is he armed?"

"I don't know," I said. "I couldn't see. He ran out of the barracks and straight up this way."

Tim nodded. "I don't think he had a weapon."

Kelsey and her cameraman came flying up the hill in the news van. She jumped out and ran over to us.

Kenny stopped her. "Wait right there, miss. This is a secure perimeter."

"I broke this story. This is my story. I'm not going anywhere."

"You don't have to go anywhere." Kenny kept his voice calm, but his stance firm. "But you're not coming any closer."

Kelsey unzipped her warm-up jacket farther and stuck her chest out. Is that how she usually scored exclusive features? I couldn't believe it.

Kenny folded his arms across his chest. "Don't come any closer."

Kelsey fumed. She furrowed her brow and whipped around. "Great. Thanks a lot, Meg." She glared as she pushed past me.

I didn't bother to respond. I knew it wouldn't do any good, and Kelsey was already distracted with trying to get the tightest shot of the action. "Hurry up," she ordered her cameraman. "We've got to get in position before anyone else gets here. Block this area off, it's mine."

She was right. As the police held their ground, news vans began to arrive on the scene.

"Why aren't you doing anything?" I asked Kenny. All the officers looked like pieces on a chessboard trying to decipher their next move.

"We've been ordered to wait for the hostage negotiating team to arrive."

"Really?"

Kenny nodded. Kelsey directed her cameraman to zoom in. Kenny shook his index finger at the camera. "You can't film this. You'll have to wait until our spokesperson arrives. She's on her way. She'll brief all media."

I started to ask Kenny for clarification. Did he think that Dylan had taken the creepy old woman hostage? Before I could ask more, his radio crackled and he walked away from the perimeter.

"Have you ever seen anything like this?" Tim asked.

"No, I thought this kind of thing only happened in the movies. I can't believe it was Dylan. He is such a hippie."

"It kind of fits," Tim said. "No real hippie would partner with someone like Billy."

He had a point. I'd thought that Billy and Dylan were an unlikely match from the first day. Why hadn't I trusted my intuition more?

Jenny ran over to us. She was out of breath and dripping with sweat. "What's going on?" She panted as she bounced on the tips of her tennis shoes. "I did the waterfront loop early. I figured if I'm not going to be getting an extra weight-loss boost from the supplements anymore that I had better add in some extra training."

Tim looked at me in disbelief. Jenny really had become addicted to exercise. Oh well, probably better than illegal drugs.

She wiped her forehead with the back of her

arm. "I got back to the barracks for warm up and no one was around. Then I noticed the police lights and sprinted up here. What happened?"

We filled Jenny in on everything she had missed.

She finally caught her breath and stopped bouncing. "Dylan, really? He was so Zen."

Tim chomped on a Snickers bar. "The Zen guys are the most dangerous. That's life. I've worked in the corporate world long enough to know that you don't have to worry about the guy who goes into a rage when the coffee is out and no one has refilled it. It's always the guy who walks away quietly, seething inside, that you have to worry about."

I considered his point. It made me think about Sheriff Daniels. He was outwardly calm and steady, but could that be because he was concealing something much more sinister?

We watched in silence as the police standoff continued. Two new squad cars arrived. One held the police spokeswoman. She wore a business suit and heels. The other was the hostage negotiating team—or at least I assumed so.

Kenny and two other officers gathered around the spokeswoman and negotiators. Detective Bridger, who I hadn't seen since the day Billy was murdered, pulled the spokeswoman close and whispered something in her ear. They both looked in our direction. After a quick briefing the woman walked over to the swarm of media near us, while the police team crossed the street and joined forces with the waiting officers.

Kenny started to cross the street with the rest of the team, but Detective Bridger grabbed his arm and held him back. I couldn't tell, but I had the sense that Kenny was pleading with the detective to let him go, but I could tell that Bridger wasn't budging and wondered if that was because the other officers were trained in hostage negotiations. I'd have to ask Kenny later. Detective Bridger's stock rose in my book. I didn't want Kenny involved in the standoff. I was glad that his boss was watching out for him.

After the team was in place, the lead negotiator spoke into a bullhorn. "Dylan, we're ready for you to surrender. Come out with your hands up!"

Nothing happened.

I thought there might have been slight movement with the curtains, but I wasn't sure if it was my mind playing tricks on me.

"Did you see that?" I whispered to Tim.

"Shhh." He pointed to the officer with the bullhorn.

The officer tried again. This time he told Dylan that if he cooperated they would be able to offer him a deal.

There was no movement inside.

For the next hour the police attempted to communicate with Dylan. I wondered if he was even inside. Maybe he'd snuck out the back while the police were getting in formation. The sky lightened with the rising sun, but thick clouds blocked it from view. Light rain began to fall as we all watched the standoff from the relative safety of the bandstand.

The crowd grew. Neighbors and morning exercisers stopped to watch the chess match play out. Every news outlet from Portland and Vancouver had reporters on the scene. The police had to constantly quiet the crowd and make sure no one attempted to cross their barrier. "We've established this perimeter for your safety," the media spokeswoman said, as an officer stretched police tape across the park's wooden fence.

Kelsey, who had retained her front row position, thrust a microphone into the woman's face. "Is the suspect armed? Does he have a hostage?"

The spokeswoman replied in a calm but commanding tone. "At this point in time I cannot share any details about the case for the safety of everyone involved."

Kelsey turned to me after the woman left for another update. "That's code for Dylan has a hostage."

"Do you think so?"

"I know so."

"That's not good," I said. "There's a little old lady who lives in that apartment."

"Really?" Kelsey's eyes widened. She moved closer to me and stuck the mic in my face. "What do you know about the hostage?"

"Nothing." That wasn't a lie.

Kelsey looked like she didn't believe me, but at that moment a team of police officers formed a line and forced the crowd of bystanders and reporters, including me and Tim, down the hill.

"Do you think something's happening?" I asked Tim.

He nodded toward the apartment. "They're going in."

Chapter 35

Tim was right. The officers broke down the front door and swarmed inside. I could feel my chest tighten as I waited for the sound of gunshots. It gave me a new appreciation for the kind of danger police officers like Kenny put themselves in every day.

After what felt like an hour, but in reality was probably five minutes, a team of officers escorted Dylan outside with his hands cuffed behind his back. The next thirty minutes passed in a blur. Dylan was carted off in the back of a police car. The spokeswoman briefed the press, praising the team for bringing the standoff to a peaceful end.

Everyone parted in a foggy haze as the sky unleashed. Fat rain drops splatted on the ground. Thunder rumbled overhead. Tim pulled out a bag of chips as we walked down the hill to our cars. "I guess we're off the hook this morning. Wonder what tonight will bring?"

"I'll be here," Jenny said. "We have to finish this. We

have to run Mud, Sweat, and Beers this weekend—for Billy."

"Jenny's right," I agreed. "Now more than ever, we owe it to Billy to finish. I'll see you guys here tonight. We'll help each other finish." I pulled off Tim's sweatshirt and handed it back to him. "Thanks for letting me use this."

"No problem." He stuffed it back into his heavy bag. I wondered if the sweatshirt was a layer of protection for hiding his stash. If his wife was as intense about his exercise regimen as he made it sound, I was surprised that she hadn't thought of searching his bag.

"It's a deal," Jenny said. "We'll finish together—for Billy."

Tim crunched a chip. "Okay. I guess." He lumbered to his car.

Jenny watched him. "Do you think he'll really show up now that he doesn't have to?"

"I do."

Kelsey and her cameraman had taken position in front of the barracks again. I had a feeling she was going to be reporting "live" from the scene of the standoff for the next few days. At least she had the story she was looking for.

"Have you talked to her?" I asked.

Jenny frowned. "Yeah, she told me about the FDA investigation. I should have listened to you, Meg. You were right. I got so caught up in feeling good about losing weight that I lost sight of why I was doing this in the first place."

"It's okay. What's next for you? You're not going to keep taking the hCG, are you?"

"No way. I turned it all over to the FDA. I'm done. It's back to good old-fashioned diet and exercise for me."

"I'm glad to hear it, Jenny. I really am."

"Thanks for being a good friend."

"Of course." I gave her a hug. "Listen, I'm getting soaked. I'll see you later tonight."

"Sounds good. I'm going to get in a quick run. See you later." She jogged away.

I continued to my car. On the drive home I realized that I had stopped holding my breath. At least one of the investigations haunting me had been solved. There was still so much I wanted to know about the FDA's involvement and Dylan. Fortunately, I didn't have to wait long. Kenny texted late in the morning asking if I wanted to meet for lunch.

We met at a pub in Northwest Portland. The rain continued. It streamed down the sidewalks spilling into the storm drain. There's nothing better than a summer rain, in my humble opinion. I drank in the smell of the wet pavement and humid air.

Kenny was waiting at a table in the back of the pub. He stood when I arrived. "You look different."

I had showered and changed into a pink striped sundress with a mint green cardigan and matching sandals. After weeks of being sweaty and muddy, I spent time applying makeup and styling my pixie cut. I even clipped one side back with a vintage silver hummingbird hair clip.

"Is different good?" I bit my bottom lip.

"Different is really good. You look great." He pulled out a chair for me.

"Thanks." I sat down. He hadn't changed out of

his uniform, but he smelled like he'd doused himself in cologne.

"Are you hungry?" he asked, handing me a menu. "Because I'm starving. I could eat everything on here."

"Me too. Why is that?"

"The adrenaline. Now that's it worn off, I've got the shakes."

Our eyes met across the table. "I was thinking about you while watching that all go down. I can't believe you put yourself in those kinds of positions all the time. I guess I never really thought about it before."

"That was my first standoff. That doesn't happen all the time."

"Right, but you know what I'm trying to say—you have a really dangerous job."

"Sometimes." He changed the subject. "What sounds good?"

"Burgers?"

"A girl who eats. I love it." He ordered burgers and beers for us.

"Did you talk to Dylan?" I asked after the waiter left.

He smiled. "I had a feeling you were going to want an update."

"Who me? Never." I winked.

"You're plucky and I like it."

"Plucky?" I wrinkled my nose. "Is that some sort of chicken reference?"

Kenny looked amused. "You figure it out."

Did he think I was really plucky, as in gutsy and adventurous, or was he teasing? I couldn't tell.

He changed his tone and became serious. "Dylan confessed. I mean, not to me personally, but yeah he came clean. He'd been adding hCG to his natural supplement product line. Billy was taking the supplements but didn't realize that Dylan was still using hCG. Billy had a pre-existing heart condition. He began having serious side effects and suspected what was happening. He sent samples into the FDA to be analyzed."

"And Dylan found out and killed him? That doesn't make sense. The FDA would still have come after him, right?"

"Definitely. Dylan didn't confess to killing Billy. He said that Billy collapsed in the locker room that morning. He was worried that hCG would be found in his system, so he wrapped a bandana around his neck to make it look like murder."

"So it wasn't murder?"

"It depends on how you define murder. The coroner thinks the hCG exacerbated Billy's heart condition."

"What will happen to Dylan?"

"He probably won't be charged with first degree murder. More likely second degree or voluntary manslaughter."

"Will he go to jail?"

"Definitely. He's also facing charges from the FDA for illegally selling hCG. He's going to have a lengthy court case."

"Did you know that Kelsey was working with the FDA?"

"Yeah, that came out early on in our investigation."

"Why didn't you tell me?"

"Mary Margaret Reed." He furrowed his brow. "You are one of the most interesting girls I've met in a long time, but a case is a case."

"Fair enough." I grinned. "Hey, whatever happened with the bandana? Did you ever find it?"

Kenny nodded. "Yeah, Jenny turned it over, but it doesn't matter. I guess she found it in the locker room. We think Dylan came back for it and she interrupted him. Lifting a fingerprint off of fabric is a formidable task under the best circumstances, but a wet and muddy bandana that a bunch of people touched—impossible."

"Right." So Jenny had given the police the bandana. I wondered why she hadn't told me, then in the same breath I chided myself. She had done the right thing by going to the police.

"You know I'll have to see if I can arrange a tour of our forensics lab for you. I've never met a girl who's so into police procedures before." He gave me a coy smile.

Our food arrived, saving me from his overt flirtation. I had to admit that I liked the guy. He was funny, obviously good at his job, and attractive. What was wrong with me? I liked Matt. Mother said once that I used to be boy crazy when I was a teenager. I thought I had outgrown that phase, but maybe I hadn't.

We scarfed down our burgers and beer. Kenny told me about how he'd grown up in Seattle and moved to Vancouver after graduating from the police academy.

"I like the slower pace of things here," he said, dipping a fry in ranch dressing.

"Except for huge police standoffs with hostages," I joked.

"Except for that. Which reminds me, Dylan said that he didn't have a hostage. Apparently that's his mother's place. She confirmed that."

"The creepy old lady is Dylan's mom?"

"Creepy old lady?"

"Yeah, I kind of met her. Well, technically I stopped by her place to ask her a couple of questions. She gave me the creeps." I thought about my strange meeting with the woman and the picture of the fat kid I'd seen on her mantel. It was Dylan! Of course. His face had lengthened and thinned out over the years, but that's why I recognized it, and that's why she had snapped it out of my hands.

"I don't know about creepy," Kenny said. "But she stood up for her son. She was hiding him in a secret room below the floorboards. We almost didn't get him. That's why it took a while. Fortunately, one of the guys spotted the carpet turned up."

"Seriously? That's like something out of a movie."

"The whole morning was like something out of a movie."

We finished our lunch.

"Sorry to have to cut this short," Kenny said as he paid the bill. I protested, offering to pay for my half, but Kenny wouldn't hear of it. "What kind of date would this be if I let the woman pay?"

"Is this a date?"

Kenny frowned. "It's kind of a lame date. I'll tell you what. I'll make it up to you. How about if I take you to dinner and a movie one night this week?"

I hesitated.

He looked hurt. "If you don't want to, don't sweat it."

"No, it's not that I don't want to. It's just that I have my last few days of training every night this week."

"Ah. No problem. My week is going to be stacks of paperwork. How about a celebratory dinner after your race?"

"Sure." The words escaped my mouth before I could think about them. What would Matt say about me going on an official date with another guy?

"Saturday night, then? I'll pick you up at seven."

"It's a date."

Meg, you're an idiot. Now you're officially dating two guys.

Chapter 36

The rest of the week was blissfully uneventful. As promised, Jenny continued our training regimen. Tim showed up for each workout, and none of us complained—even about crawling through the mud. By the time Friday rolled around I actually felt ready for the race.

I might have been a bit overconfident. Saturday morning ended up being a scorcher. I arrived twenty minutes early to meet the team and stretch. The sun beat down on the giant inflatable arch that marked the entrance to the Mud, Sweat, and Beers course. Runners wearing felt beer hats and beer goggles jogged in place to warm up. A group of moms wearing T-shirts reading TOUGH MUDDERS had painted their faces and plastered temporary tattoos on their arms.

The energy was pulsing, as was the music blasting from two speakers where Jenny and the rest of my teammates had gathered.

"Don't worry, you guys," Jenny cheered over the music as we reached our elbows behind our heads.

"Remember we're doing this for Billy. It doesn't matter where any of us finish. It just matters that everyone crosses the finish line."

She had us all put our hands in the middle of our circle after we finished stretching. "On three— for Billy. One, two, three."

We all shouted "For Billy" and threw our hands in the air.

When the race gun sounded, my legs moved as if someone else was controlling them. I breezed through the first half of the course, vaguely aware of the spectators shouting motivating phrases at us from the sidelines. Tim, Jenny, Kelsey, and I ran in parallel strides. I had a feeling that Kelsey and Jenny were intentionally slowing their pace. I appreciated the effort and sense of team spirit.

Once we got to the first mud pit things took a turn for the worse. I dove face-first into the muddy lake. Mud shot up my nostrils. I forgot to close my mouth and ended up with a mouthful of watery mud. Jenny yanked me out of the pit with both her arms and shoved me forward to the giant inflatable slide in front of us.

Climbing up the slide was not my proudest moment. I kept slipping back down the plastic stairs. Tim finally pushed me up by my derriere. I landed on the top sideways and shot down the waterslide face-first.

At the bottom I caught sight of Jill in the crowd. She jumped up and down and yelled, "You got this! Go, Meg!"

Her enthusiasm paired with my teammates' insistence that we were all going to finish the race together, spurred me on. We scaled walls, army-crawled through muddy flats, and ran until my lungs burned. Forget the punny name—the race should have been called Blood, Sweat, and Tears. By the time we crossed the finish line, hand in hand, blood dripped from a gash on my forearm. Mud and sweat poured from my forehead. The crowd erupted as each team crossed the finish line where we were greeted with plastic pints of beers and medals.

My teammates huddled in a group hug. "We did it!" Jenny high-fived us. "Billy would be so proud."

"But you didn't finish first," I said, pointing to the leader board. We had come in a respectable twenty-second place. I was glad we hadn't finished dead last, but I knew Jenny wanted to finish first.

"I did, though. This experience has taught me so much about myself. Thanks to all of you for doing it with me." She wiped mud—or maybe a muddy tear—from her eye.

Kelsey waved her cameraman over. "Everyone pose."

She had us pose for photos and did thirty-second spots with each of us.

Great. Just what I needed, everyone in Portland to see me drenched in mud. Kelsey promised to share the photos and footage with us. I had a feeling that when I posted them on *Northwest Extreme*'s social media they would get a lot of shares and likes. Oh well. *You're taking one for the team, Meg,* I told myself.

We said our good-byes, agreeing to meet for a celebratory beer after we'd all had a few days to recover.

Jill ran over to greet me. She stopped short of hugging me. "You are a muddy mess, Meg."

I spun in a circle. "What do you think? It's my new look."

"I love it." She handed me a six-pack of canned IPA. "This is from Matt. He texted me this morning to make sure I told you congrats. He wanted to be here."

"I know. He texted me this morning." I took the beer.

"What is it?" Jill asked.

"Nothing."

"Meg, come on. It's me."

"Well, I kind of have a date tonight, and now I'm feeling bad about it."

"With whom?"

I told her about Kenny as we walked to the after-party in a giant tent at the end of the course. A band played onstage. Muddy racers danced to the beat with beers in hand. It was a real party.

"You know what, Meg, I think this is a good thing."

"You do? But you've been trying to get me and Matt together since college."

"That's true," Jill said, holding out her wrist so that the bouncer could stamp it.

I tried to wipe my arm on my muddy pant. "Don't worry about it," the bouncer said. "You're good. Go in."

Jill and I headed to the snack table. "I think I moved too fast with Will." She handed me a banana. "We got serious right away. Looking back I don't even know why. I guess because I was on track to do exactly what my parents wanted me to do—graduate from college, go to law school, get married."

I couldn't believe Jill was being so open about her relationship with Will.

"Meg, I owe you so much."

"What are you talking about? You don't owe me anything."

"I do. If it weren't for you I wouldn't be going to Italy. I'd probably be getting engaged to Will right now. Watching you follow your dreams and take risks—big risks—has shown me that I can do the same."

She offered me a granola bar. I declined. "You know, watching you and Matt has also really opened my eyes."

"It has?"

"You both care so much for one another. I realize I want that too. I don't want to settle for someone like Will."

"That's good. That's really good. You deserve the best."

"I do." She threw her head in the air in a mock princess stance.

"If watching me and Matt made you realize that things weren't working with Will, then why are you telling me it's okay to go out with Kenny tonight?"

"Because I think Matt's *the one*, Meg."

"Okay?"

"But you have to realize that Matt's the one. That's not going to happen if you don't date a few other guys."

"You think?"

"Trust me. And it's not like you and Matt are officially dating. Unless there's something you haven't told me?"

I shook my head.

"Good. Then go out with Kenny tonight and see how it goes."

"Should I tell Matt?"

"If it comes up, I would. It might light a fire under him too." Jill grinned. "Let's go dance!"

We danced to the pulsing beat on the muddy floor for an hour. It felt good to release all of the negative energy in my body. After the party, I took a long bath that afternoon in preparation of my date with Kenny. Matt texted to see how the race went. I didn't tell him about the date.

Kenny arrived promptly at seven with a bouquet of flowers and a box of chocolates. I hadn't seen him out of his uniform. He looked completely different and much younger in his jeans and a dress shirt.

"You look amazing." He handed me the flowers and chocolate.

"Thanks, you want the tour?" I invited him inside. The tour took two minutes. Kenny had to duck under the arched doorways in the 1920s bungalow.

We had a great time together. I wasn't sure if Jill was right or not. My heart definitely flopped when he walked me to the front door at the end of the evening. He leaned one arm against my front door. "Can I see you again, Mary Margaret Reed?"

I wondered if I sounded as nervous as I felt when I said, "Sure."

He bent his head down and kissed me lightly on the lips. Then he turned and called over his shoulder. "I'll be in touch."

I skipped inside and shut the door behind me. My heart thumped in my chest. A second later my phone dinged with a text from Kenny: **Thanks for a great evening. Can't wait to see you again.**

Unlike my relationship with Matt, Kenny was very clear about how he felt, and I liked it. I wasn't sure if that was because I really liked him or because I liked the attention. I was going to have to give that some serious thought. But there was definitely a little spark between us.

It had been a long week. I felt proud of my accomplishments. I had followed through on my commitment and completed a mud race. Tomorrow, I would put the finishing touches on my feature and deliver it to Greg on Monday.

Monday loomed heavy on my mind. Our all-staff meeting was scheduled for nine sharp. Greg had sent an e-mail to the staff letting us know that the meeting was mandatory. I wondered what the news was going to be. Was this the end of *Northwest Extreme* as I knew it, or had Greg found a way to save the magazine?

The start of a new week and the close of my training with Mind Over Mudder also meant that it was time to focus on Pops' death. I needed to have a heart-to-heart with Mother. I owed her an apology, and it was time for me to really listen to what she wanted to tell me about Pops. I needed to pay a visit to Gam. I was fairly confident that she and Sheriff Daniels were through, but I wanted to make sure that she was okay. I needed to check in with Matt to see if he'd found anything new from PDJ's friend, and figure out how Sheriff Daniels was connected to the case. Plus there was the looming issue of Greg. I had to find out once and for all why he had really hired me to write for *Northwest Extreme*, and whose side he was on.

For the moment, though, I only needed one thing: sleep. I had a lot of work ahead of me. For the first time since Pops died, I knew that I was ready for it. I also knew I probably wasn't going to like some of what I found, but I was ready for that too. The truth was within my grasp. Tomorrow I would begin the process of reaching out and grabbing it.

Meg's Adventure Tips

Rule one—Drop and give me twenty. Slowly but surely Meg is learning the importance of training. Her adventures and misadventures with *Northwest Extreme* have helped her understand that any athletic endeavor requires time and effort. She might not have enjoyed it when Billy told her to drop and give him twenty, but without his training protocol she never would have crossed the finish line. Before competing in a mud run or an obstacle race like the fictional Mud, Sweat, and Beers, experts recommend training for a minimum of four weeks. Training should involve both strength and conditioning, as well as plenty of cardio work. To be in fighting shape by race time, practice running on hilly terrain, uneven ground, and up and down stairs. Meg dreaded burpees, but veteran competitors swear that doing sets of burpees, lunges, and sprints are sure to guarantee that you'll cross the finish line. For novices, start by sprinting one lap around a track followed by ten burpees and lunges. Repeat six to eight times, being sure to rest between sets. Before you know it you'll be scaling walls and sailing through the mud!

Rule two—No magic pills. Meg comes face to face with a weight-loss supplement that is supposed to give her magic results. Nutritionists, physicians, and trainers all concur that long-term and lasting weight loss requires a combination of diet and exercise. Small changes can make a big impact, like walking one to two miles a day, drinking at least sixty-four ounces of water, and adding more fresh fruit and vegetables to your diet. Slow and steady wins the race when it comes to making lifestyle changes that will benefit your overall health and well-being. Additionally, it's extremely important to notify your doctor before taking any new vitamins or supplements—whether for weight loss or nutrition. Doctors say that even naturally occurring supplements can have unwelcome side effects and interactions with other medications.

Rule Three—Mind Matters. Many professional athletes implement a practice of mindfulness in their training routine. Meg is fortunate to have Gam in her life as a guide and model for the importance of taking a moment of pause each day. The act of meditation (even for short periods of time) has been shown to reduce stress, lower blood pressure and heart rate, improve the immune system, speed up metabolism, and sharpen focus and your ability to concentrate. Meditating is easy and can be done anywhere. To start, find a quiet place to sit or lie down for ten to fifteen minutes. Focus your attention on your breathing, inhaling through your nose and exhaling through your mouth. Try to keep a slight smile on your lips as you breathe and release any tension in your body. If thoughts appear, simply acknowledge them and return your focus to your breath. You can hold a stone or crystal to help ground you as you meditate, or work on visualization by imagining an object (e.g., a flower or heart) or repeating a word (like *peace* or *calm*) over and over again as you breathe. Start by meditating for a few minutes a day and see what impact it has on your health and daily life. As you continue to practice you'll find yourself being able to maintain a calm and relaxed state for longer and longer periods of time.

Meg's *First Degree Mudder* Scenic Tour

Follow along on Meg's muddy adventure through some of the West's most historic grounds. You'll definitely get a glimpse into the Pacific Northwest's rich and rugged past. Mud is entirely optional!

Stop One—Fort Vancouver National Historic Site, Vancouver, Washington

Established in 1824 by the Hudson's Bay Company, this national monument is a testament to our pioneering spirit. The 366-acre site encompasses the fort, Officer's Row, Pearson Field and Air Museum, and the U.S. Army Barracks. Stroll through the parade grounds and stop for a picnic in the bandstand where you'll be greeted with views of the mighty fortress to the south and Mt. Hood to the east. Take a walking tour along Officer's Row where you can visit the museum at the Marshall House or refuel with a delicious cocktail or dinner at the stately Grant House. Fort Vancouver is a living history museum offering many events throughout the year including candlelight tours, cultural demonstrations, and archeological digs. You'll feel like you've stepped into the nineteenth century when costumed volunteers showcase blacksmithing and wood-fired baking techniques. The fort is open throughout the year for daily visits. For current hours and information, check out www.nps.gov/fova. Don't forget to take a peek at Building 614, the old Army Hospital, while you're on the grounds and decide for yourself whether it's haunted. Meg is sure that she spotted a ghost peering down at her from the third floor.

Stop Two—Food Carts, Portland, Oregon

No trip to Portland is complete without a visit to one of the city's many food cart pods. It's almost impossible to travel anywhere in Portlandia—or better yet Cartlandia—without bumping into a food truck, cart, or pod. With upward of six hundred carts and counting, you're sure to find something scrumptious to satisfy your palate and any picky eaters in your group. What makes the Portland food cart experience unique is that most of the carts are not mobile, rather they're grouped together in pods, which means you should plan to come hungry as you'll have a plethora of tiny kitchens to choose from. Additionally, many of the pods offer extra amenities like full-service bars with rotating beer, cider, and wine taps, outdoor seating, beer gardens, dog-friendly areas, and heated tents where you can take shelter from the rain during the soggy winter months. From Koi Fusion to German brats, the food cart scene is legendary and not to be missed. Don't know what you're in the mood for or where to start? Read the Portland Food Cart Adventures Blog for what's trending in the cart scene.

Stop Three—Migration Brewing and Hopworks Urban Brewery, Portland, Oregon

Meg and her pals puzzle over the clues to Billy the Tank's murder at Migration Brewing and Hopworks Urban Brewery. Migration's patio is one of the best spots to grab a pint in the spring and summer. Located in Northeast Portland, the popular pub is housed in a converted garage and is a favorite gathering spot for locals. Meg tried Blood, Sweat and Red, a gorgeous rose-colored amber beer with a nice balance of malt and a hint of citrus flavor. Grab a pint and a seat at one of the many outdoor tables where you can soak up some sun and mingle with craft beer lovers.

Hopworks Urban Brewery, better known as HUB, is a quintessential Portland pub. The organic brewery is committed to sustainability. They walk the talk by using organic, salmon-safe hops, canning their beers in order to reduce fuel consumption, and opening an energy-efficient pub, the BikeBar in North Portland. Go green at the BikeBar where you can take a spin on one of their stationary bikes and offset your carbon footprint while waiting for your beer. Meg's a fan of Rise Up Red, a seasonal

IRA (India Red Ale) with tangy grapefruit notes and a lovely sweet bready finish.

Stop Four—BrewCycle Tour, Portland and Vancouver

If hopping on one of Hopworks' stationary bikes sparked your pedal prowess, try your hand—or feet—on Portland's BrewCycle or Vancouver's Couve Cycle. The concept is simple: You and your pals put in the legwork as you collaboratively pedal from pub to pub. Sure you'll look like a tourist, but who cares? This is one of the most fun ways to see the Portland/Vancouver area and sample some of the region's best brews. Plus all that pedaling burns calories, which means you can go ahead and have another pint. If you're on the Washington side of the Columbia River, take a ride on the Couve Cycle. This pedal party will take you and thirteen friends through Vancouver's charming downtown and burgeoning beer scene. On the Oregon side of the mighty Columbia, check out BrewCycle. Tours run for approximately two hours with stops at three local pubs. Custom tours can be arranged, or if you're feeling really adventurous you might consider their newest offering: the BrewBarge. You'll pedal a fourteen-person paddle boat on the Willamette River. For this river brews cruise it's BYOB, and don't forget your sunscreen!

Stop Five—Mud Race

If you've mastered all of Meg's mud tour, then it's time to take it up a notch. What better way to end your adventure than with a little dirt? Mud runs and obstacle races are equally entertaining and challenging. Most runs cater to both uber fit competitors and first-time racers of all shapes, sizes, and athletic ability. Sure you'll have to scale a wall or two and slosh through some sloppy mud, but nothing will beat the feeling of achievement when you cross the finish line. The only problem is choosing which one. Mud runs take place throughout the year and all over the country. Find one near you, or consider signing up for a mud run in Meg's beloved Portland. It's the perfect excuse to come out West. www.mudrunguide.com has a free listing of adventure runs and obstacle races in other parts of the world and here in the United States. Happy running!

Connect with Us

Visit us online at
KensingtonBooks.com
to read more from your favorite authors, see books
by series, view reading group guides, and more.

for sneak peeks, chances to win books and prize packs,
and to share your thoughts with other readers.

facebook.com/kensingtonpublishing
twitter.com/kensingtonbooks

Tell us what you think!

To share your thoughts, submit a review,
or sign up for our eNewsletters, please visit:
KensingtonBooks.com/TellUs.